THE GIRL WHO KILLED YOU

Shee McQueen Mystery-Thrillers
Book Three

Amy Vansant

Vansant Creations, LLC / Amy Vansant
Annapolis, MD
http://www.AmyVansant.com
http://www.PineapplePort.com

Editing/Proofreading by Effrosyni Moschoudi & Meg Barnhart

Amy Vansant

The Girl Who Was Forgotten

CHAPTER ONE

"Check inside the iguana!"

Shee McQueen shouted the words as her cell connection dropped, and her father's voice snapped off mid-word.

Damn.

She dropped her head into her hands and let her phone slide onto the white beach sand.

Did he hear me?

The phone didn't have far to fall—she'd been squatting behind a tropical bush, in the dark like a stalker, when her phone had vibrated against her hip.

The iguana.

She realized it had been the *iguana* crawling around her brain—always just out of reach—since she'd searched Xander Andino's bedroom back in Florida. She'd been seeing flashes of green in her mind's eye. She should have pieced it together.

The damn iguana.

She'd been cranky and sloppy the day she met the iguana. She'd wanted to take a few more days off—wanted to spend time with her daughter, Charlotte, where the girl lived on the West Coast of Florida. When Shee's father, Mick, called and insisted she return home *immediately*, she assumed her old man had a meaty mission for her. Something important enough to abandon Charlotte earlier than planned.

Hardly.

Xander Andino, the son of a United States senator from Florida, had run away with some of Daddy's valuables. The senator wanted to keep the embarrassing incident quiet, so he'd hired Mick to find Junior and haul him home. Mick, in turn, summoned *her* because she'd spent her life tracking bad guys.

Did it matter she was busy reuniting with her daughter? The daughter she'd been kept from, through bad luck, bad decisions, and circumstance, for twenty-odd years.

Apparently not.

Rude.

Sure, it made sense on paper to have the tracker come home to track.

It just wasn't what she wanted to do.

Who cared about an AWOL spoiled brat, anyway? A *fortunate son* throwing a hissy fit?

Pssht.

She was sure Mick considered the cushy job a boon—the staff at his Loggerhead Inn had thinned in recent weeks. Half touristy beach hotel, half haven for ex-military mutts, Loggerhead was in need of adopting a few more strays. Mick provided "fixer" services for people with problems only covert, military-trained specialists could solve. The hotel was Mick's way of making up for all the bad things he'd done in the past.

If that's the way forgiveness works.

Shee hoped so.

She had a few sins of her own to work off.

Like the fact it was *her* fault the hotel was short-staffed. Her return home had been, um...

...eventful.

She'd made life difficult for her dad by putting his staff in harm's way. Guardian angels, mercenaries, soldiers of fortune, whatever you called them, it was a tough business to be in when half your army was dead, injured, or gone. If Loggerhead was hired for a mission that required, for example, someone who could split a toothpick with a knife from fifteen feet away—they were shorthanded.

They'd had that person before she showed up.

As it stood, Mick's posse boasted a young Naval Academy grad-gone-AWOL with a grab bag of tech skills and abundance of attitude, a giant who only spoke gibberish, a British landscaper-slash-sniper who may or may not have been MI6, a retired FBI agent, and Shee's ex-boyfriend, Mason—a one-legged retired SEAL.

And, of course, herself, the prodigal daughter—Shee McQueen, age forty-six, tracker, skip tracer, bounty hunter, and jack-of-all-investigations.

Throw in her father's sixty-something, poker-playing con artist of a girlfriend and two dogs—one barely larger than a Guinea pig—and it was clear Loggerhead wasn't prepared for any major assaults.

Mick's mish-mash of broken soldiers was even more mish-mashy than usual.

Mick himself was nearly seventy and had recently narrowly survived a bullet to the head. He was little help. He'd been reduced to rambling around the hotel, barking orders, and wondering why no one ever did things as well as him.

Even with all the shortages, the Loggerhead could handle a missing young man. Shee tracked Xander Andino to the *YOU* resort—a Bahamian-based playground catering to the rich and young. Miffed to be recalled from Charlotte's for a fluff mission, she'd improvised and invited her daughter to come with her. Charlotte was a private investigator now, and from what Shee'd seen, she was more than capable.

Together, they'd retrieve the senator's son.

What *mother-daughter bonding time* could have been more fitting? Painting ceramics? High tea with scones and white gloves?

Hell no.

Not in this demented family.

Shee had needed a twenty-something someone to infiltrate the island's resort, and Charlotte fit the bill.

Perfect.

Until it wasn't.

Until Shee's phone rang.

Until everything was a lie, and she realized she'd sent

Charlotte into the lion's den.

Shee stared at the phone in the sand and clenched a fist.

I should have checked inside the iguana.

CHAPTER TWO

Three Days Earlier

Shee McQueen knocked on the oversized front door of Senator Nicodemus Andino's Florida home. With its terra cotta roof tiles and tall Doric columns, the place looked like a Greek coliseum and a hacienda had an ugly baby.

Baby's first words were, *I'm rich.*

The place was *huge.*

Shee's mood felt as disjointed as the home's architecture. Part of her was overjoyed. Her trip with Mason to visit their daughter had gone well.[1] Getting Mason to forgive her for running off during his first deployment almost thirty years ago—and hiding Charlotte's existence from him since then—had been *step one* in her ongoing quest for redemption.

During the trip, she'd made progress.

He was still a little miffed.

Step two required Charlotte's forgiveness. After all, Shee'd given the girl away.

It had made sense at the time.

The trip enabled her to make progress there, too. Charlotte didn't seem bitter—even though she'd ultimately grown up like the Little Orphan Annie of the Pineapple Port retirement

---

[1] Want to find out what happened during Shee and Mason's trip to Charlotte's? Read *Pineapple Circus*!

community, unofficially adopted by the neighbors. All of them.

She seemed to be a happy, well-adjusted, beautiful young lady.

No harm, no foul.

Shee had had good reasons for staying away all those years—someone had been trying to kill her.

A pretty solid excuse.

There were a couple of other secrets Charlotte probably needed to know, but...*eh*. Shee could share that information during *step three* of her redemption tour. For now, she felt good about how things were going. She didn't want to push her luck.

That half of her—the half fresh off of being reunited with Charlotte—was feeling *great*.

The other half was *pissed* to be standing on the senator's architectural Frankenstein of a porch.

Shee took a deep breath.

Let it go.

The senator's front door swung open to reveal a woman dressed in a crisp, light blue housekeeper's uniform. The woman eyed her as if Shee were peddling vacuums.

"Can I help you?" she asked.

"Hi. Shee McQueen to see Mr. Andino?"

Another sweep with the eyeballs. "Is he expecting you?"

"He should be, yes. He called us."

"*Us?*"

Shee opened her mouth and then shut it again. The housekeeper's interrogation was growing tiresome, but it was another issue knocking her speechless.

Does 'us' have a name?

She wasn't sure. Dad had never mentioned how to market his little mercenary project. *Was it just The Loggerhead? Soldiers r' Us? Gimpy Guns, Inc?*

She'd have to ask about that.

"He'll recognize my name," she said in the meantime.

"Sheila?"

"*Shee*. McQueen. He's been in contact with my father, *Mick* McQueen."

The woman took a step back and motioned to one particular square of oversized tile at her feet. "Wait *here*."

Shee stepped inside the square and watched as the housekeeper shut the front door and disappeared into the bowels of the mansion.

What a fun lady.

She stepped past the invisible prison wall of the tile's edge and roamed the foyer.

Nothing bad happened.

Emboldened, she strolled a short hall leading to a large living room, stopping to stare at a family portrait on the wall. The senator, a woman she presumed to be his wife, and their renegade son, Xander, stared back at her. They were all dressed in white, posing beneath the local pier on a cloudless day. The kid looked seventeen in the photo. He seemed happy enough. No shifty eyes or *Daddy-doesn't-understand-me* pout. No *look-how-different I am* tattoos or piercings visible. He looked like an All-American Kid, with short dark hair and a big toothy grin—even though his parents had dressed him like an evangelical preacher and dragged his butt to a public pier.

Nothing about the photo said Xander was a rebel.

Maybe since then, he'd fallen in with the wrong crowd.

It was always *the wrong crowd's* fault.

Shee meandered into the living room. Through the hurricane glass at the back of the house, she watched a sailboat navigate the Intracoastal waterway, sunlight glinting off the polished chrome railing and the obligatory girl-in-bikini lounging on the forward deck.

"Ms. McQueen."

Shee turned to find the senator striding toward her, hand extended. She recognized him from her preparatory Internet search. Behind him, the housekeeper skulked for a moment and then slipped away, like a bad dream in the sunlight.

"Mr. Andino. Nice to meet you," said Shee.

"Call me Nic." He shook her hand, his well-rehearsed politician's smile dazzling. "I was expecting your father. Is he coming?"

"No. I'm the tracker of the family. That's what you need, from what I understand?"

Nic's smile tightened as he swept an arm toward the opposite side of the living room.

"Let's go to my office."

He headed in that direction.

Shee stepped in line behind him, shooting a glance behind her. Nic didn't want to talk in the living room.

He doesn't want the housekeeper to know.

They entered an office wrapped in dark wood paneling. A floor-to-ceiling bookshelf supported a few wildlife statues, a collection of dust-free plaques and awards, and a smattering of leather-bound books. The ornate desk in the center of the room boasted only a blotter, a phone, and a lamp. Not a pen or scrap of paper. Not a family photo. On one wall, a small ornate frame hung empty, a glaring oddity in an otherwise pristine room.

If it hadn't been for the awards, Shee would have assumed the room was staged for sale.

"Have you been here long?" she asked.

"Almost ten years." Nic closed the door and motioned to a chair. "Have a seat."

Shee sat in one of two leather chairs as the senator took his place behind his desk.

"I assume your father told you about my problem?" he asked.

"He said your son's missing. That's all I know."

He nodded and remained silent long enough that Shee took it as a sign to continue.

"When did you last see him?" she asked.

"Xander came back from a camping trip with his girlfriend a week ago—"

"Have you talked to her?"

"No."

Shee paused, surprised by the answer. Talking to the girlfriend should have come six steps before calling Mick McQueen.

"Is she in town?"

His cherub cheek twitched upward, causing him to squint one eye. "I'm not sure."

"Any chance they're back camping wherever they were?"

"They could be..." This idea seemed to lighten the senator's burden, but a moment later, he was scowling again. "Why would he come home and then go back again?"

"I don't know. It wouldn't be the strangest thing a kid ever did. Can I get the girlfriend's name and any other info you have for her?"

Nic opened a drawer to pull out a small stack of yellow sticky notes. "Her name is Isabella Candella. I don't know her exact address, but she lives somewhere out in the Vida de Playa community, I believe." He jotted down her name and then tore off the note before stuffing the cube back into his drawer as if it pained him to have it visible.

She took the note. "Thank you. Go on. He came back and then...?"

"Xander was here for two days, and then he was gone again—it's been four days. We haven't been able to reach him. His phone goes to voicemail."

Shee hooked her mouth to the side. "Not to talk my way out of a job, but four days isn't long for a young man to fall off the grid—"

"It is for Xander."

Nic snapped the words with absolute certainty.

She nodded. "Okay. Have you or your wife checked his social media accounts?"

"My wife is dead."

"Oh. I apologize."

"It's okay," he sighed. "I had my assistant check his accounts. Nothing. No posts."

"Does he usually post a lot?"

"No. She said no. I don't know. I don't encourage it."

Shee cocked her head. "How old is he again?"

"Twenty-one." The senator cleared his throat, holding her

gaze for a beat too long. "I see your point," he added.

"My point?"

"You're suggesting he's too old for me to be watching over his Internet use, but as long as he's under this roof and the son of a public figure, there have to be *rules*."

"Of course. I assume there was no ransom request?"

"No."

"Any other oddities? Any reason you're particularly worried?"

Nic's gaze floated over Shee's shoulder, and she suspected she knew what he was looking at.

The elephant in the room.

The empty frame.

He motioned to it, and she turned.

"My Picasso sketch went missing the same day he disappeared. Cut right out of the frame." He paused as if wrestling with himself over sharing his next bit of information. "So did cash I keep in my drawer here." He tapped the desk with an open palm.

"How much?"

The senator scowled.

"Not to be nosey," she added. "I'm wondering how much he thought he needed—might be a clue to how long he thought he'd be gone."

Her reasoning seemed to make sense to him.

"About four thousand," he said.

"Has he ever stolen anything before?"

Nic's head jerked back as if she'd slapped him.

"Of course not. He's—"

He paused before continuing at a more deliberate pace.

"He's a *passive* kid. He never went through a rebellious phase. He's not—"

Another lengthy pause.

"Like you?" suggested Shee, guessing the rest of his honest thought.

The senator smiled. "He's more like his mother."

"And he didn't leave any note? No message? Maybe he left

word with a friend or another relative?"

Shee made sure to add the bit about other family members. Odds were good Xander knew his father considered him weak. Kids were more perceptive than their parents gave them credit for, and Nic Andino didn't seem like the sort of man who hid disappointment well. It could be he felt closer to another member of the family.

Nic shook his head. "He didn't leave any word. Nothing. He was here and then he was gone."

Shee turned her head to the side, feeling the presence of the rest of the cavernous house looming behind her.

"Would you say you have a good relationship with Xander?"

"Of course. He's my *son*."

"Plenty of sons don't get along with their parents."

The scowl etched on Nic's face deepened. "I don't know how many other ways I can tell you. He's a *good* boy."

She looked away, scratching her neck.

I get it. You wouldn't have it any other way.

She had to ask.

"Whose decision was it to call my father? Why not the police?"

She'd been worried she'd offend the senator with such a direct question, but instead, he seemed to relax a notch.

"I'm in the public eye," he said, smiling. "People know me. They expect me to have a certain amount of *order* in my life. They entrust me with their government. They voted for me, and in doing so, asked me to be their representative."

His tone grew overly serious. Shee sniffed to quash the snort of laughter tap-dancing in her nose.

Nic didn't seem to notice. He continued.

"I wanted to keep things quiet and, to be honest, I don't think it's time to panic."

"But you called us?"

"Yes. On the recommendation of a friend, I contacted your father to put my mind at ease."

Shee realized what she'd been reading as controlled emotion on the man's expression wasn't *concern* at all. The senator didn't think his boy was in trouble—he was *furious* about the painting and livid his boy would embarrass him. He needed Xander back in the fold before the press caught wind of things.

"You think he ran off with his girlfriend," she said, more as a statement of fact than a question.

The senator held out both hands, palms to the ceiling. "I can't deny it's a possibility. They went camping, fell ever deeper in love, made plans, came home, gathered seed money for a new life, and eloped."

Shee nodded. That scenario explained why the senator hadn't contacted the girl. He didn't think for a second she was anywhere but with his son. It would also mean admitting to the girl's family that he'd lost control of the boy.

"Any reason why he wouldn't take a more traditional route to marriage? Get you involved?"

"The *girlfriend*." He leaned forward as if sharing a secret. "I think she has a mind of her own."

Shee blinked at him.

A *girl* with her *own mind?*

How terrible.

"You don't approve of her?" she asked.

He leaned back. "He can do better." Apparently pleased with his choice of platitude, he settled into his chair like a nesting bird.

His answer surprised her. Not that she hadn't assumed it to be the truth, she just hadn't expected him to be so honest.

"I'm hoping you find him before he does anything stupid," he added.

Shee again turned to the missing Picasso. "If you don't mind me asking, how much was the painting worth?"

"*Sketch*. Pencil. Less than you'd think. A few thousand dollars." His chin lifted. "My father knew him."

"Picasso?"

He nodded. "The sketch was of me as a little boy. Not that it looked like me, as you can imagine."

"It must have meant a lot to you."

His suddenly dreamy expression darkened once more. "Yes."

"Does Xander have an interest in art? Any reason to think he knows someone willing to buy your sketch?"

"If he *sold* my—" Nic poked the desk with an index finger, too apoplectic to continue.

Shee pushed on. "Did the sketch mean anything to *him*?"

"To Xander? No." The senator ran his hand over his graying temples and released a long breath. "He broke the frame once with a ball, being careless. Tore the paper in the upper right-hand corner. That's how much he cared about it. He wouldn't know what to do with *art*. He has *no* appreciation."

Shee nodded. She couldn't help but think Xander's choice of loot had more to do with pissing off Daddy than money, but she didn't see the point in riling the man any further. If the vein in his forehead throbbed any harder, it might burst and *ruin* her white camp shirt.

"Could I see his room?" she asked.

The senator seemed happy to stand. Taking a moment to compose himself by running a hand down his chest, he proceeded to lead her to the second floor. Halfway down the hall on the upper level, he opened a door.

Shee entered.

Xander's room had the same barren vibe as the office. A made bed sat between two windows, a clean desk stood tucked in the corner. No posters or sports memorabilia adorned the walls or tabletops, other than a row of three small trophies lining a shelf attached to the wall.

Shee walked over to read the inscription on one with a golden man on top. In his molded, mitten-like hands, he held a gilded baseball bat.

"Participation," she read aloud.

Ouch.

"Nothing special," said his father, echoing her thoughts

and sounding even less impressed. "They give trophies for anything these days."

She looked at him.

He'd thrown the boy under the bus faster than she could say *everyone's a winner.*

Shee wandered the room. Sliding open the desk's only drawer, she found a collection of pens. Usually, she could get a feel for a person by studying something as intimate as their bedroom, but Xander remained a mystery. The closet had enough empty hangers in it for her to surmise he'd packed to leave. Two jackets remained—he'd have needed them if he'd headed *north.*

Twenty minutes on the case, and she'd already narrowed the search to, more or less, the center ring of the planet.

I am worth every penny.

"What does he like to do? What are his hobbies?" she asked.

"He's a good student, but he's aimless. That's why he's still here. I'm counseling him toward a career."

"In what?"

"I'm not sure yet. He's attending college at FAU, trying different things."

Shee nodded. Florida Atlantic University was over the bridge, not far. Good way to give the kid freedom *and* keep him close.

Shee's gaze bounced from what looked like an expensive lamp to a rubber iguana perched on the windowsill, tucked behind a long silver drape. A toy. The only sign of any personality.

She peered at a framed painting of the sea hanging above the bed. The art seemed better suited for a hotel room than a boy's mancave.

Her attention pulled back to the iguana.

It stared back at her, open-mouthed.

Hm.

Everything in the room felt sterile and impersonal except for the trophies and the rubber iguana.

Catching movement from the corner of her eye, Shee

turned to find the delightful housekeeper at the doorway.

"Your two o'clock is here," shouted the woman. She frowned in Shee's direction.

"Just a second." The senator held up an index finger for Shee before disappearing into the hall with *Frau Blücher.*

Shee was about to move toward the iguana when she noticed something sticking out from behind the bland sea painting. Pulling the bottom edge away from the wall, she slid a piece of paper out from behind it. A folded piece of tape had held it to the back of the art, but the glue had failed, sending the paper sliding down the wall.

The note had a word and a string of numbers scrawled on it.

YOU 2-2-3-7-3-3-3

Nic Andino strode back into the room. "I apologize. I'm afraid I'm going to have to ask you to leave for now," he said.

"Does this mean anything to you?" she asked, holding the slip of paper up for him to see.

He glanced at it and shook his head.

"No. Should it?"

"I found it behind his painting."

He made a non-committal grunt and checked his watch to be sure she saw how busy he was. She suspected he had people coming and didn't want to explain her to them.

"Can I keep it?" she asked, still holding the paper aloft.

"Of course." He walked back into the hall and stared at her, waiting for her to join him.

She glanced back at the gaping reptile.

Sorry, Iggy, guess it's time to go.

She joined Nic in the hallway to find the housekeeper still lurking.

The senator headed down the hall to the stairs. "Yolanda will see you out. Anything else you need, let me know," he said, a hand waving over his head as he hustled away.

Shee nodded. She'd been dismissed. Meeting over before she'd given the room a good sweep.

She glanced at Yolanda and pointed to Xander's door. "Do you mind if I—"

"I'm to see you out," she said.

Shee nodded.

I saw that coming.

Never ask Yolanda for quarter.

There would be none given.

CHAPTER THREE

Leaving the grand home, Shee held her phone to her mouth and recorded notes from her time with Senator Nic Andino. She had a few ideas. She needed to figure out what the cryptic note behind his hotel art meant. She wanted to talk to the girlfriend. If the girl didn't know anything about Xander's escape, she could take the whole *he did it for love* theory off the table.

Escape.

She slowed, rolling the word around in her mind.

Why did I use *that* word?

Maybe the home's impersonal feel reminded her of a prison cell. The Andino's palace felt like an alien had created it to mimic a human dwelling. No clutter, no knickknacks other than a smattering of awards. Bad enough Nic's office felt like that, but for a boy barely out of his teens to have such a barren room—

The sight of a black Nissan parked across the street jerked her from her thoughts. The mid-range sedan seemed less fancy than the other vehicles in the neighborhood, less utilitarian than the landscaping and contractor trucks...

Someone inside the car moved.

Continuing to add notes to her phone, Shee crossed the street at an angle sharp enough to narrow the distance but not *so* direct as to be obvious.

The car's engine was running, and it pulled from the curb as she approached. She stopped and watched as a girl—maybe mid-twenties, wearing large sunglasses—passed without looking at her.

Dark hair. Maybe Isabella Candella herself?

Hm.

She spoke the car's license plate into her phone and stopped recording.

Slipping into her vehicle, Shee sat in the air conditioning long enough to search the girlfriend's name online. She found a few of the girl's social media accounts and forwarded them to Croix back at the Loggerhead to explore.

This is Xander Andino's girlfriend. See if you can find anything about where she or he is, she texted.

Ooh, can I?, returned Croix.

Shee lowered her phone.

Smartass.

Normally, she liked to do her own research, but she never tired of sending her father's young protégé mindless tasks to remind her who was in charge. After all, she was Mick's *real* daughter. By coming home, she'd instantly bumped Croix down the pecking order, much to the girl's chagrin.

Croix never missed a chance to push *her* buttons. She was only returning the favor.

Totally immature.

A lot of fun.

She couldn't let the girl know how much she respected her. That would be a *total* disaster.

Shee checked online and found a *Robert Candella* not far away in the neighborhood the senator had suggested she search.

Good place to start.

She'd gotten lucky with the name. If Xander had decided to date a Maria Lopez or Jennifer Jones, it might have taken her a month to narrow down the possibilities.

Shee drove to the Candella address and pulled to the curb across the street from a neat, French-country-style home in an upper-middle-class neighborhood. From the senator's description of the girl, she'd expected less.

Another surprise sat in the driveway of the home—the car she'd seen parked across from the Andino residence.

She smiled.

Two birds, one stone.

Maybe *three* birds. The boy could be holed up at the house. The girl might have been casing the Andino house, maybe to clue Xander in on a safe time for more looting.

Shee tapped her steering wheel, thinking. She had two options. She could lay in wait, hoping to catch a glimpse of the boy, or she could knock on the door and *demand* to see him. Could be the girl's parents weren't privy to their daughter's shenanigans and would cough him up at the first sign of trouble. Worst case scenario, she could always *still* case the house...

Yep. Time to knock.

Shee left her vehicle and walked along the home's flagstone path, feeling upbeat.

This might be the fastest case ever.

She knocked on the door. A few seconds later, a female voice called out something, and the door opened on the young woman she'd seen in the black Nissan.

The girl paled.

"Can I help you?" she asked, straightening.

Shee smiled.

We're pretending I didn't see you. Cute.

"I'm here about Xander," she said.

The girl's eyes saucered. "Are you police?"

Now it was Shee's turn to be surprised. The girl looked...*relieved?*

Before Shee could answer, a voice called from deeper inside the house.

"Who is it?"

A woman hurried around the corner. Shee wasn't sure if she'd ever seen anyone so disappointed to see her.

"It's not her, Mama," said the girl. "It's the police."

"I'm not police," said Shee.

The woman's expression drooped another inch. She looked as though she might cry.

Shee grimaced.

I can't stop breaking this poor woman's heart.

The girl seemed angered by Shee's admission.

"Then you work for the Andinos?" she asked.

Shee nodded, seeing no point in pretending otherwise. "They've asked me to find Xander. Are you Isabella?"

The girl shook her head. "I'm her sister, Carolina. And it's *Izzy* who's missing, not that ass—"

The mother walked up to place a hand on her daughter's shoulder, effectively shutting her up.

"If you find him, will you find her, too?" she asked.

Carolina jerked from her mother's touch. "She works for the *Andinos*. She doesn't care—"

"Shush." The mother eased her daughter aside to make way for Shee's entry. "Come sit down. Could you find her? Have you found *anything*?"

The woman took Shee's wrist and pulled her toward the kitchen at the back of the house as Carolina closed the door behind them. The mother motioned to a wooden kitchen chair.

"Sit."

Shee did as she was told. The women claimed chairs across from her.

"She didn't come home," said the mother.

"From camping. They went together, but he came back alone," said Carolina. She seemed to have resigned herself to Shee's presence.

"You haven't seen her since they left together?" asked Shee.

Mama wrung her hands together. "No. Nothing. Not a phone call since the second day."

"How long ago was that?"

"Almost a month."

Shee's eyes popped wide. "A *month*?"

Carolina nodded. "They were walking the Appalachian Trail. But *he* came back, and I saw him—on *accident* or I wouldn't have even known he—" The girl's anger seemed to reignite. "Why are you looking for *him*?"

"His father said he came back and then left again. When

did you see him?"

"I saw him in his camper van a few days ago. The one he took with Izzy. I assumed she was with him, but I didn't see her. When she didn't come home, I went to his house, but he wouldn't come out. I couldn't get past the housekeeper."

Shee sympathized. She knew something about Yolanda's hospitality.

"Xander wouldn't talk to us," said the mother. "And the big senator thinks he's too *important* to talk to us."

"You've tried to talk to him?"

"We've knocked. We've called. We've *begged* him to help us find Izzy, but he won't answer. And the police—they won't consider her missing because she's with *his* son. He tells them they're camping."

"Do you think they could be camping again?" asked Shee.

"No way. She stopped posting." Carolina pulled her phone from her pocket and navigated to an account Shee recognized as Izzy's. "The last post was a few days before he came back. She *never* stops posting. It's her *life*."

Shee considered this. Maybe Izzy went dark in preparation for Xander's theft and their eventual elopement. She didn't want to tell the Candellas about the Picasso. Not yet. As much as she hadn't warmed to Nic Andino's charms, he *was* her client.

"Can you think of a place they might run off to together? A place they might elope to?" she asked.

"*Elope*?" The mother seemed horrified. "She would *never* do that to me."

Carolina smacked the tabletop. "*He came back.*"

Shee nodded. "I'm not saying that isn't weird, but he left again. She might have been waiting for him somewhere."

"Why would he go home on his own?" asked Carolina.

Shee shrugged. "Maybe to pick up some things. What do you think of him? Do you think he could hurt your daughter?"

She expected the women to grow angry, but they seemed confused.

"No," admitted Carolina. "He's kind of..." She looked at her mother for help with her thoughts.

"He's a nervous guy," said her mother.

Carolina nodded. "That's it. He's jumpy. Shy."

She wasn't surprised. She suspected his father's austere love had been sucking the confidence out of him his whole life.

Izzy's mother mumbled to herself. "Do you really think they eloped? Why? Why would she do this to me?"

"Young love rarely makes smart choices," offered Shee. "Let's assume they're together. Can you think of anywhere they might go?"

"No, no, no..." The mother's head shook, but she didn't look up. She seemed to have checked out.

Shee directed her attention to the sister. She seemed strangely still.

"Did you think of something?" she prompted.

Carolina frowned. "When you said elope..." She glanced at her phone and swiped around for a moment. "I found this place in her browser history."

Shee took the phone and scrolled through a website for a vacation destination—an expensive-looking resort on a private island in the Bahamas, specializing in "fun and freedom" for twenty-somethings.

Tagline: *It's all about YOU.*

It took Shee a moment to realize the *name* of the resort was *YOU.* The word sat at the top center of the page in all caps, flanked by what looked like off-kilter angel wings on either side as if the logo were struggling to become airborne.

YOU. Just like the scribble on the scrap of paper she'd found.

She scrolled through a gallery of photos featuring young people grinning, both poolside and seaside.

Flipping to the next page, a large, colorful banner slid into place at the top of the page.

BECOME *YOU*.

It seemed like a great place to launch a new life.

A great place for a honeymoon.

"She had it bookmarked on her school laptop. She didn't

take it with her," said Carolina.

Shee forwarded the link to her phone. "I'm going to look into this. I'm sending myself a text so you have my contact information. I'll let you know if I find anything, and you let me know if you think of anything else. Deal?"

She returned Carolina's phone and stood. As she did, the mother grabbed her wrist again.

"Anything. *Please*," she begged, squeezing.

Shee put her hand on the woman's. "I'll keep you in the loop. I promise."

Isabella's mother nodded and released her.

Shee headed for the exit as Carolina rushed ahead to open the door for her.

"Call or text me anytime," she said. "*Anything* you need."

"Will do."

Shee said her goodbyes and left the house, the Candellas' desperation palpable on her skin.

The women were scared.

She didn't blame them.

Something wasn't right.

CHAPTER FOUR

Eighteen Years Ago, New York City

Ollie Lopes spotted his mark, a brown-haired man in a shiny suit, walking toward him on the corner of Wall and Broad Streets.

Just a little further. That's it...

This sucker was *perfect.* Cell phone in hand, distracted, yapping, suit jacket flapping open—honestly, Ollie could walk away with the idiot's tighty-whities, and the man wouldn't notice.

Ollie adjusted his ill-fitting police uniform and stepped from his spot to clip the man with his shoulder.

"Sorry, buddy," he said, righting the man as they jostled. He kept his voice low and gruff.

The man's expression lit with anger. He glared, his attention dropped to the police uniform—and then his fury dissipated as fast as a shallow puddle on an August day.

"Excuse *me*, officer," he said. He flashed a nervous smile and moved on.

Ollie grinned. The marks always looked flustered when a cop knocked into them—like they might be hauled to jail for the trespass. It didn't matter that Ollie was at least twenty-five years the man's junior—his father's uniform changed the power dynamic.

Ollie rifled through the wallet he'd plucked from the Wall Street schmuck's jacket pocket.

Like candy from a—

"Ollie."

A cop—a *real* cop—appeared in front of him so suddenly Ollie stumbled back to avoid smacking into him. As he lurched, he slipped Mr. Wall Street's loaded wallet into his pocket.

Ollie stretched his smile as wide as he could without breaking his face.

"Hey, Uncle Jim. How you doin'?"

Jim Paretsky, Ollie's father's ex-partner, glowered at him from beneath patches of graying eyebrow hair so thick only a gas-powered weedwhacker could make a dent in them.

"You little prick. Don't *Uncle Jim* me," said the officer.

"Sorry. I meant, *Officer Paretsky*."

"You know that's not what I mean." Paretsky poked him in the chest hard enough that it made him cough. "Whatcha got on there, Ollie?"

Ollie looked down. "This? I'm going to a costume party."

"Like Halloween?"

"Yeah."

"It's *May*."

Ollie held out his palms in mea culpa and shrugged, holding his shoulder against the side of his neck as if it had stuck there. "You know kids. We're *crazy*."

Jim explored the inside of his cheek with his tongue and squinted as if he could melt Ollie with the heat of his glare.

"You know what's crazy? We got a report of a young man dressed like an officer pickpocketing people on Wall Street."

Ollie gasped. *"Really?"*

"Really. You wouldn't know anything about that, would you?"

"No..." Ollie peered past the officer to a place far away, where he wished he could be.

"Put out your hands," said Jim.

"Hm? Look. I've got nothing—"

Jim clamped his hands on Ollie's arms, forcing out his hands for inspection. The officer slapped a pair of cuffs on one wrist.

Ollie hadn't seen the cuffs coming. He whistled, impressed.

"Damn. That was pretty good, Jim."

"You're not the only one with moves." The old man continued to scowl at him, but Ollie could tell he'd been pleased by the compliment.

But enough is enough.

"Well, that was fun. Let me go. I'll head home."

Ollie raised his captured hand, presenting the keyhole of the cuff for easy unlocking. His other hand, he tucked behind his back to keep it from joining its partner's fate.

Jim held Ollie's cuffed wrist, wrapped in his fat sausage fingers.

"Give me the other hand."

Ollie's eyebrows bobbed skyward. "No way."

"Give it."

"*No.*"

They remained deadlocked, staring at each other as passing pedestrians sneaked glances at their drama. One man parked himself a few feet away to watch the exchange as if they were on stage.

Ollie rolled his eyes in the direction of the gawker.

"You want me to get you some popcorn?"

The man looked at Jim as if asking for permission to stay.

"Beat it," said the officer.

With a huff, the man wandered off.

Ollie smiled at Jim. "See what we can do when we work together?"

Paretsky didn't seem to appreciate the sentiment.

"Ollie, damn it, I promised your dad I'd watch out for you."

Something about the man's tone struck Ollie as strange. It made a googly feeling pass through his stomach.

Clearing his throat, he doubled down his *tough kid* act. "Are you arresting me?"

"I am. If that's what it takes."

Ollie grimaced to hide a smile.

Jim said *if.*

He wasn't arresting him.

Ollie relaxed. "I didn't even *do* anything," he muttered.

That was a mistake.

Paretsky jerked the cuffs, and with his opposite hand, grabbed the fabric of Ollie's upper sleeve.

"Shut up. Stop it. I mean it, Ollie, it's time to *stop it*. You're wearing your father's *uniform*. It's a disgrace."

"It's not a crime."

"Actually, it *is*. It's called *impersonating an officer*."

"I haven't told anyone I'm a cop—"

Eyes flashing white, Paretsky shook him. Ollie thought his eyes might tumble out of his head.

The officer spit words at him like bullets.

"You're wearing the f—"

Paretsky stopped.

He hung his head, shoulders rising and falling with each measured breath.

His stillness frightened Ollie.

When the officer looked up again, he seemed less angry.

Ollie swallowed. He thought he and his father's partner had a good thing—he broke the law a *little*, Paretsky gave him *the speech*, and then they went on their way to do it all over again later.

Something had changed.

Paretsky started over his voice low.

"If I check your pockets, am I gonna find any wallets with other people's names in them?"

Ollie's battery of smartass comments, unstoppable as a sneeze, failed to find his lips. The hairs on the back of his neck started to dance.

Is Jim crying?

Paretsky slapped at his eyes as if angered by his tears.

"You've used your last pass, kiddo," he said. "I can't do it anymore. Your mother's at her wit's end, did you know that?"

Ollie looked away. His cheeks felt hot. It wasn't fair of Paretsky to bring up his mother.

"Unless..." Jim cocked his head to the side as if an idea had just occurred to him.

A sense of foreboding draped over Ollie.

"Unless what?" he asked.

"I need you to stop this. *Permanently.*"

Ollie nodded. "Done. I'll stop."

Paretsky shook a finger back and forth in front of his face. "No, *no*, buddy. I'm not taking your word. Not again. I can only think of two ways this ends."

"What ways?"

"Option one, you go to jail."

Ollie laughed. "I'll take option two."

"Option two, you enlist."

Ollie's grin died on his face.

"Enlist? Like in the *Army*?"

Paretsky nodded. "Army was good enough for your dad. If you like water better, try Navy. I don't care."

"How 'bout Boy Scouts?"

"I'm serious. I'm *done*. I can't let you float around breaking your mother's heart like this anymore."

Ollie's shoulders slumped.

Again with his mother. It made him wonder...

Am I breaking my mother's heart?

She'd said as much before, but he hadn't taken her *seriously*. That was something mothers said, like *put on a coat* and *have you eaten anything?*

Had she been crying on Jim's shoulder?

When he didn't answer, Jim pulled a key from his pocket and unlocked the cuff.

"Take off the uniform. Give it to me," he said.

Ollie rubbed his wrist as Jim hooked the cuffs to his belt.

"Take it off *here*? Are you crazy?"

"At least the jacket. Hand it over."

Scowling, Ollie removed his jacket and handed it over, shivering in his white tee shirt as the November wind funneling down Wall Street cut through him.

Paretsky tucked the jacket under his arm. "I'll give you a day or two to think. I'll check in with you and your mom a week from today. Either you're packin' to ship out, or I'm taking you in." He paused and then added, "I'll make sure you're convicted, too. Don't worry about that."

"You've got nothin'," muttered Ollie.

"You wanna take the chance? They *love* fresh young meat like you in prison."

Ollie recoiled. He *was* a pretty kid. He'd been told as much his whole life. At a buck-fifty soaking wet, Paretsky had one thing right: prison would eat him alive.

The officer put one of his giant paws on Ollie's shoulder. He didn't shake him this time. He peered into his eyes.

"One of these days, you're going to scam the wrong person and end up dead, kid. You're not a scrapper."

Ollie swallowed. "I'm fast."

Jim chuckled. "Right. I just caught you, and I'm built like an air conditioning unit."

Ollie's gaze dropped to the pavement.

The old guy had a point.

With a knuckle, Paretsky lifted Ollie's chin until he couldn't help but make eye contact.

"You're at a crossroads, Ollie. Make the smart choice." The big man took a step back and held out an open palm. Ollie stared at it a moment, confused, and then, with a healthy dose of resigned indignation, fished in his pants pocket for the wallet he'd lifted from the Wall Street guy. He handed it over.

Paretsky stared at him a moment longer, slapping the wallet against his open palm as if it were a blackjack sap. Shaking his head, he turned and strolled away without another word.

Ollie leaned his back against the building beside him and wrapped his skinny arms around his chest. Paretsky *had* found the perfect way to end his day's activities. He'd have to get home before he froze to death.

His father's partner would have to return the uniform. He'd get a chewing out, but then his mother would hide it in one of her usual hiding places, and he'd find it again. He'd stay away from Paretsky's beat for his next fishing expedition. Maybe try downtown.

Ollie took the subway back to the Bronx, Paretsky's words running in his head no matter how much he tried to think about other things.

Army.

He scoffed.

The guy was *crazy.*

He rushed the half-mile walk from the subway to his house, the wind chapping his cheeks.

Two blocks from his house, the first punch struck his jaw.

The blow knocked Ollie's head sharply to the left. He stumbled off the curb into the street. Before he could turn and focus on his attacker, he heard footsteps approaching. Someone was coming from the other side of the street. *Running.*

This is bad.

He tried to scramble away. The new guy tackled him at the waist, and he flew forward, the skin on his palms peeling as he blocked his teeth from the cement.

The first guy kicked him. Had to be the first guy—the second guy was still on top of him, trying to flip him on his back.

"You think you're funny stealin' wallets?" asked one of them.

Ollie raised his arms in time to block a punch aimed at his left eye, only to take a smack in his right. The blow came out of nowhere.

How many guys are there?

"We catch you griftin' again we're going to break every finger on both yer hands," said a different voice.

Another kick to the side. Someone had hold of his wrists. Ollie fought to ball up, to keep the blows from his fragile internal organs and that *pretty* face. No one would fall for a toothless con man covered in battle scars. He had to protect his assets.

After another minute, the blows stopped raining.

"What a waste," said one of the men. The voice was farther

away. "You or me coulda handled that skinny Spic. Didn't need us both."

Ollie peeked through his forearms.

He was alone.

His mouth throbbed. Ollie touched his lip, and his fingers came back crimson.

Groaning, he sat up.

What was *that?*

He didn't make a habit of lifting wallets from thugs for a myriad of obvious reasons. Maybe one of his victims hired them? They talked as if that was the case.

Rich people did all sorts of crazy stuff.

Ollie wiped the blood from his face as best he could. If his mother saw his fat lip, she'd either burst into tears or smack him herself. He never knew which.

His eye throbbed. He sighed.

Pathetic.

He hadn't gotten one swing in. Not one punch. He'd balled up like one of those pill bugs, and they'd stomped on him like one.

Maybe Paretsky had a point.

He had no plans to stop grifting—that would be like Babe Ruth quitting baseball in his prime. He *could* use some fighting skills, though. Maybe the Army would provide.

His dad had been a badass.

Enlisting would make his mom *and* Paretsky happy, keep them off his back, teach him skills, and cost him nothing. Hell, they'd pay *him.*

Maybe it's not such a crazy idea...

He wouldn't be giving in.

He'd be playing the long con.

CHAPTER FIVE

Retired Navy Commander Mason Connelly slid his notepad to the side. Reconsidering, he moved it back in front of him. He shifted in his seat and squeezed the spot where his right leg entered the cuff of his prosthetic, a habit from when his stump had ached on a more regular basis.

His curly-haired mutt of undetermined lineage, Archie, popped up from beneath the table. Throwing Mason a stink-eye, he wandered across the room to flop back down in the corner. Mason guessed he'd bumped the sleeping dog with his fake foot.

Sorry, buddy.

He glanced at the clock on the wall and compared it to his watch. The clock was off by a minute. He took a deep breath and tapped a drum solo on the table with his fingertips.

Why am I so nervous?

He'd led SEALs into battle. Why would interviewing someone for the Loggerhead's team have him flustered?

Only one answer made sense:

Mick McQueen.

Mick had entrusted him to make decisions on hiring. He hadn't thought much about the responsibility until he sat in the breakfast room—half an hour too early—and waited for his first interview to arrive.

Back at the Naval Special Warfare Training Center in Coronado, California, a million years ago, Mick had been *his* teacher. He didn't want to disappoint, and Mick wasn't always the easiest guy to impress.

He didn't want to lose the Loggerhead now that he'd

landed. He'd never admit it, but he'd felt a little *lost* after retiring. He'd only known the Navy, and it didn't help to suddenly find himself one leg short of a pair.

As Shee would joke, for retirement, he needed a leg up.

Ha.

She was another complication. Disappoint Mick and he'd be disappointing his daughter, too. Unlike his legs, those two came as a pair, whether *they'd* admit it or not—

Mason's attention flicked upward as a head popped through the entrance.

"You Mason?" asked the man attached to the pointy beard leading the way.

Mason stood and cleared his throat.

"Ollie?"

Beard nodded and took three long strides to move in for a handshake. Halfway through the interaction, he bumped past Mason to squat next to Archie and rub the dog's ears.

"He yours? Good-lookin' dog."

"Yes. Thank you." Mason motioned to the chair next to his spot at the head of the wooden dining table. "Have a seat."

Ollie left the dog and sat at the table, his head bobbing as if a catchy tune reverberated inside his skull. He wore an untucked high-end polo, khaki shorts, and loafers.

Mason wasn't sure what to make of him.

The guy was slim but fit, average height. Olive skin with striking light-hazel eyes. He hadn't dressed for an *interview*, per se, but looked put-together. The dossier Mick provided him with said Ollie had been career Army, but nothing about him said *military*. The sculpted beard and longish hair slicked back from the widow's peak of his forehead—sides short but not *military* short—no visible scars or tattoos... The man sported none of the usual soldier clichés. In addition, Ollie had a *lightness* about him. Career soldiers rarely felt so *breezy*.

"So, uh, Army, hm?" said Mason, looking at his blank legal pad as if the words were printed there.

Ollie's head-bobbing accelerated to a full nod. "Yup.

Eighteen years, believe it or not."

"Eighteen? It says here you finished a captain?"

Mason read the line again.

That can't be right. After eighteen years?

Ollie shrugged a shoulder.

"I might have gotten knocked back a few times."

Mason frowned.

What's Mick's interest in this goofball?

He tapped his pen, trying to manifest a tactful way to ask Ollie what was *wrong* with him, besides the fact he was a bozo. The Loggerhead Inn collected broken soldiers who still had something to prove. This guy looked as if he'd be heading right to the golf course following the interview. He'd come in on two good legs, shook hands with two good arms, had no head scars, and didn't seem depressed...

Only now did he realize Mick had provided him with precious little information about Ollie.

Nothing to do but ask.

"So, Ollie, what brings you here?"

"Cook," said the man.

Mason scowled. He'd expected a little more than an inscrutable one-word answer.

"You want to *cook*?

Ollie shook his head. "No, *Cook*. Capital C. He said this might be the place for me."

Oh.

They'd recently lost the hotel's chef, Cook. He'd gone to live with his son out west. The Loggerhead's tendency to attract bad-guy attention had been more than Cook had bargained for. He wanted to stamp waffles for tourists without worrying about getting caught in the crossfire.

The *nerve.*

"Do *you* want to cook?" he asked.

Ollie laughed. "No. I can't boil water. My nickname was Pony."

Mason stared at him. When no further comment followed, he bit.

"I don't know what that means," he said. "*Pony.*"

"Oh. I'm a one-trick pony. Cooking isn't it."

Mason frowned as another silence ensued.

Bastard. He's going to make me ask.

Mason grit his teeth. "So what's *your* trick?"

Ollie sat back, smiling. His gaze shifted to Mason's hand and then back to his eyes.

Mason waited, mulling the different ways he could kill the guy.

Ollie's eyes shifted again, this time with a subtle head nod. Drawn by the action, Mason glanced at his hand.

The tan line where his watch usually perched stared back at him.

No watch.

His attention snapped back to Ollie.

"You took my watch?"

Ollie grinned and produced Mason's black Luminox from beneath the table, dangling it from his fingers.

"Cheesy, I know," he said, handing it back.

Mason clasped the watch back on his wrist, wondering if Ollie wanted to see the trick where he made the idiot's *teeth* disappear. He guessed the theft had happened when Ollie bumped him on his way to the dog.

"So you're a *thief*," he said.

"The prestidigitation's a hobby." Ollie beamed as if he'd been waiting all day to use the word *prestidigitation*. He paused, apparently waiting to see if his million-dollar word pulled a reaction from Mason.

Mason didn't flinch.

Ollie continued. "In the Army, the term for me is *procurement officer*. I get things people need, one way or another."

Mason nodded. That made more sense. He'd known more than his fair share of sneaky procurement officers.

"Gotcha. Handy talent to have in the Army."

Ollie shrugged. "I enlisted with low expectations—turns

out Army life fit me like a glove."

"You're a conman and thief." Mason made a peace sign. "That's *two* tricks."

Ollie's expression broadened. "That's an *excellent* point. You can still call me Pony."

Mason nodded. He had no intention of calling the guy *Pony*.

A cagey way to inquire about Ollie's shortcomings popped to mind.

"I imagine your skills would be useful in a lot of places," he said. "Did Cook mention why he thought *this* would be a good place for you?"

Ollie's permanent expression of amusement flickered like a faulty movie strip. His smile returned in no time, but Mason had clocked the droop in his grin.

"You want to know what's wrong with me," Ollie said, more as a statement than a question.

"We only have so many beds. We like to help the soldiers and sailors who need it most."

Ollie's gaze lingered on the large, gnarly scar peeking out from the sleeve of Mason's upper right arm. He leaned to the side to glance under the table.

"Guess there's no hiding your handicap," he said, motioning. "Is that all it takes to get in this joint? A quick dance on a landmine?"

Mason bristled but refused to take the bait.

"You're *more* qualified?"

"You could say that." Ollie looked away.

Mason waited for more. Nothing came. His patience packed up and left town.

"Are you going to make me ask again?"

He felt sure Ollie heard the annoyance in his tone, but the soldier didn't flinch. Instead, he leaned forward, his gaze locked with Mason's.

"I think for now I'm going to leave that between me and Mick, Commander."

Mason realized Mick had already talked to Ollie. Someone—Mick, maybe Cook—had talked to the guy *enough* that he knew

Mason's retirement rank.

The guy knows more about me than I know about him.

Why would Mick ask him to interview the idiot if they'd already talked? Any way he tried to spin things, he looked out of the loop.

He and Mick needed to talk.

For now, he decided to wrap up with some standard questions.

"How are you with a weapon?"

Ollie looked sheepish. "That might be how I originally got the nickname. I'm not great. I'll hit center mass in a pinch, but if you're looking for someone to shoot the flame off a candle, I'm not your guy."

Mason lost the will to continue. It was clear Mick had already given Ollie the thumbs up. Maybe the old man just wanted to make him feel *involved*. Maybe he wanted to make sure Mason didn't *hate* Ollie.

He supposed he didn't hate him.

He didn't *like* him...

A phone rang, and Mason recognized the tone. He patted his pocket before realizing the sound had come from Ollie's direction.

"I have the same ring," he said.

He winced, already realizing the truth.

Ollie chuckled as he produced Mason's ringing phone from his pocket.

Sonuvabitch.

CHAPTER SIX

Shee rolled into The Loggerhead Inn's parking lot, parked, and left the air on while she called YOU to work her best lead.

She felt the stretch of a tiny smirk on her face.

I might be able to wrap this up before I even get out of the car.

"Good morning. It's all about YOU," answered a woman.

After a lifetime of responding to questions like *How can I help you?* or a nice neat, *Hello?* Shee found herself fleetingly baffled as to how to continue.

So corny...

"Hello?" prompted the woman.

Shee snapped from her spell. "Oh, hi, yes—I'm looking for Xander Andino, please?"

"I'm sorry. We don't have anyone by that name here."

Shee frowned. The woman had answered *immediately.* No time to tap on a keyboard. Either she'd memorized the guest list, or she'd been instructed to never let anyone know who was staying on the island.

Rich kids.

She tried another angle. Maybe someone less famous?

"How about last name, Candella?"

"I'm sorry."

Miffed, Shee squinted at the scrap of paper she'd taken from Xander's. The number didn't match the phone number of the resort.

Reservation number?

"Hold on, I have a reservation number," she said, rattling

off the digits.

"I'm sorry," said the woman on the other end of the line, cheery as could be. "That's not one of our reservation numbers."

Shee huffed.

Well, this isn't turning out like I'd hoped.

If Xander and Isabella were on the run after robbing his father, they might have used a fake name. In her experience, people on the lam tended to stick with their first name and only changed the last...

"Anyone named Isabella or Xander, maybe with a different last name?"

"I'm sorry, ma'am."

Shee glowered at her steering wheel. The woman had called her *ma'am,* which meant she sounded old on the phone. How depress—

Hold on.

That gives me an idea.

"Listen," she said, trying to find a tone that blended both haughty anger and concern. "This is his *mother,* and it's very important I talk to him."

The ruse didn't even ding the woman's armor.

"I'm sorry," she answered without hesitation.

With a grunt of insincere thanks, Shee hung up and glared at the inn's front porch.

Foiled again.

It seemed cracking the case wouldn't be as easy as making an international phone call. She'd have Croix call back later when the next shift might be manning the phones. Maybe they'd get lucky and connect with a newbie, less adept at thwarting inquiries.

Shee headed back into the hotel, stopping to high-five their enormous doorman as she entered.

"Hey, Bracco."

The big man grinned. "Flappy back."

Shee pointed at him. "Hey, pretty good. Making progress."

Bracco suffered aphasia from head trauma during his last

tour of duty. His body made an excellent sentry at the door, but his brain scrambled words inside his basketball-sized skull. Little he said came out the way he meant it. He'd been going to speech therapy, and she thought "flappy back" was pretty close to an appropriate response to being high-fived. Progress, no doubt.

Shee strode to the front desk. Croix looked up from her perch behind the counter.

"Oh, it's you," she said.

Shee ignored the open hostility.

"Do you know how to flirt?" asked Shee.

Croix scowled. "You're not my type."

Shee pulled out her phone and held it up for Croix to see. "What do you think of this place?"

Croix took the phone from her and scrolled through the YOU website, her lip curling higher with every swipe.

"*Ew*," she said, handing the phone back to Shee. "It's like a hookup resort for douchebags. Going trolling for fresh young meat?"

"Yeah, *no*. I'm sure they wouldn't let my old ass within two hundred yards of the place."

"Obviously. But why would you *want* to go there? It's probably covered with venereal diseases."

"That's a lovely thought." Shee sighed. "You might not be the person."

"For what?"

"I might need someone to go in there. Undercover."

"Oh." Croix perked and then deflated almost as quickly. "And pretend to be *into it*?"

"That would help. Mingle. Flirt."

"You mean, like, *talk* to these people? Play volleyball in a bikini and do keg stands? That sort of thing?"

"If that's what it takes."

Croix chewed her lip and grunted. Any interest the girl had in the assignment seemed to fade.

Shee took back her phone. "I'll get back to you. Where's Mason?"

"In the break room getting ready for an interview."

Shee took a few steps in that direction and then stopped.

Hold on...

She had a *great* idea.

Shee went to her room to use the larger screen of her laptop as she scrolled through the YOU website. The story behind the place seemed pretty straightforward, though it related a 'history' without sharing any *real* information at all. All it revealed was that someone with a stupid amount of money had bought the Bahamian private island and turned it into an exclusive resort, catering to the spawn of the rich and famous.

The more she swiped through the website's photo gallery, the more she wanted to return in her next life as a billionaire's daughter. The place was *amazing*. As a rule, Bahamian islands were little more than coral outcroppings covered in scrubby pines and shrubs, but somehow YOU looked like a lush jungle retreat. How did they keep all the greenery alive? There had to be mega-expensive desalination equipment to keep the plants watered. That's *before* they built the network of private bungalows, the three infinity pools, or hired the chef poached from the King of Belgium's private staff...

YOU took pains to hide the identities of its guests, though she did find a testimonial from a young Arabian prince gushing about how YOU was the only place he felt at peace.

Heartwarming, but it didn't matter for her case.

How had Xander afforded YOU? Isabella's family appeared upper middle class but not chillin'-with-the-prince-of-Jordan rich. She couldn't have been much help with the finances. Nic said his Picasso sketch was only worth a few thousand. A few thousand more had been taken from his drawer. It probably cost that much just to *get* to the island.

YOU didn't have prices listed on the website, but she imagined a bungalow cost more than all of Xander's birthday and Christmas gift savings combined.

And if the couple was running off to start a new life together—to live a life presumably far away from Nic Andino's largess—why would they drop a sizable chunk of their nest egg on a vacation?

Granted, no one would think to look for them at YOU. And maybe Xander had saved up more than she, as a Naval officer's daughter, could comfortably imagine. She'd have Croix call the Andinos and do a little digging on the kid's allowance and resources. Maybe Xander had a side hustle they didn't know about.

Still, YOU seemed like an excellent lead. It had shown up behind Xander's creepily impersonal artwork *and* on Isabella's computer. And if they could crack the cone of silence over the place or sneak someone in there for a day, they could either solve the case or check it off the list of possibilities.

Shee searched the website for a place to book a room, discovering instead what amounted to an *application*. YOU wanted to know a little bit about her before they shared any more information—name, address, age, who referred her.

Hm. This might be tougher than I thought.

She needed to invent a girl YOU would love.

First, a rich-sounding name...

She did an Internet search for "rich girl names."

"MacKenzie" stood out.

Perfect.

She typed it into the 'name' field and then tapped the side of her phone, pondering a last name for her fictional rich girl.

Kennedy? Hilton? Too obvious and too easy to crosscheck. She hated to lock into a last name. It paid to remain fluid when it came to backstory—

She smiled.

What about *no* last name.

MacKenzie fancies herself more of a *Beyonce, Madonna,* single-name type girl.

Of course, she does.

Shee snorted a laugh as she moved to the rest of the short form.

"Just MacKenzie" was twenty-five, landing smack in the middle of YOU's acceptable age range. For address, she moved one island north of the Loggerhead's home in Jupiter Beach to Jupiter *Island*—a favorite home base location for sports figures, celebrities, and captains of industry. She left off street name and house number. MacKenzie didn't have time for things like that.

She stopped short on the next field.

Referral.

That would be more difficult. They wanted a name and an email, which implied they'd check the validity of the referrer.

Hm.

She couldn't use Xander—after all, if he was *there*, they could ask him if he knew the enigmatic MacKenzie.

She hopped to social media and searched for people posting about their vacations to YOU. Nothing came up.

How is that possible?

Young people and social media were like chocolate and peanut butter.

Time to try another angle. She uploaded a photo pulled off the YOU website to *image search*. The shot of an infinity pool anchored by a large winged-man statue seemed specific enough to trigger a match.

Bingo.

The YOU website itself popped up, but so did *Piper's Fashion Passion* at PipersFashionPassion.com, the personal fashion blog of a wealthy Texas financier's daughter. Shee clicked through.

Can't tell you where I am, but I am forever changed! read Piper's post caption. In the photo, the girl toasted the camera from her spot at the foot of the winged statue.

And there's our referral.

The post was a few years old, so chances were good Piper wasn't currently at the resort.

Shee logged into her domain registrar account and bought the domain *PipersPassion.com*, which happened to be available. Once it cleared, she created an email alias, so any email sent to piper@piperspassion.com would be forwarded to Shee's own *real* email address.

Eat your heart out, Croix. You're not the only one with some tech-savvy.

Now, anyone at YOU checking with Piper to see how she felt about MacKenzie would be sending an email to Shee, who would give MacKenzie a *glowing* recommendation.

Returning to the YOU form, she typed Piper's name in the referral section and added the newly created email alias as Piper's contact information.

Now she needed an email for MacKenzie. Setting up a free Gmail account didn't feel like something MacKenzie would do, so she popped back to the domain registrar. MacKenzie.com was taken, of course. She grabbed MacKenzieRules.com—suffered a moment of regret wondering if kids still said *rules*—and then set up another email to forward to *her* address.

She added Mac@MacKenzieRules.com to the form.

She'd decided Mac was MacKenzie's nickname.

She hit SUBMIT.

Ta da!

The page refreshed to a message nestled between two palm trees.

Thank you. We'll be in touch.

Shee smiled.

Lucky me. I'm so honored.

She snapped shut the laptop, snatched her phone from where she'd tossed it on her bed, and called Charlotte.

She'd had another *amazing* idea.

"Hi," said her daughter on the opposite side of the line, like a normal person.

Shee grinned. She couldn't help it. The whole *having a daughter* thing was surprisingly wonderful.

"How would you like to be an insanely wealthy girl named MacKenzie?" she asked.

"Uh... I think I'm pretty happy with being me..."

"I need someone in their twenties to pose as a rich kid on a tropical resort."

Charlotte squeaked like a stepped-on dog toy. "Ooh—In that case, I'd *love* to be MacKenzie. This is for a job?"

"Yep. Bonafide Loggerhead mission. Not dangerous. Just need you to look around, and I'm afraid in a resort full of twenty-somethings, I'd stick out like an aging thumb. You're in?"

"Call me *MacKenzie*," said Charlotte.

She sounded excited. That was the response Shee'd been hoping to get from Croix.

You snooze, you lose, Croix.

"Great. I guess I need to clear paying for all this with Mick, but I'll give you a call to confirm. We'll probably fly out of Ft. Lauderdale, so I'll need you to drive here."

"How soon?"

"Maybe as soon as tomorrow?"

"Sure. Anything you want me to bring with me?"

"Do you have anything in *rich girl resort wear*?"

Charlotte snorted a laugh. "Probably not."

"I'll figure it out. What size are you?"

"Six." Charlotte paused and then added. "Thank you for thinking of me for this..."

"Thanks for being a badass daughter." Shee raised her hand to her mouth.

Whoops. Are you supposed to call your daughter a badass?

Charlotte giggled. "I'll see if I can borrow anything from the fashionistas in the neighborhood. See you soon."

Shee hung up, beaming until she realized she still had to run her plan past her father, who'd then have to run it through Nic to be sure he got reimbursed for entry to YOU.

Better get on that.

CHAPTER SEVEN

Shee left her room and walked down the hall to knock on her father's door.

No answer.

Her phone dinged, and she saw YOU had already responded to her reference, Piper, with a letterheaded email.

Dear Piper,
We have a visit request from:
MacKenzie
Who has listed you as her referral. Please confirm this is the case.

Thank you,
YOU

Form letter. The response had come too fast. No doubt they had their site set up to automatically forward the confirmation note using the information from their form.

No human had looked into Piper or MacKenzie yet.

That's good.

Leaning against the wall, she prepared and sent a short email to YOU, posing as Piper. To keep complications to a minimum, she kept the content short and breezy.

Hi!
MacKenzie is the BEST. I know she'll love it there.
Love, Piper

She added a collection of upbeat emojis and hit send.

That oughta do it.

She took the elevator to the lobby and paused before disembarking to avoid smashing into Angelina, her father's on-again-off-again girlfriend, as the raven-haired hotel manager-slash-concierge clacked down the hall in her trademark black heels, black tights, and moody blouse.

If people were supposed to wear bright clothing and comfortable walking sandals in Florida, Angelina never got the memo.

"Hey—have you seen Dad—?" Shee called after her.

Angelina held up a hand as she headed for the front door. "No time."

Harley, Angelina's miniature Yorkie, barked from down the hall where she remained locked in her mommy's bedroom. She barked a second time and then whined, slowly accepting her fate.

Angelina strode through the front door as Bracco opened it with seasoned timing.

Shee wandered to the front desk, watching through the front windows as Angelina slid into her Jeep.

"What's up with her?" she asked Croix.

Croix's attention never left her phone. "I stopped asking a long time ago."

"Have you seen Mick?"

"No."

"Great. Good talking to you."

"Wish I could say the same."

Deep in thought, Shee walked into the Loggerhead's breakfast room. The morning's donuts had been devoured, but most of the fruit remained. The large silver coffee urn looked as if it had been manhandled by a swarm of sticky-fingered children. An obligatory torn creamer cup and swizzle stick sat discarded on the table beside it.

Shee tossed the trash in the clearly labeled garbage can

sitting not two feet away.

"*Tourists.* I swear—"

Someone cleared their throat in the opposite corner of the room and Shee spun to find two sets of eyes staring at her. Mason perched at the end of their custom-made aqua-painted dining table. Beside him sat a handsome, golden-tanned man in a blue polo, smaller-built than Mason but muscular in his sinewy way. His neck had the tight shiny look of a man who knew his way around a gym.

The stranger flashed a toothy grin nestled in a fantastically groomed ducktail beard. He seemed amused.

Mason looked...*agitated.*

"I'm sorry, my bad," she said, holding up a hand. "I didn't see you."

"We're done," said Mason.

"We're done," echoed the stranger, his gaze still locked on her.

Mason's dog appeared at Shee's feet, begging for pets. She squatted to oblige.

"Hello, Baby Bubba," she said, running her fingers through Archie's face fur. All her nicknames for him had something to do with his size. *Bubba, Gigantor, Goonytoons...* the pup had gained forty pounds since arriving at the hotel. She snuggled with him while inspecting the stranger from the corner of her eye.

New hire?

Whoever he was, he wasn't a terrible person to have around from an eye-candy point of view. She'd have to keep Angelina from corrupting him. Even in her sixties, the woman was a temptress.

Mason stood. The stranger remained seated long enough to make it seem as if Mason had stood too soon. The SEAL cleared his throat again.

"Are you Shee?" asked the man, seemingly oblivious to the glare Mason was burning into the top of his head.

"I am." Shee stepped around Archie to shake hands as the man stood. "And you are?"

He bowed with a flourish. "At your service."

He looked up at her from his bent position—another flash of that hungry grin.

Oh my.

"He's *Ollie*," said Mason. "Your father's new hire. Keep an eye on your watch."

"Hm?" Confused, Shee glanced down at her wrist.

Ollie feigned offense and then returned his attention to Shee. "It's nice to meet you. Your father told me a lot of impressive things about you."

Shee snorted a laugh. "Did you record it? I'd like to enter it into the record."

"Croix will get you a room," said Mason, a little louder than necessary. "She's at the front desk."

Ollie turned to him. "Aye aye, Commander."

Mason's expression remained rigid. Ollie offered a single head bob in Shee's direction, before walking out of the room in a relaxed, hands-in-pockets gait.

Shee watched him go before turning to Mason.

"Nice guy."

Mason remained staring at the door.

"Hm," he grunted.

"You couldn't have been ruder to him," she said.

That got his attention.

His head snapped in her direction. "*Me?*" He lifted his arm to show her the back of his wrist. "He stole my *watch*. He's lucky I didn't—"

His outburst faded to an unintelligible grumble as he registered Shee squinting at the watch on his wrist.

"He gave it *back*," he added, lowering his arm.

"So what is he? A magician?"

"A *thief*. A con artist. That's all we need. I don't know what Mick's thinking."

Again, his sentence was reduced to muttering.

Shee chuckled. "I don't know. We already have Angelina. Speaking of Mick, any idea where he is?"

"No." Mason picked up his empty notepad. "How'd your thing go?"

"Good. I'm sixty percent sure the kid eloped to YOU with his girlfriend."

"To where?"

"YOU. All caps. It's a resort for rich kids. Their slogan is *It's all about—*"

"*You.* Got it. Sounds perfect for a spoiled rich kid."

"Yup." She chewed on her lip, realizing she hadn't bounced her *Operation Undercover Charlotte* idea off of Mason, either. *Crap.* Maybe as her father, he should get a say? No rule said she *had* to get his permission; it's not like they were sharing parenting duties of a twenty-seven-year-old girl in any *real* way, but she had a vaguely guilty feeling tightening her chest.

"I'm too old to sneak in there myself," she said, laying the ensuing argument's foundation.

"You have to *go* there?" he asked.

"Maybe. I tried calling. It didn't work. They're either hiding him, or he checked in under a pseudonym."

"Or he's not there."

"That's possible too, but both he and his girlfriend had been researching the place before they disappeared."

Mason glanced at the door again. "You sending Croix?"

Shee squinted one eye. "She didn't seem interested, and I'm a little afraid she'd find it too hard to hide her loathing for everyone." She paused as Mason waited for her to continue. She'd been hoping he'd grab his notepad and rush out before she could finish.

"Uh, but I had this great idea—"

Mason's bulgy shoulders slumped an inch. "Oh."

"What?"

"I know what *I had a great idea* means."

She scoffed. "You don't know *anything*."

"Right. *Newsflash*—in the last thirty years, you haven't changed as much as you think."

She took a step toward him, leaning forward to punctuate her point. "For your information, *I had a great idea* means *I had a great idea."*

"Uh-huh. Like when we got caught drinking off Coronado, and you had the *great idea* of throwing a dead fish at the police boat chasing us."

Shee crossed her arms against her chest. "It's not my fault flounders are Frisbee-shaped."

"Nope. Not your fault at *all.* I spent the night in jail."

"No, you didn't. Dad came and picked us up."

He poked a finger at her. "He picked *you* up. He left me there overnight."

Shee giggled. "Probably worried you'd get me pregnant or something."

Shee watched a wash of red rise on Mason's cheeks and realized her face felt hot.

They tittered like school children.

Speaking of daughters...

Time to strike.

"I'm sending Charlotte," she said, as a sort of aside, as she headed for the door.

Mason's chuckles cut short.

"*Our* Charlotte?"

Damn. Almost made it.

She turned.

"Yes. She's *perfect.* She's gorgeous. It's a cushy mission. She can infiltrate the compound and locate the kid, and then, when she's safely back, we'll go in and pick him up."

Mason's mouth pressed into a hard line.

"You know she's capable," she added.

His jaw started working.

Is he grinding his teeth?

She plowed on.

"She's super excited about it. I'm telling you, this is a *cushy* case. Zero danger. I'm sending her to a *resort.* And it will give us some quality mother-daughter bonding time."

The visible tightness in Mason's shoulders eased a notch.

Ah. There it is.

How could he be mad about mother-daughter time?

He turned his palms to the ceiling. "I guess she's perfect for it. She's got good instincts." He nodded to himself for a moment. "She reminds me of you—the way you assess risk."

Shee cocked an eyebrow. "You make me sound like an insurance adjuster."

"She's coming here?" he asked.

"Tomorrow."

He smiled. "It'll be nice to see her."

Shee grinned.

"I know, right?"

CHAPTER EIGHT

Angelina drove her black Jeep to the Tempest Café's parking lot and pulled beside Mick's identical vehicle. The Loggerhead's staff had access to four Jeeps, though no staff member who wanted to stick around *ever* touched the one Angelina had claimed as her own.

She spotted Mick at a white plastic table overlooking the parking lot and headed in that direction. Tempest Café didn't have the most scenic outdoor dining, but Mick was a fan of the thick-cut maple-glazed bacon. Bacon obsession was a trait he'd passed to his daughter. Given the chance, she imagined he and Shee would strip a salted, roasted pig to bones in minutes like a pair of hungry piranha.

She lowered her baggy purse into one of the unused plastic chairs and sat.

"So what's with all the cloak and dagger?" she asked.

Mick raised his coffee mug to his lips. "I already ordered. I figured you weren't getting anything."

"Good guess. Little early for me." The server stopped by, and Angelina requested coffee before returning her attention to Mick, whose gaze had wandered to the bacon-covered plate of a nearby diner.

"Don't make a scene. Yours is coming," she said.

Mick seemed to wake from a dream. "Huh?"

"Nothing. What's going on? Why am I here?"

"Oh. Your sister's coming."

"Snookie?" Angelina straightened. Her retired-FBI sister

had arrived in town a few weeks earlier. She was staying at the Loggerhead, so it was even more strange all three of them were arriving at Tempest in separate vehicles.

"What's going on? Are we talking about her working for the Loggerhead? I thought that was a done deal."

Mick rolled his eyes. "Yeah, that's all I need. You two cackling witches, under my roof, twenty-four-seven—"

Angelina squinted at him. "Mick, we talked about this—"

"I'm *kidding*. Of course, she can work for us if she wants to, but this is about the *reverse*. She wants us to work for *her*."

"I don't get it."

"For the FBI."

"But she's retired."

"She's contracting."

Angelina leaned back in her chair. "Why didn't she mention this to me?"

He shrugged.

The waitress served Mick his breakfast as Angelina absorbed this new information. Mick had a strip of meat in his mouth before her steaming mug of coffee hit the table.

She opened a small creamer container and dumped it into her brew, giving Mick a chance to get the worst of his berserker-munching out of the way.

"Why, when Snook's living in the hotel, did we have to take separate cars here?"

Mick shoveled a spoonful of eggs into his maw. "Shee."

"Shee?"

"She's forbidden me to work."

Angelina mouthed the word *Ooooh...*

That made more sense. Shee had caught her father acting a tad disoriented and made him swear he wouldn't work for a while. Of course, asking Mick to quietly convalesce was like asking a two-year-old boy to sit still after mainlining sugar.

She took a sip of her coffee. "Got it. Still, this seems a bit much, don't you think?"

Mick grunted. "You don't know her the way I do. She'll probably smell the bacon on the three of us and put the pieces together anyway."

"Then maybe you shouldn't have ordered bacon."

Mick laughed. "Yeah, right."

"Morning, staff," said Snookie, appearing from nowhere to take a seat beside her sister. She looked like a photographic negative of her raven-haired sister—short blond hair, cream shorts, bright floral top. Snookie had embraced the Florida lifestyle.

"The power's already gone to her head," muttered Angelina, loud enough for her sister to hear.

Snookie smacked her sister's shoulder as she sat, but Angelina was having none of it.

"Why didn't you tell me you were back working?" she asked, motioning to Mick. "Before *him*?"

Snookie shrugged. "I bumped into him on my way to see you, and he made me realize this could work for *both* of us."

Angelina glared at Mick. "Oh he did, did he?" she drawled.

Mick looked away, munching on his toast like a beaver with a stick.

Snookie waved down the waitress to order coffee and an untoasted croissant before side-eyeing Mick and his ever-dwindling pile of food.

"Thanks for waiting," she said.

"Thanks for being on time," said Mick between bites.

The server brought Snookie's order, and after a sip of coffee, she got to business.

"The FBI's offering me a chance to contract with them in the South Florida area, and I'd like you and your group to act as an arm of my operations."

Angelina squinted at her sister. "And the FBI is good with that? We'd be official?"

"Does it matter?" asked Mick, though it sounded more like *Duddit natter?* filtered through his mouthful of home-fried potatoes.

Snookie shrugged. "We can maybe cross that bridge when we come to it."

"What's in it for us?" asked Mick.

Snookie grinned. "Bags of government money."

He popped the last hunk of bacon into his mouth. "Then we're in."

CHAPTER NINE

The boat drifted as Xander Andino jumped from the vessel onto the pier. Four people stood staring at him, frozen smiles on their faces.

"Where's Zeus?" asked Xander.

He felt the strain in his voice and cleared his throat for fear his greeters could hear it. The two largest men, members of a security detail who greeted every visitor to the island, remained expressionless. The eyebrows of the girl holding a tray of beverages bounced at the sound of Zeus' name.

Gregory, the concierge who'd greeted him during his first visit, cocked his head to the side.

"Do you have an appointment?"

Xander swallowed. He'd felt sick the entire flight to Andros Island, and he'd thrown up once during the boat ride to Tantalus. He felt the rising tide approaching again.

Scampering to the edge of the dock, he doubled at the waist and dry heaved. In his head, he chanted.

Don't do this. Don't look weak. Zeus doesn't like weak. Don't do this.

He willed his legs not to buckle.

"Boat ride was choppy," he croaked. "No appointment. It's an emergency."

"I see," said Gregory, sounding much less accommodating than he'd promised to always be. "I'll make a request as soon as we get back—"

"It's not a *request*." Xander's nausea passed, and he snapped straight again. "It's an *emergency.* I *have* to see him. I have to—"

Xander raised his arm. He wanted to grab Gregory and shake him. Struck with another wave of nausea, he diverted his hand to his mouth and ran past the concierge to the end of the pier to gag again. He'd lost the crackers from the plane during the boat ride. There was nothing left.

He felt a hand on his back.

Gregory.

"It's okay. I'll take care of it," said the concierge.

"I think I have food poisoning."

"Mm-hm. Do you want something to drink?"

Xander wiped his mouth, turned, and nodded. "Water. Cold."

The girl took a step forward with her tray. Selecting the bottled water, Xander swished and spat and then slugged back the rest.

"Oysters," he lied.

Gregory winced and nodded with apparent empathy.

Standing still, bottle in hand, Xander took a few deep breaths, feeling a little better.

Gregory would get Zeus. Zeus would fix everything.

I have to calm down.

Gregory produced a phone from his pocket and stood with it pressed against his ear, his gaze never leaving Xander.

"It's Mr. Andino. He says it's an emergency."

Gregory put his hand over the phone. "Can I ask the nature of the emergency?"

Xander grimaced as his throat tightened again.

"It's bad," he said. "It's really, really *bad.*"

CHAPTER TEN

Shee checked her phone to find YOU had responded to MacKenzie's form response with questions of their own. They wanted to know more about MacKenzie and her family, her hobbies, her ambitions—all so they could personalize her experience.

Right.

They want to know how rich I am.

Shee huffed at the length of the request.

Favorite books? Is that a trick question?

"I'm trying to vacation, not take out a second mortgage," she muttered, scrolling through the questionnaire.

On the upside, the questions meant she'd passed the first test by providing a referral.

Score: Shee: one, YOU: zero.

She forwarded the email to Croix even as she approached the front desk.

"I need you to fill out the form I just sent you," she said.

Croix's thumb danced around the screen of her phone before she paused to read what she'd been sent.

"What is it?"

"I'm trying to get Charlotte into YOU, but to prove she's worthy, they're asking for everything except her favorite Beatle."

Croix scowled. "Who has a favorite bug?"

Shee closed her eyes. "Just *stop* being so young, will you?"

"Wait." Croix lowered her precious phone. *"Charlotte*? This is the thing you were talking to *me* about. I thought you wanted *me* to go."

Shee reopened her eyes. "Sorry. I was underwhelmed by your enthusiasm."

Croix's nostrils flared. "What was I supposed to do? Jump up and down at the prospect of hanging out with a bunch of rich kids?"

"*Yes*. That's *exactly* what I was hoping for."

Shee suffered a tinge of guilt, realizing she'd leapfrogged past Croix as a candidate to advance her *look, I'm a great mom now* agenda.

She needed to atone...

She had an idea.

Clearing her throat, she leaned toward the cranky receptionist as if she were sharing a secret. "To be honest, I need you to organize the extraction. I need someone *in charge of the mission*."

She used the phrase *to be honest* the way it was most often employed.

In a lie.

Croix straightened. "I'm *in charge*?"

"Yes. On the home front, one hundred percent. You're logistics. I'm the handler. I'll get Charlotte in, locate the kid, and then you send in the troops to get him if she can't convince him to leave on his own."

"I can do that." Croix paused and then added, "Aren't you getting *old* for fieldwork?"

Shee offered a cold smile. "I'll do extra stretching in the morning."

Croix approved.

Shee pointed to the girl's phone. "Before we do anything, I need you to get her an invite to this elitist island. Don't screw it up."

"I'll make sure to give them what they want." Croix dropped her attention back to the email. "Looks like so far you've told them a first name—No last?"

"Left that open."

"*Nice.* Age, referral—" She looked up. "Where'd you get the referral?"

"Found a rando who'd been there before through image search."

Croix's eyes widened. "Not bad, old lady."

"*Gosh*, thanks. So we're good?"

"Yep. Let me do a little research and figure out the best angle. This email, *MacKenzieRules*, works?"

"It does. Forwards to me."

"Website?"

"Hm?"

"You have a domain name. Is there a website?"

Shee scoffed. "*No.* She's too cool for a website."

Croix laughed. "Oh. My bad."

Shee turned as the sound of Angelina's approaching heels echoed behind her.

"You're back. Where'd you go?" Shee sniffed. "You smell like bacon."

Angelina placed her tiny terrier in the dog bed sitting on her concierge desk and sat. "Ran some errands."

Shee didn't believe a word. Angelina had left in more of a hurry than errands warranted. But no reason to make a federal case over it when she needed the woman's help.

"I need some fashion assistance."

Angelina nodded. "Good. The first step is admitting it."

"Ha. Not for *me*, for Charlotte. I'm sneaking her into a resort for the rich and famous and she needs to dress accordingly."

"To what end?"

"To find a runaway rich kid."

"Ah. I might have a few things she could borrow."

Shee winced. "Won't all your things smell like menopause?"

Angelina snorted a laugh before poking a ruby red

fingernail at her. "You better watch it, Missy."

Shee giggled. "Seriously, not to doubt your fashion prowess, but I need her to *look her age*."

"Then why didn't you ask *me* to shop for her?" barked Croix from behind her.

Shee turned. "You're kidding, right? I've never seen you wear anything that doesn't look like you stole it from a summer camp counselor."

Croix glowered. "It's my *uniform*."

"Whatever." Shee turned back to Angelina. "Can you help?"

Angelina nodded. "I'll shop for her and have it here tomorrow."

"Great. Thank you. Hey, have you seen Dad?"

Angelina looked her in the eye. "Nope."

Shee frowned.

Before landing at Loggerhead, Angelina had made her living as a con artist and poker shark. The woman was nearly impossible to read.

It felt like she was lying.

Shee pushed open the creaking screen door and stepped onto the back porch. Halfway between the hotel and the Loggerhead's pier on the Intracoastal Waterway, their landscaper-slash-sniper-in-residence, Trimmer, stood talking to the new guy, Ollie. Trimmer waved to her with a long pair of clippers.

She waved back and cupped her hands around her mouth to call to him.

"Love the new bushes!"

He nodded.

She suspected Trimmer didn't get his nickname from eliminating *branches*. It couldn't hurt to stay on his good side.

"Any progress?"

Shee jumped at the sound of the voice to her right. She turned to find her father tucked in one of the porch's many colorful Adirondack chairs.

"There you are," she said. "You scared me."

"I get that a lot." He sniffed. "Or I used to."

Shee leaned against the porch railing. "Sitting out here feeling sorry for yourself?"

He scoffed. "Never."

"Why are you sitting in that low-ass chair? Can you get out of that?"

He shot her a *look* and returned to staring at the water.

She sat in the chair beside him, swooping in his direction and taking a deep breath.

He smelled like bacon.

"Where were you this morning?" she asked.

"Hm?" Mick cocked his head as if her question made no sense.

"I was looking for you," she explained.

"Oh. I ran some errands."

Shee scowled.

Again with the 'errands.'

Not suspicious *at all.*

"Are you and Angelina officially dating again?" she asked.

His brows knit. "Why would you ask that?"

"Just curious."

He shrugged. "Aren't we always? To one degree or another?"

"Is dating supposed to have degrees?"

He nodded. "I think so. What about you? Have you and Mason stopped pretending you're not hot to trot?"

"*Hot to trot*?" Shee chuckled. "Jeeze, you're old. Now I know how Croix feels every time I open my mouth. Do you know she doesn't even know who the Beatles are?"

"Bunch of hippies," muttered Mick.

Shee sighed. "Hey, I need you to clear something with Nic Andino. I think his son is holed up on an island resort for rich kids. I need to confirm it and then extract him."

"What am I clearing, exactly?"

"The island is exclusive. I need to send in a twenty-something to look for him. I need Andino to okay the expense."

"How much?"

"I don't know yet."

Mick looked up. "How am I supposed to clear *I don't know*?"

She shrugged. "Let's assume it's around five thousand."

"A week?"

"A *day*."

Mick sat up. "Jeezus. For a kid to hang out on the beach? I—"

Shee held up a hand to stop him. "I know. When you were a kid, you walked to school in a blizzard, uphill both ways. We *all* know."

Mick glowered. "You kids have no idea."

"Um, I spent my childhood shuttling from cheap motel to cheap motel chasing military criminals with you. I wasn't exactly Eloise at the Plaza."

"Who?"

"Never mind."

He chuckled. "You loved every second of it."

She sniffed. "That's not the point."

Mick rubbed his eye and settled back into his chair. "How many days does Andino need to pay for?"

"Two. Three if there are complications."

Mick shook his head. "If you're sure—"

"Reasonably."

"I'll give him a call."

"Thank you."

Shee considered telling him she'd enlisted Charlotte's help but decided against it. First, she needed *mission approval*. She didn't want to complicate the approval process.

"Let me know."

She stood and reached to open the screen door, only to find it swinging towards her. Dodging, she avoided a distracted Mason from crashing into her but felt her heel catch the edge of the porch step. As she tilted backward, he grabbed her arm and jerked her toward him.

"Whoa," he said.

"Whoa," she echoed, steadying herself against his chest.

Mason's gaze met hers before dancing away.

"Letting the dog out," he said, as Archie ignored them both and trotted down the steps to the grass.

Shee took a step out of Mason's way as he released her and followed Archie. The dog bolted toward Ollie as the new hire headed in the direction of the hotel.

Shee found her father staring up at her from his seat.

"*What?*" she asked.

"You two are ridiculous," he grumbled.

Shee flung open the door and walked inside, unmolested. She took two steps and then, struck by the fact she hadn't heard the door close behind her, glanced back to find Ollie at the threshold.

"What was *that?*" he asked.

"What?" She could tell by his bemused expression he'd seen her 'dancing' with Mason.

He shifted gears. "Let's go to lunch. I'm new, and it's the neighborly thing to do."

Shee stared at him for a beat and then checked her watch. She *was* hungry and didn't have much to do until her father gave her the thumbs up for Operation YOU.

"Sure. Where do you want to go?"

"You pick it. Right now. Blurt it out. The first place that comes to mind."

"Uh, Watering Hole. They have good sushi."

Ollie leaned back to pop the upper half of his body back onto the porch.

"Hey Mick, Shee and I are going to Watering Hole for lunch. Want anything?" he asked. He sounded unnecessarily loud as if he thought Mick had a hearing problem.

Plenty of problems. Hearing isn't one of them.

"Nope," she heard her father say.

Ollie tapped the door jamb twice with the butt of his palm. "Okie dokie. See you in a bit."

"Can't wait," added Mick.

Ollie walked inside, grinning. "Ready when you are, m'lady."

Shee glanced past him to where Mason now stood at the foot of the porch steps, tossing a weathered tennis ball to Archie.

She turned and headed for the lobby.

"I'll drive."

CHAPTER ELEVEN

Shee and Ollie sat on the patio of the Watering Hole and ordered drinks. An oversized umbrella poking from the center of the table kept the worst of the Florida sun from baking their skin.

"I appreciate this," said Ollie, removing his sunglasses. His gaze swept from the water to the parking lot and back again. "Nice spot."

"No problem," said Shee. A steady breeze from an oversized fan forced her to pull her mahogany locks into a ponytail as she watched a waitress waiting on a nearby table flash a smile at Ollie.

Cheeky.

Their new soldier *was* handsome by the numbers—dark hair, tanned skin, large shockingly light hazel eyes outlined with thick lashes—but his most powerful asset was undefinable. His confidence, maybe. She imagined the roguish smirk permanently affixed to his lips paired with his quick, self-deprecating humor disarmed most he encountered.

She gave him some time to peruse the menu while she studied him for clues. His sunglasses, clothes, and watch were expensive, though not prohibitively so. His well-manicured ducktail beard and clipped, clean, even fingernails belied attention to his hygiene, as did the air of fitness she'd clocked earlier.

Everything about him said *I'm fancy enough you should trust me, but not so fancy you can't.*

He looked up and noticed her attention. "You're not looking

at the menu," he said.

She shook her head. "I always get the Rocky Roll."

"That's a sushi roll?" He put the menu to the side and tapped it to signal his search had ended. "Then Rocky Roll it is."

"You won't regret it." She slid her sunglasses to her head. "So, what brought you to us?" she asked.

"By way of the Army—and Cook said I might be of some use here."

"Our Cook? How do you know him?"

"We were stationed in Germany together. I helped him get a set of nonstick pans, fresh truffles, and a couple of other odds and ends. I was a procurement officer."

"Ah, right. Mason told me you procured his watch."

Ollie chuckled. "Just showing off. It's a hobby I started as a kid."

"As a kid? How does a child pickpocket end up in the Army?"

"My godfather suggested it. Then he hired some goons to beat me up to make sure I listened."

Shee grimaced. "Yikes."

"Nah, it wasn't a bad thing. They didn't hurt me, and I needed encouragement. Kept me out of jail. I owe him a lot."

Their server returned with a beer for Ollie and her iced tea. He thanked her and took a sip before returning his attention to Shee.

"So what's *your* thing?" he asked. "Besides being the boss' daughter?"

"I'm a tracker, mostly."

"Military?"

"No, well, I guess you could say I was *honorary* military. When Mick wasn't on some special mission, he chased criminals for the Navy. AWOLs and whatnot. He took me along." She chuckled. "His way of homeschooling me."

"Your mom was okay with that?"

"No mom. I never knew her."

Ollie nodded. "I lost my dad young."

She nodded and then straightened. "Hold on..."

"What?"

She smiled. "You're *good*."

Ollie seemed confused. "What are you talking about?"

"Mason said you're a con man. We've been talking for five minutes and you've already made a connection with me on a deep, personal level."

"What are you talking about? You think I'm *lying*?"

"I'm not sure. The Hallmark movie of the week godfather story, the single parent parallel..."

He laughed and put his hand over his heart. "I'm not lying. I swear. Every word is true."

Shee looked away, still pondering his honesty. As she turned toward the parking lot, Ollie reached across the table and took her hand in his.

"What's that scar on your thumb?" he asked.

Her focus snapped back to him, but not before she'd seen the black truck sitting in the parking lot.

Mason.

She glanced at Ollie's hand cradling her left.

Hm.

He stared into her eyes, his shoulders and expression relaxed.

As if butter wouldn't melt in his mouth.

Shee leaned toward him and put her right hand on top of the pile, creating a hand sandwich with hers as the bread.

"You knew he'd follow us," she said.

Ollie's open, innocent expression tightened a hair.

Just a hair.

She continued. "You demanded I pick a restaurant and then called the place out to Mick. You knew Mason would hear."

Ollie chuckled. "Wow. See? You're the one who's *good*. I don't think one in a hundred would have pieced that together." His eyes bounced in the direction of Mason's truck and then back again. "You spotted him fast. Almost before me, and I was *looking* for him. Did you know he'd follow us?"

"No." Her answer felt like a lie. It took her a moment to

realize she *had* been tipped. "Maybe. Your eyes. You kept looking at the parking lot."

He shook his head. "I must be losing my touch."

"How did *you* know he'd follow us?" she asked.

"You said you followed my eyes. I followed *his*. They're always on you."

Shee fought not to reveal how his statement tickled her by narrowing her stare. "Holding my hand. You're trying to make him jealous? Why?"

He laughed. "I'm not the only one."

"What does that mean?"

"We're still holding hands."

Shee jerked her hand away and sat back.

Wiseass.

"So this lunch is all to make him jealous?"

He was staring at the parking lot now. "Don't worry, you're not my type." He turned back to her, looking pleased with himself. "But you want to know *why* you're not my type?"

She rolled her eyes. "No—"

"Of course you do. It's human nature."

"You're not as smart as you think," she said, leaning back. "For one, he didn't follow because he's *jealous*. He followed because he doesn't trust you."

He pointed a finger, bouncing it from her to the parking lot. "So you two don't have a history?"

"We do. It's no secret. But I'm telling you now, I'm not a fan of games."

"Don't be offended. I did want to go to lunch with you. Throwing bait to Mason was...*fun*."

"I don't believe that for a second."

Ollie put his hands against his chest in mea culpa. "It's true. I *swear*. I could use a friend here in my new home. I picked you."

"I'm flattered. But I wouldn't make an enemy out of Mason, either."

He batted away her warning with a wave of his hand. "He'll be *fine*. You're more important. You're the sun in his little solar system."

Shee hooted. "That's what you decided? In the ten minutes you've been under our roof?"

"Yep. You have power over Mason *and* your father."

Shee snorted a laugh. "You clearly don't know either of them."

Ollie's gaze darted toward the parking lot again as their food arrived.

"He's coming. Should we ask him to join us?" He waved to Mason, who'd left his truck to stride toward the restaurant.

Shee shook her head. "You like poking the bear, don't you?"

Ollie grinned. "The forest can get pretty boring if you don't."

He stood and walked to Mason, who paused to receive him.

Shee twisted in her seat to watch.

What is this guy up to?

Ollie reached Mason and then *passed* him without pause, slapping the big man on his shoulder as he continued to enter the indoor portion of the restaurant.

Mason remained still as if wrestling down the urge to chase Ollie down like a big cat. Locking on Shee, moved forward again.

"What's he up to?" he asked, arriving tableside, clearly agitated.

"Hello to you, too."

Mason rolled his hand in the air. "Quick. Before he gets back."

"He's not up to anything. We're having *lunch*. What are *you* doing here?"

"Picking up takeout."

"*Really*... You should have let us know. We could have picked it up for you."

Mason glanced back at the building. "Something's up with that guy."

"Don't worry. I'm not his type."

"Don't—?" Mason scowled. "What's that supposed to mean? How do you know *that*?"

"He told me."

Mason's features tightened, bunching into the center of his face.

"I think that means you *are* his type," he said.

She acted surprised. "Would that *bother* you?"

He scoffed. "*No.*"

"Okay, then. Did you need anything else?"

Mason chewed his tongue for a moment and then shook his head. "No. I'll see you back at the hotel."

"See ya."

He turned and walked toward the entrance as Ollie returned in the opposite direction.

"Hey," said Ollie.

Mason nodded. "*Ollie.*"

Ollie raised a hand to a high five. "Call me *Pony*."

Mason declined on both accounts and continued to the restaurant.

Unphased, Ollie took his chair across from Shee.

"Did you tell him to call you *Pony*?" she asked.

He snorted a laugh. "I told him that's my nickname."

"But it isn't?"

He shook his head. "I just want to hear that giant call me *Pony*."

Shee giggled. She couldn't help it. "You're crazy."

He grinned. "I don't think he'd call me by my real nickname either."

"What's that?"

"Monkeypaw."

"Monkeypaw? Why does that sound familiar?"

"It's from a story you probably read in school. A family makes a wish on a magic monkey paw to bring back their son, who died in a machinery accident, but he comes back the way he was in the grave. All mangled."

"Yikes. What's it got to do with you?"

"It's a *careful-what-you-wish-for* story." He smiled. "And when you ask me for a favor, chances are, it's going to cost you."

Shee chuckled. "I don't think he's going to call you Monkeypaw, either."

"Probably not. So how'd it go?"

"How'd what go?"

"I assume you talked to Mason while I was gone? He came over here?"

"I assume you *saw* that he did?"

"I was in the bathroom."

"Sure you were."

"Did he seem jealous?"

Shee remained silent and took a sip of her tea, trying to appear as bored as possible.

Ollie grinned. "That's what I thought. You can pay me back later."

She put down her glass. "*What* are you talking about?"

Her phone vibrated, rattling against the table as it announced an incoming call from her father. She answered without waiting for Ollie's response.

"You've been cleared," said Mick.

"Andino? We can go to YOU?"

"Yep. He gave us the go-ahead for two days and two days *max*."

"Then two days it is. Great."

"Should I tell Croix?"

"Croix?"

"I assume you're sending Croix?"

Shee paused. *Now* didn't feel like a great time to tell him she was taking his granddaughter, either.

"Oh. No. I got it. Thanks."

She hung up and thought of Charlotte, eager to call her and let her know they'd be taking a trip.

"You look happy," said Ollie.

She grinned. "I am."

CHAPTER TWELVE

Shee sat on the Loggerhead's reading room sofa, her laptop resting on her thighs as she fleshed out ideas and reviewed pertinent facts about the Andino case by typing an email to an imaginary friend.

Fifteen years on the road, alone, trying to avoid being killed by a vengeful lunatic's assassins, had given her a few strange habits.

She'd made real, *living* friends over the years, of course, but her relationships were transitory—people she met when she stopped in a new town and took on a case—cops, detectives, sometimes family of the victim. Unburdening her every thought to strangers wouldn't be wise, so she'd started emailing herself as if she were bouncing ideas off a trusted friend.

Her odd habit had three benefits. First, self-addressed emails served as notes she could refer to later if needed. Second, the act of typing her thoughts helped clarify them. Faulty thinking glowed like fireworks when put in print. Third, she sometimes read the emails to herself days later and found herself *surprised* by the contents.

She didn't tell anyone about that third one. It was bad enough she was writing emails to herself.

"What are you doing in here?"

Shee closed the lid of her laptop as Mason entered the room. His dark hair slicked back as if he'd come straight from the shower.

She shrugged. "Just typing up some notes."

Not emailing them to myself. No siree.

He motioned to the cushion beside her.

"Mind if I sit?"

She shook her head.

He sat, and she felt her body tilt toward him. She didn't mind. He smelled like shampoo and body wash—a touch of coconut, a hint of lavender.

"Freshly Showered Man would make a good candle fragrance," she said.

He cocked an eyebrow. "You certainly haven't gotten any less *weird* over the years."

She chuckled. "Strange, isn't it? Being alone for long periods usually makes people so *normal*."

He looked away, but she heard him mumble.

"That was your decision."

Her scent therapy session screeched to a halt as anger flashed inside her like a grease fire.

"It wasn't *my decision*," she hissed, aware Croix sat at her front desk station in the next room. "I had people trying to *kill* me, remember?"

The muscles in his jaw tensed. "You could have come to *me*."

"Right. The guy I ran out on. Such an obvious solution. Why didn't I think of that?"

He glared at her, his turquoise eyes stormy. "You could have—"

She held up a hand to stop him. "Don't even. I heard this speech from my father. Seriously, what could you big tough guys have done? Killed a never-ending stream of assassins, like you're in some kind of video game?"

"You don't know—"

"But I *do* know, Mason. Who do you think you're talking to? Do you think Mick and I didn't try every other option? Plus, I'd already lost my sister and Charlotte—how many more people had to suffer? We needed to find the person *hiring* the killers, and we *couldn't*."

"Right." Mason nestled himself in the corner of the sofa,

crossing his arms against his chest. "I forgot. You're the tracker who couldn't track her own enemy."

Shee flinched.

"That was just *mean*," she said.

His cross expression softened. "I'm sorry. You're right. I'm frustrated and—that was low."

She nodded and looked away.

"It's just..." He hemmed a moment before continuing. "I do think you got *comfortable*."

She turned to him. "*Comfortable*? On the run?"

He nodded. "I think you got comfortable being alone. Maybe you thought you *deserved* it."

Shee barked a laugh and rested her fingertips on his arm. "I forget. Were you a SEAL or a psychiatrist?"

"Am I wrong?" he asked.

"Of *course* you're *wrong*."

She sounded emphatic, but inside, her stomach flipped.

Is he right?

It didn't matter. She could torture herself with that thought later.

She narrowed her eyes until the edges of his face grew blurry. "Did you need something? Or is this why you came in here? To revisit what a huge disappointment I am? To—" A thought occurred to her and she straightened. "Wait. Are you accusing me of wallowing in self-pity for *twenty years*?"

He stared at her, his expression unreadable.

Thoughts rushed into her head. She let them fall from her lips like a herd of lemmings spilling off a cliff.

"Are you saying I felt like I *deserved* to be alone after leaving you and giving up Charlotte and getting my sister killed? Or are you saying living under my father's shadow, I'd never developed my own identity, and that I threw myself onto the road to find it?"

His eyes widened, and he held up a hand. "*Whoa*."

"Whoa?"

"I wasn't saying that. Not all of that, anyway."

"No?"

"*No.*"

"Oh." In her head, Shee repeated what she'd said, trying to listen to it from his point of view.

Hm.

"I guess I misheard you."

He sighed. "*Have* you talked to someone about—"

She turned to cut him short. "Mason, why are you *here*?"

"At the Loggerhead?"

She suspected she *had* meant that, but adjusted course.

"No, I mean, why are you here, *now*, in this room?"

He seemed relieved. "Oh. I came to talk about Charlotte—"

Shee felt the strength rush out of her.

Not again. She couldn't say sorry for hiding Charlotte from him again...

Mason continued. "—about taking her on this job to the island. Are you sure it's a good idea?"

Shee felt the tight ropes in her shoulders ease.

Oh. Current day stuff.

Good.

She smiled. "Are we *parenting*?"

Mason's cheeks colored. "Whatever. I think we should talk about it. Shouldn't we? Isn't that what normal parents do?"

She laughed. "Your guess is as good as mine."

Shee took a deep breath and then released it as she flopped her hand on his knee. Beneath her fingers, she felt the cuff of his artificial limb, tracing it with her finger as she tried to think like a parent.

"She'll be fine. She's going to take a plane ride, wander around a luxury resort, and report what she sees. That's it. It's more like a Christmas present than a job."

His attention dropped to her hand. "I suppose. I worry about her."

"I know. I do, too. I mean, a lot. It's crazy—"

"I worry about *you*, too," he added.

She smiled. "I'm sorry. I didn't mean to say all that nonsense. I—"

She stopped.

Those eyes. It felt as if Mason was staring into her head, seeing her thoughts spinning like unlucky cows in the twister of her mind.

The *earnestness* of his expression snapped something inside of her. She had no warning to brace against it.

She looked away, her throat too tight to continue.

It was happening.

Shit.

I'm going to cry.

His hand touched hers—the one still resting on his knee, not the one pretending to wipe dust from her eye.

"Come here," he said, slipping his arm around her.

She sobbed once, unable to stop it. Loud and dorky.

What the hell. Don't do this to me...

Then it was done. The twister ripped through her emotional barn and everything blew to pieces. Splinters were everywhere. She collapsed toward him, and he wrapped his big arms around her, pulling her tight against his chest. Her head fell against his shoulder as if it weighed a thousand pounds.

"I really couldn't come back," she said. "I swear."

"I know. I'm sorry."

She felt his lips moving against her head and snuggled a little tighter.

"So much time," he whispered.

"I know."

"And I love Charlotte so much it *hurts*, you know?"

"I *know*."

"And you—"

She felt his chest rise and fall.

He fell silent.

Shee wanted to ask him if his words meant he was ready to forgive her. She wanted to ask him if her lunch with Ollie had made him jealous.

No. Shut up for once.

His body against hers felt *so good*—as if she could curl up and sleep for a thousand years—

"*Ew.*"

Shee pushed back from Mason to find Croix staring at them.

The girl's lip curled as she gawked.

"Get a *room*," she said.

Teeth gritting, Shee turned her head to hide her tear-streaked face.

Nice timing.

"Can we do something for you?" asked Mason.

"No," said Croix, motioning for someone in the lobby to come her way. "But maybe her."

Shee turned for a glimpse.

Charlotte appeared, suitcase in hand.

Charlotte.

Shee's mental twister dissipated, giving way to a clear, pink-hued sunrise.

"I'm ready for my assignment," Charlotte said, grinning.

"Wow, you got here *fast.*" Shee sniffed and sprang to her feet. Charlotte wouldn't be able to see her face if she were hugging her.

Mason seemed to have contrived the same plan. They jostled to stand and hug her.

"Are you okay?" asked Charlotte, as Shee released her.

Shee nodded.

"Sorry. Allergies."

CHAPTER THIRTEEN

Shee was lying about having allergies.

Charlotte wanted to ask about her mother's tears, but it was awkward with her father there—especially when he looked a little misty himself.

Something between the two of them. Not her business. From what she'd gathered, their relationship was complicated.

They seemed okay. Whatever had upset them wasn't something they felt the need to share and, for now, she still felt trapped in a sort of strange parent-child limbo.

What level of nosey was appropriate in a relationship with your parents...*when you just met them?*

She needed to check Amazon for a handbook, like, *What to Expect When You're Not Expecting to have Parents.*

No time now. Shee was already hustling her to Angelina's room to try on designer duds for her assignment. The assignment had her squealing with excitement the whole three-hour drive from her side of Florida.

"If you hate what she has, we'll find more," said Shee, knocking on Angelina's door.

The door opened, and little Harley shot out to run circles around their legs. Charlotte was careful to stand still to keep from stepping on her.

Angelina stepped back to let them in. "Just getting things ready. Come in. Nice to see you again, Charlotte."

"You, too." Charlotte eyed the clothing spread across Angelina's bed and draped over her furniture as if she were throwing a trunk show sale.

Angelina waved her hand over the collection, red nails flashing like slot machine cherries.

"Pick in any order you like—the bathroom is there for changing."

Trying not to appear giddy, Charlotte plucked shorts, a blouse, and a belt from the corner of the bed. It appeared Angelina had grouped them there for a reason, so she went with it. She wasn't exactly a fashionista. Suggestions were welcome.

She changed and popped back into the room to twirl for Shee and Angelina, who had set themselves up on the end of the bed to judge.

"I'd say *yea* on the shorts, but *nay* on the blouse. It's a little old for you," said Shee.

"What do you know?" muttered Angelina. She cast a critical eye across Charlotte's ensemble and sighed. "Agreed. Keep the shorts, lose the blouse."

Charlotte peered down at the Gucci belt circling her waist. "Doesn't a leather belt seem a bit *heavy* for a Caribbean resort?"

Shee shrugged. "Rich people don't sweat."

Charlotte laughed. "I'll have to work on that."

She grabbed a spaghetti-strapped floral dress and returned to the bathroom.

When she returned for her next sashay around the room, someone knocked on the door, and Harley exploded into furious yapping.

"Come in," called Angelina, her eyes never leaving Charlotte. "I like that," she said.

Shee nodded. "Me, too."

Mason poked his head into the room, using his foot to block the Yorkie from escaping.

"Fashion show?" he asked.

"This fabric feels *amazing*," Charlotte said, doing a pirouette.

"Rich people's clothes are spun from unicorn tails," said Shee.

"Spiffy," interjected Mason.

Shee looked at him. "*Spiffy*?"

He ignored her and spoke to Charlotte. "Hey, sorry to interrupt, but I'd like to show you some self-defense before you go."

Charlotte stopped preening. "That would be *awesome*."

Shee threw him a withering glance. "She's going to a resort, Mason, not Afghanistan."

Mason returned a stiff smile. "That's why I'm teaching her self-defense and not how to disarm an IED."

"That would be cool, too," said Charlotte. "I mean if we can fit that in." She scanned the remaining items left to try. "Maybe fifteen minutes?"

He nodded. "I'll meet you out back."

Mason withdrew.

Shee caught Charlotte's eye.

"Such a *dad* move, right?" she said.

I wouldn't know, thought Charlotte, but she kept the thought to herself.

Instead, she grabbed another dress and popped back into the bathroom.

"Do you have any training in Krav Maga?" asked Mason.

Charlotte's eyebrows bobbled toward the sky.

"In *what*?"

They were standing in the grass behind the hotel. A large oak tree blocked the sun and kept them from bursting into flame. Charlotte had changed back into her boring old shorts and top.

Nearby, Trimmer toiled on a collection of flowering bushes, and Shee watched while leaning back against an oak. Charlotte couldn't see past the sunglasses, but it looked as though her mother was staring at Mason with some degree of incredulity.

"Why would she have Krav Maga training?" Shee asked. "She grew up in a fifty-five-plus community, not practicing to become Batman."

"I did take some kickboxing classes," offered Charlotte.

Mason's attention remained on Shee. "Plenty of people take all kinds of martial art lessons. I volunteered to teach a few self-defense courses, and I had all *sorts* of people show up."

Shee chuckled, muttering. "*Krav Maga...*"

Mason pointed from her to Charlotte. "Why don't you step in there and be her sparring partner?"

Shee pulled off her sunglasses and set them at the foot of the tree. "Sure."

Stretching her arms she moved to stand next to Charlotte.

"I'll be gentle," she said in an exaggerated whisper.

Charlotte laughed.

"Face each other," said Mason.

Shee and Charlotte pivoted.

"Now, Shee, swing at her with your right hand in slow motion. Charlotte, while she's doing that I want you to block her by sweeping outward with your left hand and punching forward with your right." Mason demonstrated the move in the air.

"Like this?" asked Charlotte as the two women beat each other up in slow motion. Shee provided sound effects. Charlotte giggled.

"Not bad," said Mason. "Tell you what. Switch places and watch for a sec. It might make more sense."

Charlotte stepped back and Mason stepped in to take her place across from Shee.

"You forgot to tap in," said Shee.

Mason ignored her. "Now, if I were to attack like this—" He swung in slow motion with his right fist. Shee swept with her left to knock away his blow, punching forward with her right fist at full speed. She stopped a hair's breadth from his nose.

He grimaced. "Right."

Shee offered a large grin.

Mason turned to Charlotte. "You can see my punch pulled me forward—"

Fist still hovering near his face, Shee flicked him on the side of his nose.

Mason flinched.

"Very funny—"

Shee stepped back and took a fighting stance, beckoning him forward.

He made an eye-rolly face at Charlotte and then turned his attention to Shee. "You're kidding, right?"

Shee motioned again. "Bring it."

Mason licked his lips and made three lightning-fast moves to doff Shee on the head with his fingertips. She blocked two. He caught her with the last on the forehead.

Unphased and without delay, Shee kicked for his groin. He blocked by grabbing her ankle. Shee dropped, sliding her opposite leg into Mason's metal appendage.

Mason swore. Wobbling, he released her and stumbled back to catch himself against the tree. Shee jumped to her feet and moved in like a woman possessed.

He sniffed. "Oh, we're playing like that, are we?"

"What's going on here?" said a voice with a British accent to Charlotte's right. She turned to find Trimmer beside her.

"They were teaching me self-defense, but I think there's something else going on now," said Charlotte as her parents sparred.

Trimmer nodded. "I'll teach you self-defense. Hold out your hand."

She did as she was told. Trimmer reached into his pocket, pulled out a small gun, and placed it in her palm.

She looked at the gun and then at him.

He smiled.

"Thus endeth the lesson."

CHAPTER FOURTEEN

The next morning, Shee and Charlotte left early for Ft. Lauderdale airport. It offered direct flights to Andros Island, the closest Bahamian Island to YOU boasting a decent airfield. Croix had arranged for them to take a boat from Andros to the resort.

As they waited to board the plane, Shee slipped a pain reliever from her purse and popped it into her mouth. She felt vaguely achy everywhere after showing off her fighting skills for Charlotte.

Or, maybe she was showing off for Mason.

Or maybe trying to prove to *herself* she still had skills.

Honestly, she wasn't sure for *whom* she'd been showboating, but she was paying for it now.

She scrolled through her email. Croix hadn't sent much she didn't already know, other than the travel itinerary, but what was there to report? Either her hunch about Xander's whereabouts was right and he was holed up at YOU, or she was wrong and would have to start looking for additional leads.

She thought *finding* Xander would be the easy part. They'd also have to reunite him with his father, whether the boy wanted to see Daddy or not.

That could prove more difficult.

The contract didn't say she had to bring the girlfriend home, too, but Shee planned to make the effort. The pain of Isabella's family had permeated their brief meeting. Girls tended to be more reasonable—certainly not in every case—but she might get lucky. She hoped telling Isabella how upset her mother and sister were would inspire the girl to go home. It might even motivate Xander to join her.

Wouldn't that be nice.

"They're boarding," said Charlotte.

Shee nodded and, flashing their tickets to the agent, the two walked onto the tarmac to board the small plane.

The very small plane.

They shuffled into the belly of the aircraft, sharing the tiny space with another couple and a single man.

"What's the name of the island?" asked Charlotte, as she buckled into the seat of the small prop plane. "The one YOU is on?"

Shee sat beside her. "That's a good question. I've been calling it YOU."

"YOU is on Tantalus Island," said a short, small-boned flight attendant as she adjusted the safety materials at the front of the plane. Both the front and back of the aircraft sat ten feet from their seats, a fact Shee found unsettling.

"Ah, thank you," said Charlotte.

"Have you been?" Shee asked the attendant.

"To YOU?" The woman laughed. "How much do you think they pay me to sit on this little plane?"

Shee smiled. It was worth a shot. She glanced at Charlotte, who seemed deep in thought.

"What's up? Something wrong?"

Charlotte snapped to. "Hm? Oh. No. *Tantalus* sounds familiar, but I can't place it. Something from mythology?"

"I don't know. Mythology isn't my strong suit."

Charlotte shrugged. "I'll look it up later."

The attendant took her place in the jump seat, and soon they were taxiing for takeoff, engines roaring in their ears. Shee peered out the tiny window opposite Charlotte and watched the whirling prop, quietly doubting any science claiming they could keep them airborne.

The flight to Congo Town International Airport on Andros Island took an hour. Thanks to the noise, they spent the bulk of that time in silence to avoid losing their voices.

Arriving before noon, thankfully in one piece, they disembarked directly on the tarmac. Shee stretched as they waited for their luggage to be extracted from the belly of the aircraft. An attendant jerked her backpack and Charlotte's Gucci suitcase free, the latter provided by Angelina. The case was old, but they'd collectively decided *old* Gucci was *vintage* Gucci and something MacKenzie would consider cool.

They took a cab to the pier where their small private charter boat promised to wait. A large cabin cruiser bobbed at the end of the dock.

"That must be it," said Shee, pointing.

They walked past a shabby center console craft on their way to the shiny cruiser. Shee watched Charlotte's gait shift to something more *swishy*. She walked like an unimpressed rich girl, in no hurry to convenience anyone.

The man lounging on the cruddy center console sat up as they passed.

"MacKenzie?"

Shee turned, eyeing both the man and the sad little boat. Rough fiberglass patches on the back of the craft suggested the engine had once fallen into the sea, taking half the transom with it. Someone had hand-painted the vessel's name in capital letters meandering like a drunk beneath a pockmarked cleat.

MASTER BAITER

Shee's eyes narrowed.

Croix.

She should have known better to put a pissy twenty-something in charge of her travel arrangements. The jalopy boat was payback for taking Charlotte instead of *her*.

"Are you MacKenzie?" the man asked when neither of the women had navigated past their shock to answer.

Charlotte nodded. "I am."

He clapped his hands together, rubbing them before thrusting one out. "I's Captain William. Hop in."

Charlotte looked at Shee, her expression awash with alarm. Shee wasn't sure if the look was part of her daughter's *MacKenzie* persona or true horror. Either was justified.

The Captain kept his hand outstretched.

"Gimme yer tings, Bey."

With hardly a nod of acknowledgment, Charlotte placed her bag on the dock instead of handing it to him, as if any accidental touch might infect her with plague.

Shee smirked.

Turned out her daughter made a heck of a brat.

Untroubled by her revulsion, the captain stowed her bag behind his seat and again extended a grubby mitt to steady the girl as she stepped into the boat. With little other option, short of jumping into the vessel like a paratrooper, she deigned to accept his assistance.

Once Charlotte was safely aboard, Shee moved forward, preparing to join. The captain shook his head and side-chopped his flattened palm through the air.

"Guests only."

"But Agatha is *always* with me," whined Charlotte, who sat on the back bench, legs crossed and hands on knees, looking as prim as a British princess.

Shee shot her a look.

Agatha?

The captain shrugged. "Sorry. YOU make da rules."

"I say she can come," said Charlotte.

He poked a finger toward open water. "*YOU.* Da place. *Dey* make da rule."

Charlotte tried again. "Can she just take the boat ride? She won't get off."

He shook his head.

"Dem doan allow it."

Shee stared at him, considering her options. Reaching into her tiny traveling purse, she fingered the wad of cash she'd brought with her for emergencies. Counting off two bills, she slid them free.

"Is there a way around the rules?" she asked, thrusting the money toward him.

The captain smiled, his gold front tooth glinting in the

sunlight.

"Dems a good customer. You need ta go *furder* to get 'round *deez* rules."

Shee peeled off another hundred and handed it over.

Captain William pocketed the cash and held out a hand.

"Welcome aboard."

Shee stepped into the boat as he opened a door in the console beneath his steering wheel to retrieve a yellow polo identical to the one he wore. A stitched logo reading *Captain William's Tours & Fishing* covered the left chest.

"Go and put dis on," he said, handing it to her.

Shee understood. For her three hundred dollars, she'd be masquerading as staff.

She held up the shirt. In addition to being six sizes too large, sweat stains circled the pits, and grease spotted the fabric. It smelled like a seafood joint's dumpster.

Lovely.

The engine roared to life as *Master Baiter* pulled from the pier. Bracing to keep her balance, Shee slipped the shirt over her tee, her skin recoiling from the stiff fabric.

Captain William tore across the glistening turquoise water toward Tantalus Island. At some point, laughing to himself, he produced a logoed cap and turned to slap it on Shee's head before giving her a thumbs up.

Having inspected the shirt, she didn't want to know what lived in the cap. She thumbed back, dreaming of the ways she'd make Croix pay.

Steadying herself against the staccato bouncing of the boat, she dropped onto the bench beside Charlotte.

"You good?" she asked over the roar of the outboard.

Charlotte nodded and tapped her chest with an open palm before offering a thumbs-up of her own. Shee understood her pantomime to mean *nervous but good.* Her daughter pointed at her new *uniform* and held her nose. Sheepish, Shee shifted her seat farther away to spare her daughter the stench.

Lounging in his captain's chair as if he had no bones, Captain William pointed to an island rising from the sea on the horizon.

"YOU," he screamed at them, dragging out the vowels for several seconds.

Shee found herself confounded by the vision. The island looked as though a silver pyramid rose from the center of it.

They skipped across the water, slowing as they entered a small egg-shaped cove on the west side of Tantalus. Now closer, Shee confirmed there *was* a sparkling pyramid rising from the trees. Huge wooden doors embedded at the edge of a jungle stood sentry at the end of the receiving pier. A gray rock mountainside, unlikely to exist on a Bahamian island, nevertheless flanked the door on either side.

"Is that where they keep King Kong?" asked Shee, as the engine's roar dropped to a sputtery hum.

Captain William howled with laughter.

Shee guessed the wooden doors to be thirty feet high. The rock and jungle stretched as far left and right as she could see. Shee shielded her already shaded eyes with a hand and spotted a window facing them near the top of the gleaming pyramid.

A lookout? Offices?

She wished she'd thought to bring binoculars.

"Nothing on the website said the place was a walled fortress," she said to Charlotte.

Charlotte shrugged. "Gotta keep out the riffraff."

Shee chuckled. "You might be enjoying this role a little too much."

Four people in light blue linen shorts and tops stood waiting on the pier to receive them. Captain William sidled his craft against the pilings.

"Here goes nothing." Charlotte squeezed Shee's hand and then released it.

"MacKenzie?" said a small, wiry man, somewhere near Shee's age, sporting tightly cropped blonde hair. "I'm Gregory. I'll be your personal concierge."

Charlotte nodded and held out a hand to engage his eager assistance. A dark-haired, younger woman holding a silver tray leaned toward her as she stepped onto the dock. From Shee's vantage, it looked as though her daughter had her choice of Bellini, bottled water, or a neon red slushy concoction with a colorful paper umbrella poking from the top. Charlotte waved them away and the woman retreated to her original position.

Shee turned her attention to two powder-blue-clad sentries. The impressive pair stood with their hands folded in front of them, still and expressionless. From the size of them, she guessed their purpose to be *paparazzi defense.*

Gregory motioned down the pier. "Let's get you inside where you can relax, Miss MacKenzie. I know the trip was long."

The giants split to make way.

Without another word or a glance back at poor long-suffering *Agatha*, Charlotte sashayed toward the island. The bouncers followed behind her, and the woman with the tray fell into line behind them, Charlotte leading the parade like a drum major.

Gregory moved to follow and then turned to eye Captain William.

"New hire?" he asked, his gaze darting in Shee's direction.

"I's need a vacation, too," said William, jovial as always.

Gregory gave Shee another arched-eyebrow glance and then headed down the pier after the others.

Captain William wasted no time pulling away.

Shee steadied herself at the back of the boat, watching as YOU's great wooden doors opened and Charlotte and the others disappeared inside. She couldn't make anything out beyond the doors other than additional greenery.

"Have you ever been inside there?" she screamed at the Captain.

He laughed.

Throwing back his head, he continued to cackle as they tore toward Andros.

CHAPTER FIFTEEN

Charlotte fought the urge to turn and catch one last glimpse of her mother as she followed the hulking men in powder blue down the length of the pier to YOU.

Be cool.

She couldn't put into words how excited she was to be on a mission.

Undercover.

Was there anything cooler?

She felt herself growing giddy and took a deep breath to better keep the *I've-seen-this-all-before* persona serving as the base for her MacKenzie character.

Blasé. Been here, done this.

The huge wooden doors to the island creaked open. Though they resembled doors from a forties monster movie, she could see they moved mechanically, not cranked by islanders.

"Did you have a good trip?" asked whippet-thin Gregory as he appeared at her side.

She gave a single nod without looking at him. It made her ill to be so rude to everyone, but chumming with the staff could jeopardize her cover.

She had a plan. She'd remain aloof at first, and then, when she'd identified a likely candidate, she'd *confide* in them some personal "MacKenzie" facts—make them feel as if she'd singled them out for her attention. Hopefully, this basic psychological trick would open the floodgates and get her mark talking.

Croix had said it appeared YOU had two tiers of guests. She

was tier one—typical rich kid. Tier two was so expensive it could only be populated by royalty, Hollywood elite, and the spawn of mega-millionaires. The son of a senator didn't make the cut for Tier Two by birth, and she didn't imagine Xander had been able to afford an upgrade.

Hopefully, Xander hadn't weaseled his way up the food chain. She didn't have the budget to follow him.

Charlotte and her entourage walked down a sandy path bordered by lush tropical jungle. The money spent on YOU's landscaping was mindboggling. Why would someone convert a Bahamian island into a jungle you could get for free in St. Lucia or Mexico or South America?

Proximity?

That had to be it. They wanted to keep the island paradise close to the States for the convenience of their American guests.

Or maybe they just had more money than they knew what to do with.

Must be nice.

A large, modern, single-floor building armored with what looked like polished teak hardwood appeared as they rounded a turn. Above her, the jungle opened like a morning glory to reveal a crystal blue sky. The sun blasted down to greet them. Beyond the teak building, there appeared to be another line of trees, followed by the upper third of the silver pyramid. She could see from this distance the "silver" of the pyramid was created by rows and rows of solar panels.

Ah. Smart. Free energy for the island.

The group mounted the steps to the porch where fans spun overhead—silently, at top speed—a novelty she found almost as fascinating as the resort itself. Having grown up in Florida, she'd sat beneath a *lot* of wonky fans in her day.

She paused, straining to spot a brand name.

"Would you like a quick tour of the property or to go directly to your room?" asked Gregory as they entered what appeared to be the main lobby.

The question threw her. She wanted a tour of the property, but she couldn't help but think a spoiled rich girl would want to freshen her makeup or something *me-oriented* after the plane and boat ride.

After a moment of hemming, she decided she didn't have to try so hard to be MacKenzie anymore. She'd made it into the compound. The primary objective *was* to find Xander, not win an Oscar. Best to take every opportunity to search the grounds.

She smiled. "I'd like the tour, thank you."

The tray-toting woman and the heavies peeled away. Charlotte's luggage disappeared with them.

Gregory opened his arms wide, motioning to each area as he began her tour.

"This is our main clubhouse. To the right are the Jupiter Club, a community lounge and game room."

"I'm from Jupiter Island," she piped. The line was delivered in too chipper a tone for apathetic MacKenzie, but at least she'd remembered to lie about her hometown.

Seemingly unimpressed, Gregory continued.

"The main gaming area features a pool, ping pong, shuffleboard, and other larger-scale games, but there are several smaller rooms for gaming and poker."

"And this area is available to *all* the guests?"

Gregory nodded. "Our Deities have additional facilities, so they rarely use these."

"Deities?"

"There are Deity and Demigod levels. You may have seen that when you booked?"

Charlotte blinked at him.

Whoops.

She rolled her eyes. "My assistant booked for me.

"Of course."

She sniffed. "Which am I?"

"You're a Demigod." He smiled. "Between you and me, I'm partial to the Demigods. They're a lot more fun."

She smiled.

Smooth. Gregory knew how to keep his spoiled clientele happy.

He was on the move again, leading her to a large dining

area featuring open seating and a smattering of secluded booths.

"Back this way, to the left of the entrance is our main dining area..."

Enticed by a glorious scent wafting from the kitchen, Charlotte raised her chin to get a better whiff. She scanned the area for Xander as her stomach growled.

"That smells *amazing*," she said.

Gregory agreed. "The hoisin glazed duck breast, I believe."

Charlotte swallowed to keep from drooling as Gregory led her outside. Two feet onto the back patio, she stopped.

Oh my...

She ogled an infinity pool, around which a dozen half-dressed, flawless bodies draped across loungers and oversized daybeds.

Did I just walk into a designer perfume commercial?

She suspected only her sunglasses had kept her eyes from falling out and rolling across the Travertine tiles.

"Are these Deities or Demigods?" she asked.

Gregory swept his gaze over the crowd. "Little of both, I think."

Many of the sun-worshippers had their backs to her or were tucked away inside gauzy tents, making it impossible to search for Xander from her vantage point.

"Mind if I take a quick stroll around?"

Gregory folded his hands in front of him as if he were putting himself into sleep mode. "Of course. It's all about *you*."

Charlotte sauntered around the pool, pretending to admire things like the landscaping, flowers, and views while sneaking peeks at the guests. A few seemed familiar, but none matched the photos of Xander Andino she'd studied.

Of course not. That would be too easy.

Circling back, she rejoined Gregory, who reanimated.

"Ready to see your cottage?" he asked.

She nodded, and he led her through the clubhouse again to a stone paver path weaving through the jungle.

"So what do you do?" asked Gregory, as they strolled past

an offshoot of the path marked *102* by a polished teak sign.

"As little as possible," she said, dodging the question with a giggle.

He pressed on, undaunted. "How about your parents?"

She cringed. Seems he was going to force her to lie to him.

"My mother's thirty-second in line to the throne of the Netherlands," she said. It sounded ridiculous, but Croix had assured her there was no way the resort could confirm or refute the claim.

His brow knit. "But you're American?"

"Yes. My father's in tech."

He took a few more steps before continuing. "Any tech I'd recognize?"

She huffed. "I dunno. He moves around. I don't ask." She tried to sound annoyed. While Shee and Croix had concocted an elaborate backstory for MacKenzie, she didn't want to share too much. The more facts the resort possessed, the easier it would be to catch her in a lie.

It worried her that Gregory's nosey questions felt like a pop quiz.

They turned onto a path marked *106* and approached a peach-hued Key-West-style cottage.

Gregory moved ahead to mount the stairs to the wide front porch and punch in a key code. As he opened the door to the cottage, Charlotte felt herself blasted by air conditioning and a scent she could only describe as *citrus and heaven.*

He handed her a small envelope as she entered.

"Your keycode is in here. I'd recommend memorizing it if you can."

She pulled a small white card out of the envelope, surprised to see three numbers staring back at her.

778.

Memorize them *if I can?*

How stupid does he think the guests are?

She glanced at Gregory, but he'd dipped to pluck a piece of lint off the sofa.

She took a deep breath.

MacKenzie. Be MacKenzie.

She scanned the room. The cottage was large for one person, consisting of three rooms—a main room-slash-bedroom with a large, canopied bed, a bathroom bigger than her kitchen back home, and a back sunroom filled with comfy chairs, a laptop, a Kindle, a game console, speakers, and a door leading to a patio complete with plunge pool.

Wow.

Gregory pushed a button, and an enormous television dropped from the ceiling near the foot of the bed.

"Your television is here. Anything you need, pick up that phone, and someone will be on the other side, ready to assist."

Charlotte found herself speechless. Looking bored had become *exhausting.*

Gregory stared at her.

"Oh, tip." She fished her second-hand Chanel purse for the cash Shee had provided her.

Gregory waved her away. "No tips. We're not allowed to accept them on the property."

Charlotte nodded, grateful to avoid having to calculate her gratitude.

"I do need to remind you that posting images of the other guests is prohibited. You can selfie, but you can't mention where you are. Our guests' privacy is our number one priority, and any identifying posts are grounds for banishment."

Charlotte fought off a snort of laughter.

Banishment?

She nodded. Shee had mentioned finding images of the resort online had been nearly impossible. Now she knew why.

Gregory's demeanor softened again. "Is there anything I can get you? Maybe sign you up for an activity or make a spa appointment? Everything we offer is in those brochures there."

He gestured to a collection of pamphlets on a table next to a large reading chair.

"I, uh…I think I'll take a moment here," she said, feeling as if taking a few minutes to collect her thoughts could make her

Xander-hunting all the more efficient in the long run.

Plus, she wanted to play with all the gadgets.

"Very good." Gregory showed himself to the door and, with a final nod, disappeared outside.

Charlotte's head fell back as she gawked at a blown-glass chandelier hanging above her. It looked like a turquoise-blue jellyfish.

That must cost more than my whole house.

She ruffled through the smattering of brochures and menus before settling into the giant reading chair to peruse them. The spa service menu proved as thick as a Tolstoy novel, featuring services ranging from a simple massage to facials made with ingredients so delicious-sounding she wondered if she could order them for lunch.

Sadly, the chances of bumping into Xander at the spa were less likely than finding him at one of the group activities listed on yet another bound menu. A printed insert listed the day's available special events—volleyball, diving, a walking history tour of the resort—she'd need to sign up for all of them and hope Xander showed up.

She pulled out her phone and called Shee.

"You're in?" screamed Shee. In the background, she heard the sound of Captain William's roaring engines.

"I'm in. Going out to look for him now. Might take a month..."

"What?"

"Nevermind. I'm kidding. Going to look for him now."

"Oh, good. If you can, give me a call later, when I'm not on this damn boat."

"Will do."

Charlotte hung up and found herself perusing the spa menu again.

Xander *could* be at the spa...

Someone knocked on the door, and she rose to answer. A pretty, mocha-skinned woman stood on her stoop, smiling.

"Hi. I'm Dr. Lilith."

The woman's tone made Charlotte believe she should know who she was, but she had no idea. She detected a hint of an accent, maybe Bahamian.

"Can I help you?" she asked.

The doctor squinted one eye. "Did Gregory not tell you I'd be stopping by?"

Charlotte shook her head. "No."

"I'm sorry. I'll only be a moment." She moved forward without waiting for an invite.

Charlotte took a step back to make way.

"Here at YOU, we like to talk about *you*," said the doctor. She pointed at Charlotte to emphasize her point. "We take care of your food, sleep, health and wellbeing, and also your mind and emotional balance."

Dr. Lilith paused to place an opened palm against her chest. "To that end, I'm a licensed psychiatrist and mental wellness counselor. Would you like to talk?"

Charlotte's brow knit. "*Now?*"

"Absolutely. Guests find releasing their burdens increases their enjoyment at the resort by a hundredfold."

Charlotte shook her head. She didn't have time for an impromptu psychiatric examination. She needed to start increasing her efforts to find Xander – *by a hundredfold.*

"Could we do it later? I had some plans—"

Dr. Lilith smiled, faltered, and then reappeared ten percent larger. "No problem *at all.* I'll get out of your way. Is there a specific time that would work for you today?"

Today? Why is this woman so pushy?

Charlotte released a huff without meaning to do it. Luckily, she imagined the sound of her impatience was on-brand.

She motioned to the magic phone Gregory had pointed out to her.

"Can I use that phone to call for you?"

Dr. Lilith nodded. "Absolutely."

"Great. Thank you."

Charlotte took a step forward to guide Dr. Lilith out the door. As she did, the woman put a hand on her upper arm.

"You look as if you have a lot on your mind," she said in a level tone.

Dr. Lilith stared into her eyes with an unsettling amount of *sincerity*, leaving Charlotte unsure whether to recoil or confess her deepest, darkest secrets.

Instead, she giggled.

Dr. Lilith's serious expression eased into chuckles of her own.

"I'll talk to you soon, MacKenzie."

"Thank you for stopping by," said Charlotte, watching the woman head back down her path.

"Remember..." The doctor raised a hand and called out without turning. "It's all about *you*."

CHAPTER SIXTEEN

Halfway down the island paver path, with no humans in sight, a voice spoke to Charlotte.

"Have you been invited to this bungalow?"

She stopped, her gaze rising to a camera mounted on a well-hidden vine-covered post, nestled inside the tree line.

"What?" she asked, stalling to give herself a moment to think. Visiting other cottages on the island wasn't as easy as walking down a path.

"Have you been invited to this bungalow by the current residents?" reiterated the voice.

Charlotte walked toward the camera, trying to look as confused as possible.

"This is *my* bungalow," she said, tapping herself in the chest.

"No, it isn't, MacKenzie. Your bungalow is three paths down on the left."

"Really?" She did a full three-sixty before poking her face at the camera again. "Are you *sure*?"

"We're sure. Just go back the way you came and make a left."

Charlotte rolled her eyes. "You should mark the paths better."

"I'll take your suggestion to management. Thank you."

Charlotte headed back up the path, grumbling to herself. YOU's intense security was going to make her life difficult. If Xander and his girlfriend had sequestered themselves in their room, which, considering the level of room service available, wasn't an awful idea, she might *never* bump into him during a group activity.

She only had two days. She couldn't leave things to chance. So far, she'd checked a volleyball game, strolled poolside, peeked into the gaming rooms—no sign of Xander or Isabella.

"Hey, I don't know you."

Charlotte looked up to find herself about to bump into a pink-haired girl.

"Me?" she asked.

"Yeah, you, silly." The girl said goodbye to the couple walking by her side and broke off to stride toward Charlotte.

"I'm Rapture," she said, thrusting out a hand. Tiny tattoos of stars, hearts, and cartoon characters riddled her forearm as if someone had thrown them at her, and they'd stuck wherever they landed.

Charlotte shook her hand. "Hi. MacKenzie."

The girl's lids drooped, and she stretched her neck as if she'd suddenly become intensely bored.

"How long have you been here?" she asked.

"Just a few hours."

"Well, that explains it. I basically own this joint, so I'd know if you've been here long," she chuckled, never looking at Charlotte to gauge if *she'd* found the comment funny. "Wanna get a drink at the tiki bar? I'm headed to the Cove."

Charlotte's brow knit. She hadn't seen anything with that name in the brochures or menus.

"The Cove?"

Rapture studied her own long, blue nails. "It's a Deity thing."

"Oh. I'm a Demigod."

Rapture shrugged. "It's cool. You can go with me. I'll be your *chaperone*."

Laughing, she skipped forward, pulling Charlotte's hand, and dragging her into motion.

"Do you stay in the bungalows here, too?" asked Charlotte when Rapture's burst of energy shifted back to a lazy saunter.

The girl flicked a finger in the direction from which they'd come. "There are waterfront bungalows on the other side of the pyramid for Deities." She turned to walk backward in front of Charlotte, looking giddy. "But *I'm* staying in the pyramid."

"I didn't know that was a hotel," said Charlotte. Inside, she groaned, faced with a plethora of *new* possible hiding spots for Xander.

Rapture bit her lip and lowered her voice to a whisper. "You have to be *invited.*"

"Oh." Charlotte wanted to ask what one had to do to be invited, but she didn't want to get too nosey, too fast. She didn't want to scare off her valuable new friend.

Anyway, she guessed she knew the answer: be *really, really rich.*

Rapture spun to walk on, and Charlotte fell into line behind her on the narrowing path. She studied what looked like a fresh tattoo of wings on Rapture's back. The design felt familiar.

"Are those the YOU wings?" she asked.

Rapture glanced over her shoulder.

"Yep. Cool, aren't they?"

Charlotte nodded. *Cool* wasn't the word she was thinking. *Crooked* was the word. In this version of the resort's logo, the word YOU had been removed, but the off-kilter wings remained. The effect made her want to straighten them.

Rounding a bend, a large ornate gate with a keypad attached to it appeared to block their way. Rapture typed in the code as Charlotte pretended not to watch.

2-2-3-7-3-3-3

Charlotte pulled out her phone and texted herself the number. Even with all the repeats, the code was *long,* and she didn't trust herself to remember it.

The ground shifted from crushed shells to beach sand on the opposite side of the gate. The air echoed with the sounds of people at play.

Hanging a right at a tightly wrapped fence made of bamboo, Charlotte spotted Rapture's aforementioned tiki bar embedded into the side of the faux mountain surrounding the resort. It faced a wide expanse of beach, dotted with the de rigueur collection of beautiful twenty-somethings in various states of undress and revelry.

She scanned the beach, looking for anyone who might be Xander. No one fit.

Rapture perched on a barstool. "Watch for drones, if you care."

"Hm?"

"If you're worried about paparazzi drones, stay under the nets." She pointed to a gauze canopy stretching out towards the beach. "Those things scramble the photos or something."

"I'm not that kind of famous," said Charlotte, taking a seat beside her new friend.

"Lucky you," muttered Rapture, scrolling through her phone.

Charlotte studied her friend.

How famous was her new buddy? She *did* look vaguely familiar. *Rapture* certainly sounded like a performer's name.

"Do *you* have to worry about paparazzi?" she asked.

Rapture looked up at her, eyes as large and white as golf balls.

"You know who I am, *right*?" she asked.

Charlotte swallowed, worried she'd offended her way out of a Deity pal.

Was it too late to *pretend* she knew who Rapture was?

"Um—"

"You can't name one song?"

Charlotte blinked.

So she's a singer...

"Um..."

Rapture's eyes widened. "OMG, you *don't* know who I am." Rapture squealed with what looked like delight. "That's *awesome*."

A bartender approached, and Rapture hooked a thumb in Charlotte's direction.

"She's never heard of me. Isn't that *awesome*?"

The bartender laughed in a perfunctory manner.

"I'll have the usual," she added.

Before Charlotte could order, Rapture threw back her head and began singing.

"I'm the star, but he's my sun..."

Charlotte recognized the tune. She'd heard the same song on the radio during her cross-state drive to Jupiter Beach. She remembered it because she'd thought how unfortunate it was the sexy song had used the homonym *sun* to describe the singer's lover. It made it sound as if she were in love with her *son.*

"That's *your* song?" she asked.

"*Yes.* I'm *Rapture.*" She shook her head. "Are you from a convent or something?"

Charlotte chuckled.

Fifty-five-plus community. Close enough.

"I'm sorry. I don't listen to the radio much."

The bartender delivered a clear iced drink to Rapture and turned his attention to Charlotte.

"I'll have the same," she said.

Rapture sucked on her straw, eyeing a group of young men playing volleyball. Half of them had abs that looked as if they'd been chiseled from marble.

"Do you come here a lot?" asked Charlotte.

Rapture nodded. "I love it. Can't get enough. Changed my life."

"I imagine it's nice to get away."

Rapture huffed. "You have *no* idea. Fans, family, boys—everyone." She looked left and right and leaned in. "Have you talked to Lilith yet?"

"Dr. Lilith? She stopped by my room—"

Rapture put her hand on top of Charlotte's. "You've *got* to do it. She's a *genius.*"

Charlotte's drink arrived, and she slid her hand out from Rapture's to take it.

"I dunno. I'm not a big fan of psychiatrists," she said, taking a sip.

Rapture barked a bitter laugh. "I've been to a *hundred*. Lilith's different. She reaches into your mind, and your heart, and—" The girl closed her eyes as if she had, indeed, ascended to rapture. "This place is *life*-changing. *Promise* me you'll go see her today."

"I'll try—"

Rapture slapped Charlotte's knee. "*Fit it in.* She's only the first step. I don't know if I should be telling you this, but..." Once again, she scanned the area for eavesdroppers before continuing. "...when you're ready, they let you talk to *the big guy.*"

"Who?"

"*Zeus.* He lives at the top of the pyramid."

"You've talked to him?"

"Not yet, but..." Rapture puffed her chest. "I'm level *six.*"

What had to be *pride* washed across the girl's expression.

"There are *levels*? Levels of what?"

Rapture shook her head. "Can't say. But I can say Zeus changed my life. Or, he's about to, anyway."

"But I don't understand. How?"

"Talk to Lilith. I can't say any more. They'd throw me out and never let me back, and I can't think of anything worse—" Rapture's attention snapped to a man on the beach waving her over.

"Oh, it's Tandy," she said, waving back. "I've got to go see him. His dad has some kind of in with the music awards. Gotta work it." She threw her arms around Charlotte's neck for a quick squeeze. "It was nice to meet you. I'll see you around."

Rapture walked with an exaggerated hip motion toward Tandy, a passably handsome man with a rolled blanket tucked beneath one arm.

Before she reached him, she turned and called back to Charlotte.

"Don't forget Lilith. *Next level shit.*"

Charlotte nodded and held up her glass to show she'd heard, suddenly feeling very exposed. Was she supposed to be on the beach without her Deity chaperone?

Better search the beach before I get kicked out.

She stood and wandered to the water, sneaking a peek at each face she passed.

The beach wasn't long, ending at an outcropping of jungle foliage and a jetty wall. Peering over the wall, she saw another beach that was empty and much smaller. Judging by the collection of seaweed gathering on its shore, she suspected the area wasn't used for guests.

Turning, she crossed the beach to the opposite side until she was stopped by an additional rock jetty. The opposite side of that structure sported only rough coral outcroppings, and no useable beach.

She turned and put her hands on her hips.

It was official. No Xander on Deity Beach.

Her attention drew to the pyramid, standing like a colossus over the jungle, one of its large, dark windows watching over her.

Is that what Rapture meant? She was on level six of the pyramid?

"Hey."

Charlotte refocused on the present as a mopey young man nodded at her on his way to the water.

"Hey," she answered, though the word barely made it past her lips.

It was *him*.

Xander Andino.

She was sure of it. As he walked past her, she spotted wings tattooed on his shoulder.

Did that mean the senator's son had made it to Deity status, complete with branding?

Didn't matter. She had him. She had to keep him before he disappeared back into some inaccessible Deity land.

Charlotte slipped her phone from her pocket and called Shee.

CHAPTER SEVENTEEN

Appalachian Trail, North Carolina

"Want to split that last piece of jerky?" asked Lisa, speaking to the back of her boyfriend's head. They'd been walking for what felt like a year, and she was starting to think she *hated* the sight of Gage's stupid neck more than anything in the world. Whenever she tried to walk side-by-side, he sped up, and she ended up right back behind him.

Gage turned, a dark stick of beef jerky poking from his lips.

"Hm?"

Lisa gawped. "Seriously? You're eating the last stick?"

He plucked the meat from his mouth to offer it to her. "You want the rest?"

She stared at the saliva-covered jerky. It looked as if rats had been gnawing on it.

"No, thanks."

He popped it back into his mouth. "There's a stop not far from here. We'll stock up. Do you want some nuts?"

Lisa stuck out her tongue as if gagging. "If I eat another pecan, I'm going to turn into a pie."

"That doesn't make any sense."

"A *pecan* pie."

"Yeah, but—"

Lisa pressed her lips into a tight white line to keep from shouting every thought in her head. When they'd talked about hiking the Appalachian Trail at home in Virginia, it'd seemed an adventurous and romantic thing to do. Now, forty-two miles into the trip, the only thing she knew for sure was she was breaking up with Gage the *second* they got back. She couldn't risk a fight with him on the trail—if he left, she'd be alone, and that wasn't cool.

She'd wait.

But, dude...

She stopped and stared into a clump of trees. Gold, red, and yellow leaves carpeted the forest floor.

"I have to go," she said.

Gage turned. "Again?"

She shrugged and tromped into the forest for privacy.

Gage snapped his tongue on his tooth, sucking until it made a loud *crack!* and then slurped again. She could hear him from fifteen feet away.

What did I ever see in him?

In an attempt to rid herself of Gage-noises, she continued toward a clearing visible through the oaks. A shaft of light pierced the canopy there, making it feel like a haven.

She squatted near the edge of the clearing and pondered her situation. Maybe she'd call home and see if her parents would come to pick her up in Hot Springs, North Carolina. It looked like a pretty cool town. She might even enjoy a day there with Gage, and then—

Lisa cocked her head as her meandering gaze fell upon a clump of mushrooms. The pale, blue-tinged stems struck her as strange. Finger-like. Back when walking the trail seemed like an exciting idea, she'd researched mushrooms in case she and Gage got lost and needed to forage to survive.

Now, brushing up on survival techniques seemed a little *dramatic*. Her imagined *wild adventure* had been supplanted by exhaustion and blisters. At the time, she'd thought, *who knows? People are always falling into ravines and getting lost.*

But these mushrooms... They didn't look like any she'd studied.

Lisa finished her business and snapped her shorts shut before wandering toward the cluster of stems. One had a bright orange cap she hadn't seen before. It looked like something out of *Alice in Wonderland*—

She stopped.

Her cheeks tingled as two words popped into her head.

Nail polish.

Like an evolving Rorschach test, her mind translated what she'd initially perceived as mushrooms into something entirely new.

Fingers.

One finger with orange polish on the short nail. The tips of the others looked as if they'd been gnawed away.

Lisa stumbled back.

"Gage!"

"What?" came the call from the trail.

"Gage!"

"What?"

The panic in her voice proved sufficient to motivate even her sluggard boyfriend. She heard him stumbling through the woods behind her.

"What?"

She pointed to what now could never look like anything to her but a human hand. Adult-sized, but small. Definitely a girl.

Gage followed her line of sight.

"Wha—oh shit. Is that—?"

Gage moved toward the body, reaching slowly towards it like Indiana Jones discovering the lost Ark of the Covenant.

Lisa's incredulity snapped her from her panic.

What is he doing?

"Don't *touch* it," she snapped.

He continued to tip-toe forward as if he were afraid he'd wake the girl.

"I need to see if she's dead," he said.

"She's *dead*, idiot."

"Maybe not—"

"She's *blue*, buried under a foot of leaves, and her fingers are all chewed up. What about that says *taking a nap* to you?"

Gage found a stick to flick away some of the leaves.

"It looks like something dug up her hand," said Gage.

"Shut up. I'm going to be sick," muttered Lisa, pulling her phone from her pocket. She dialed 911 and glowered at Gage as she raised the phone to her ear.

"*What?*" he asked, apparently annoyed by her attentions.

She spoke without unclenching her teeth.

"This trip is so *over.*"

CHAPTER EIGHTEEN

"I've been looking into it, and something doesn't feel right," said Croix, talking as Mick opened his Loggerhead apartment door.

"What doesn't?"

"YOU. The island is owned by a shell company that's owned by another shell company—something's fishy."

Mick shrugged. "Not our problem."

Croix peered past him into his open-plan living room. He watched her gaze scan until it hit the box of donuts on his counter.

"Mind if we talk through this a little?" she asked.

He took a step back. "Come in. I'm just watching the news."

"Thanks."

Mick dropped into his lounge chair as Croix snatched herself a donut and a single-serving bag of bright orange cheese sticks.

He watched in envy, his hand resting on the paunch he'd recently discovered around his middle.

If only I still had her metabolism.

Croix returned to flop onto the sofa.

Mick muted the news playing on his enormous wall-mounted television and rubbed his eyes. He'd been asleep when she knocked, but she didn't need to know that.

He peeked to see if she was watching him. She seemed more pensive than usual.

"You wanted to go?" he asked.

Croix pulled her attention from the silent glowing screen.

"Huh? Oh. To the island? No. Well, *yes*, but I get the whole mother-daughter bonding thing."

"That's very mature of you."

"It happens." She flashed a crooked smile. "Anyway, something doesn't feel right about this place."

"So you said. You don't think the kid is there?"

"It isn't that. It's the resort itself. There's like *no* information about it. I blew it off as rich people stuff at first, but then it started to get weird."

"It *is* a secret place for celebrities, right?"

"Yeah, but, *nothing*? This place is like Atlantis."

Mick shrugged. "We only care if the kid is there. Money like that can be pretty squirrelly."

"I guess. I—" Croix gaped at the television. Animating, she gestured at the screen as if poking an elevator button. "Quick, turn it up."

Mick turned. Senator Andino's son and the boy's girlfriend stared back at him, both smiling, arms around each other.

Frozen smiles on the news.

Never a good thing.

"Uh oh."

He fumbled for his television remote and turned up the volume.

"—last seen together at—"

"They're dead," said Croix.

"*Sshhh*," he hissed, waving her quiet.

The voiceover continued as more happy photos rolled onscreen.

"—Xander Andino is missing—"

"*Rewind it*," said Croix, clearly exasperated.

With a grunt, Mick tossed the remote to her. "*Here*, you take the clicker."

"The *clicker*..." Croix sniggered as she rewound to the beginning of the breaking news report.

The report began with a red banner confirming half of Croix's prediction. Isabella "Izzy" Candella, the girlfriend of Senator Andino's son, had been found dead.

Xander Andino was missing *and* a person of interest.

"They found her the same place where they went camping," said Croix. "But didn't his father say he came home?"

Croix jerked her phone from her pocket, finger alternately swiping and hovering.

"Girlfriend of Florida senator's son found dead in North Carolina," she read aloud before looking up at him. "If he came home and left her there dead..."

Alarm bells were already ringing in Mick's head.

Shee. Charlotte. They weren't chasing some senator's kid now. They were chasing a suspected killer.

"Call Shee. *Now*," he barked.

Croix made the call.

"Voicemail," she said.

"Leave one."

Croix did and then hung up.

"This isn't good," she said.

"No. The kid isn't missing. He's *running*."

"It looks like the first stories hit the news an hour ago. You had the news *on*. How did you not see it?"

"I don't know," he said, his voice laced with irritation.

"Were you sleeping?"

"*No*. I was *thinking*."

"With your eyes shut?"

"Croix, I swear to—" He stopped himself. No time for back and forth. He had to think. "You've got the story there?" he asked, motioning to her phone.

Croix scrolled. "They found her in the woods near the Appalachian Trail. Seems like she's been there a little while..."

"So she was dead *before* he came back here?"

"Probably."

"Not good."

"Nope."

Mick stood and wandered to the kitchen where he'd plugged in his phone. He had three missed calls from Nic Andino.

Shit.

He returned the calls, but Nic's phone went directly to voicemail.

He's probably in the thick of it now. Cops, press...

Mick caught Croix's attention. "Go to the Andino's. Search the boy's room again. Talk to Nic. Get anything you can out of him."

"What do you want me to ask? *Hey, did your son happen to mention killing his girlfriend?*"

"Tell him anything he tried to hide from us doesn't matter anymore. Ask him if he'd ever seen a possibility like this in the boy. Tell him we need to know *everything* if we're going to keep the kid from dying in a car chase or a blaze of gunfire."

"Dramatic." Croix stood. "What about Shee? I can't keep trying to call her *and* interrogate the Andinos."

"I'll get her."

"And Mason? Should I tell him?"

Mick considered this. He didn't want Mason going into savior mode and heading for the island before they knew more. "Hold off. Let me see if I can get Shee on the horn."

"Okay. Hey, how much do you think Nic knows?"

"He knew Xander came home. He knew the girlfriend didn't. Shee said he'd been avoiding the girl's family—*Huh.*" Mick hooked his mouth to the right as a thought occurred to him.

"*Huh*, what?" asked Croix.

"I wonder if he only hired us for an alibi?"

"For Xander?"

"For *himself.*"

Croix took a moment to process. "You mean so he can say he isn't hiding Xander—that he even hired a detective to find him."

"Right."

"He might be stalling while the kid gets away."

"Could be."

Croix grunted. "Pretty sneaky."

Mick nodded.

"Well, he *is* a politician."

CHAPTER NINETEEN

Charlotte lowered her phone as she watched Xander drop his towel to the sand, pause, and then walk into the sea. He'd chosen a spot away from the other bathers, far from the lifeguard sitting in his tower closer to the jetty on the opposite side of the beach.

Charlotte watched. Something felt off. After initial hesitation, Xander didn't slow or hurry. He walked methodically into the placid water until only his head bobbed above the waterline.

Charlotte had intended to dial Shee, but she found herself mesmerized by Xander's progress. He wasn't swimming. He proceeded as if he intended to continue walking until he reached the next island.

He paused as she squatted to set her phone on the sand, water lapping at his chin.

Is he trying to drown himself?

Charlotte jogged to the water's edge.

"Xander!" she screamed, waving her hands over her head.

He turned.

Drawn by her call, the lifeguard stood and whistled in their direction, motioning for Xander's return.

Xander glanced at the lifeguard and then back at Charlotte. Following a third warning whistle, his body emerged from the water as he trudged ashore.

She backed up as he exited the sea.

"Who are you?" he asked. His eyes were rimmed with red.

Charlotte hemmed. "MacKenzie. I—you looked like you—"

"How do you know my name?"

Charlotte bit her lip. She'd completed the first half of her mission and located Senator Andino's errant son. Calling him by name hadn't been the best way to earn his trust for phase two: *getting him home.*

Xander appeared both spiritless and annoyed. He *didn't* seem like a guy open to suggestions. Now wasn't the time to dive into her case for returning home.

"Do you want to get a drink?" she asked.

His brow knit. "Did Zeus send you?"

Charlotte shook her head.

"No."

He looked disappointed.

She noticed.

"Not *directly*," she added.

Xander buoyed. "Is he ready to meet me? I thought he might be mad—"

He stopped to rub his eye with his knuckle, and Charlotte noticed the slackness of his expression and the droop of his eyelids.

Is he drunk?

She nodded in a non-committal fashion. "Let's get a drink."

His gaze bounced to the beach bar where the men who had been playing volleyball now gathered. Two were dragging a giant beer keg through the sand toward the others. He frowned with unmistakable disgust. The volleyball crowd looked as if they'd been coughed up by an Olympic village—each trim, glistening, hairless body more perfect than the next.

Xander was stocky, hairy, and long-nosed.

"I don't want to be around all these people," he grumbled. "Are we just *waiting*? Did he send you to talk to me or to sit with me until he's ready?"

"We could go somewhere else. Pick a spot," she said, deflecting his questions.

He glanced at the bar again and shrugged. "My room?"

Charlotte considered the offer. Xander seemed harmless

enough. She didn't want to give him the wrong impression, but the privacy of his room might make him more pliable to listen to her suggestion that he head home. Plus, she'd implied she was with the resort, so he'd be on his best behavior.

He had a girlfriend, and anyway, he seemed more interested in her as an envoy of YOU than anything personal.

"Okay," she said.

His miserable expression loosened. "Cool."

She dipped to pick up her phone as he gathered his towel.

"Oh," she said, pretending her phone had vibrated. "Two seconds while I get this."

She took a few steps away to call Shee.

"I have him," she whispered into the phone when her mother answered.

"You do? Is he willing to go?"

Shee sounded excited, too.

"I'm not sure. He's drunk."

"Good. That could work in your favor." Shee paused. "Or *not.* Is he calm?"

"Mellow…" Charlotte considered telling Shee about Xander's odd stroll into the water but decided to save it for later. She needed to get her mother a location for pick up.

"On the south side of the island, there's a guest beach with a tiki bar, but to the *right* of that, on the other side of a jetty, is a smaller beach," she said. "How about I meet you there? How soon could you get here?"

Shee clucked her tongue several times. "I need to find a boat, plus the trip…Two hours?"

Charlotte eyed Xander, who was now standing with his chin pressed against his chest as if he were sleeping on his feet. She could get him back to the room, let him pass out, and then wake him up at the right time with promises of going to meet Zeus.

That could work.

"Perfect," she said to her mother.

"Great. See you soon. Oh, and *great* job."

Charlotte grinned. "Thank you."

She hung up and tapped her phone against her hand as she watched Xander sway like seaweed in a stiff current. All she had to do was keep him pliable for two more hours.

Easy peasy.

"Ready?" she asked.

His head snapped up.

"Hm? Oh. Yep. Let's go."

He led the way toward the gate, giving the rowdy volleyball players a wide berth. He walked with his head down, shoulders hunched, as if he were leaning into a cold winter breeze.

She hadn't known him long, but she couldn't say Xander seemed in a positive state of mind.

And where was Isabella?

Maybe they broke up.

That would explain a lot.

CHAPTER TWENTY

One week ago...

"We shouldn't go to YOU anymore," said Isabella.

Xander poked a stick into the fire, sending a shower of sparks towards the heavens.

"What are you talking about?"

She moved closer and put her hand on his, effectively ending his fire-poking fun.

"That man is *evil*," she said.

"Who? Zeus?"

"Whatever he calls himself."

Xander scowled at her. "He's trying to *help*."

"Is he?" Isabella pulled out her phone. "I searched online to find out more about him."

"*Why*?' Xander could hear the anger in his voice. Everything about Izzy was annoying him. Doubting Zeus. Poking around online. That earnest look on her face—like she was *so* much smarter than him.

It reminded him of his father.

Dr. Lilith had warned him against people like her. People trying to trick him under the guise of "protecting" him. He hadn't understood what she meant at the time, but now that he was *aware*, it seemed like *everyone* was trying to use him.

"*Why*?" She swiped through her phone. "Because he asked you to steal from your own family, Xander." She held up her screen for him to see. "I showed you that list I made, and *look*, I found this article—"

Xander slapped the phone out of her hand.

"Hey!"

Isabella scrambled after her phone as it narrowly missed the fire and skittered across the dirt.

Xander froze, surprised by his reaction.

"What the hell do you think you're doing? You could have cracked it," snapped Izzy, brushing off her screen as she glared at him.

"I won't be a victim," he said.

Her expression twisted.

"*What?*"

He poked a finger at her. "I won't be *your* version of me."

She scoffed. "Oh, *please*. Stop spouting Dr. Lilith shit. You sound like an *idiot*."

Xander felt his ire rising.

"You're trying to ruin *everything*." He stomped to his backpack, where he kept his bottle of tequila. Uncorking it, he took a long swig.

"You've had *enough*," said Izzy, shaking her head. "You're drinking *way* too much. Who are you? You're not even yourself anymore."

He shook the bottle at her. "You know what? You're just *jealous*. You know Zeus doesn't even want you on the island."

She turned away. "Give me a *break*."

"He said I should get rid of you."

She spun back around. "What? When?"

Xander shrugged. "He said you're not right for us."

She squinted. "*Us*? Who's *us*?"

He took another hit from the bottle.

Forget it.

He couldn't explain everything to her. She wouldn't understand. He wasn't supposed to tell her anything anyway.

Isabella folded her hands in front of her face as if she were beginning to pray and spoke in a measured tone.

"Xan, don't you see? He's trying to separate you from the people who *love* you. He's trying to *control* you."

Xander barked a laugh. "*Control* me? He's trying to *free* me. My father's been controlling me my whole life—"

"Your father is your *father*. He's hard on you, I know, but he's still your *father*. He loves you."

Xander coughed as the booze burned his throat. "No, he doesn't. You don't know anything. You're a stupid sheep."

"*What did you call me?*"

The shock of Izzy's shriek echoing in the quiet forest night made Xander jump, but he was in it now.

No time to hold back.

Time to command the now.

He'd tell her the truth and be done with it.

"I'm sorry, but you're a *sheep*. You people who follow your parents around and do what they say—"

"*You're* the sheep, you *idiot*," Izzy stormed toward him, her eyes flashing white. "Don't you get it? YOU is a *cult*. You're so stupid—"

He struck her. The moment she entered his space, he backhanded her with his left hand.

She whirled and fell near the fire, clipping one of the outer logs with her hand. A burst of burning orange embers exploded into the air around her.

He gasped and jerked back the hand still hanging in the air in front of him.

Isabella shielded herself from the bits of fire as they rained down on her.

"You *hit* me," she said, slapping at the embers on her clothing. One side of her face had darkened with ash.

She tried to rise. Her arm gave way. She collapsed to the ground.

He smelled burning hair.

"Help me," she said.

Xander shook his head.

Was her face red? Swelling? Black and blue?

This is bad.

Everyone would know he hit her. He'd go to jail. Worse, his father would know. It would be all over the news how the senator's son hit his girlfriend. His father would be furious. He'd cut him off.

Just like Zeus said he would.

Isabella would tell everyone about YOU, too. He'd be banished. His father *and* Zeus would leave him in jail to rot, now, when he was *so close* to freedom.

"*There.*"

The word came from behind him.

Xander turned.

The trail.

People on the trail. They hadn't camped far from the Appalachian. The damn trail walkers. They were all so chummy. They'd come to see if they could join for sure. He stared at the campfire, willing it to die.

He swallowed, listening.

Someone saw the fire.

He had to kill the fire.

"Xander," called Izzy.

The sound of her voice made him jump. He held up a hand.

"Shut up."

"You are in so much trouble..."

"Shut *up.*"

"Xander..."

His chest tightened.

This is bad.

He turned and took a step toward her.

She needed to be *quiet.*

CHAPTER TWENTY-ONE

Shee set her phone on the marina restaurant's lacquered picnic table and stabbed a chunk of conch ceviche.

Charlotte had called—she'd found the boy.

That's my girl!

Shee was thrilled and proud to hear the news, though she wished it had come ten or twenty minutes later. After lunch. She was *starving*.

Ah well.

Finding Xander was a good thing. Charlotte hadn't mentioned finding Isabella, but that didn't mean she wasn't on the island. Shee hoped she was, for her family's sake.

No time to bask in parental pride. She had a lot to do.

First on the list?

Secure a boat.

She couldn't use the same boat they'd used that morning, one with a captain terrified of losing YOU business. She needed a boat without a sweat-stained uniform requirement. A vessel heftier than a tin can center console, so her insides didn't rattle to mush during the crossing.

She watched as a pot-bellied man in his sixties waddled his way to a cabin cruiser docked at the end of the longest pier of the marina.

Hm.

She'd spotted the balding mid-life crisis earlier, picking up bar food as he ham-handedly flirted with the bartender.

One mahi-mahi sandwich, extra fries.

That probably meant no *Mrs. Potbelly* awaited him back on the boat.

Shee threw money on the table and headed for the marina, pulling her tee-shirt over her head as she moved. She'd worn a bikini for underwear in the off-chance she'd need to get wet. The boob-enhancing pushup bra might be *just* what she needed to accomplish step one.

Hustling down the pier, she slid into a hip-swinging saunter as she neared the cabin cruiser. Potbelly balanced one leg on the pier and one leg on his cruiser's gunwale as he braced himself to hop to the deck.

"That's a gorgeous boat," she purred.

She wasn't lying. The Grand Banks oozed classic charm. She guessed it to be a little over forty feet long, which meant the ride back to YOU would be as smooth as Potbelly's glistening skull.

The name painted on the aft could use some work, though. *Hedge Fun.* Apparently, her mark was a hedge fund guy with a limited imagination.

Potbelly dropped to the deck with a grunt before turning to squint through his sunglasses at her.

"Huh?" he asked. As he focused, his chest swelled, and his abdomen sucked in half an inch.

"I said, that's a *gorgeous* boat." Shee raised her voice to be heard over a passing Jet Ski. The result was much less sexy, but she wouldn't get far if he couldn't hear her.

He seemed confused but grinned. "Oh. Thank you."

She moved to where he'd hopped onto the vessel. "Permission to come aboard?"

He straightened. "What?"

Shee sighed. Flirting to get what she needed had never been something she enjoyed. She didn't consider herself particularly good at it and having to repeat every cringy line didn't make it any easier.

"I'd love to come on board if you have time?" she bellowed like a carnival barker.

He pointed to the deck. "On my boat?"

"No, on your *sandwich*," she muttered without moving her lips, her smile frozen in place. "Yes, your boat, *silly*," she added, louder. In her experience, men loved it when she called them *silly*.

No idea why.

"Um," he glanced at the carryout bag in his hand and then back up at her, looking something like a trapped animal.

Shee braced herself.

Is he about to choose a fish sandwich over my company?

She knew she wasn't in her twenties anymore, but she'd assumed she still had more allure than a fried chunk of Mahi—

"*Absolutely*," he said, putting the bag down.

He'd made his Sophie's choice.

Whew.

"I'm Richard," he added.

"Tiffany." Shee reached out a hand and let him guide her into the boat. He ran his hand down her bare back under the pretense of steadying her progress. She fought not to elbow him in the mouth.

She gawped at the boat to show him how impressed she was. The vessel wasn't new, but it was well kept. The teak floors were spotless and shiny. What looked like an untouched paddleboard hung tucked against one side wall.

Quite an upgrade from her last taxi to Tantalus.

"It's so *big*, Dick," she said.

She had to turn her head to hide a snort of laughter.

I crack myself up.

"Would you like to see inside the cabin?" he asked, motioning to the door. He stared at her unabashedly, his eyes wide with wonder.

"I *would*." She took a step forward, only to have him raise a hand to block her path.

"Wait," he said, his mouth drooping into a tight frown. "How much is this going to cost me?"

She blinked at him, unsure if she felt flattered or insulted.

"Are you asking if I'm a *hooker*?" she asked.

His jaw bounced soundlessly for a few seconds before he found his voice. "Yes. I mean. If you *are*, that's okay. I'm not judging. You're just—" He wiped his sweaty brow with the back of his hand. "You're so *pretty*."

She smiled. "I'm not out to take your money." She glanced at the restaurant to see if anyone was watching them.

I'm here to take your boat.

Richard swallowed and lowered his hand to grant her access to his floating castle. Shee walked past him into the teak-lined cabin, air conditioning crisp against her sun-kissed skin.

"This is the, uh, kitchen," he said, following.

"Gally," she corrected before she could stop herself.

. *Whoops.*

He removed his sunglasses. "Hm?"

"*Golly*," she said. "It's beautiful."

His grin grew an inch. "I had the bar area here custom made—"

She walked to the helm, delighted to find the keys dangling in the ignition.

"Do you drive this all by yourself?" she asked.

He nodded. "I do. I mean, I *can*, but I have a captain right now. He's a local. My guide around the islands."

Shee fought to keep her smile and glanced out the window.

Shit.

Wherever the captain was, he'd be back soon. Chances were good he'd be younger and fitter than Richard Potbelly.

She'd have to move fast.

"*Piña Colada*?" she chirped.

"What's that?"

"I was thinking all we need are a couple of *Piña Coladas*." She pointed her chin in the direction of the restaurant to help the gears in his head start churning.

"I can get those at the bar," he said, putting the pieces together. "But then you have to promise to stay and tell me more about yourself..."

He said the last part in a sing-song voice that made it

difficult not to cringe.

"Oh, you're a *dream*," she said, booping him on the nose with her finger.

He giggled.

"Um," he peeked outside and then back at her. "Would you mind waiting outside? It's stuffy in here."

Shee tried not to look disappointed. The guy wasn't *quite* as dumb as she hoped—he didn't want her rifling through his cabin while he was gone. He *was* aware of the age and appearance chasm between them and clearly suspected she had an ulterior motive. Luckily for her, he still wanted to play out the scenario, in case she had a fetish for older, bowling-ball-shaped men.

"No problem," she said, moving back outside.

He followed her, locking the door behind him, before clawing his way back onto the pier. Breathless, he turned to stare down at her.

"I'll be right back."

She waved. "I'll be waiting, Richard."

He beamed, seemingly thrilled to hear his name on her lips, and toddled toward the bar.

She watched until he was tucked away, ordering the drinks.

How to proceed...

She wandered, finding a smattering of tools in a hold, including a fish knife and a collection of zip ties.

What more could a girl ask for?

Looking over her shoulder, she spotted someone at the bar next to Richard.

She paused her search.

Move along. Nothing to see here...

A young man with a short blond ponytail engaged Richard. They chattered for a bit and seemed to know each other. Richard motioned to the boat, and the young man grinned and slapped him on the back.

Crappity crap crap.

The young man had to be *El Capitan*.

Shee closed the door of the hold and slipped the zip ties into her pocket. The oversized screwdriver she slid into her shorts and beneath the elastic of her bikini bottoms, which she used as a gun belt to hold it in place. To cover the grip poking from her shorts, she popped her tee-shirt back on.

The bikini top had done its job. Time for retirement.

She pretended to gaze at the water while watching Richard and his young friend from the corner of her eye. The bartender approached them with two white frozen cocktails in hand.

The moment of truth.

Don't panic.

Richard wouldn't want the captain tagging along on his date. He'd tell him to make himself scarce for a while in the hopes he's about to get lucky.

Please, please, please...

Richard took the cocktail glasses and headed toward the pier.

The captain fell into line behind him.

Shee held her breath.

No, no, no—

Richard wobbled on, chunks of coconut cream-coated ice slush sloshing to the decking in his path. A step away from the pier, the shadowing captain made an abrupt left to sit with a group of other young men, though not before everyone had been thoroughly high-fived and fist-bumped.

Richard was returning alone.

Shee's shoulders dropped a notch.

Whew.

Now all she had to do was devise a way to incapacitate him without the persuasion of her gun, which hadn't made the international trip.

"They look amazing," she said, reaching for the now half-empty, skull-sized glasses.

He handed them to her and hopped inside, as graceful as a hedgehog.

"Do you mind if we drink them inside?" she asked, nodding

her head toward the cabin. "I might have overdone it today, and the air in there feels *amazing*."

He shrugged and hooked a little smile. He seemed less flustered and more sure of himself each minute she remained on the boat.

"Sure." Fishing in his pockets, he produced his keys and unlocked the cabin.

Shee walked inside and set the glasses down on the counter by the galley sink. She heard two clicks—the glasses hitting the counter and the bolt sliding shut.

He'd locked the door behind him.

She turned and smiled.

You little shit.

"Hey, I have an idea," she said. "I'm going to read your palms."

He rolled his eyes. "I don't believe in that stuff. Let's just drink and get to know each other." He moved toward her.

Shee put a hand on his shoulder to stop his progress. "Aw, come on. I *love* doing it. Hold out your hands."

He huffed a sigh and held out his right palm.

"Both hands," she said.

He raised his left to join its mate.

"Okay, give me a second to feel your energy. Close your eyes."

His lids closed.

She slid a zip tie from her shorts.

"This is stupid," he muttered, even as his fingertips reached to brush the top of her breasts.

"Almost finished," she whispered, trying to sound as if she were wrapped in some mystical trance. "Now press your palms together."

He did as he was told, making it easy for her to slip the plastic tie around his wrists and zip it shut.

His eyes popped open.

"Hey!"

He took a step back, but she maneuvered behind him before he could get far. Jerking the long screwdriver from her hip, she pressed it into his back.

"Ow!" he yelped, twisting.

"Stay facing *front*," she barked. "Make a sound and I'll slip this knife through your fifth and sixth ribs, straight into your heart."

She had no idea if the space between those two ribs were the expressway to a man's heart, but it sounded convincing.

"What are you doing?" he asked. "Take my watch. I don't have much money on the boat."

"I'm not here to rob you," said Shee, pushing him toward the front berth. He took the hint and stumbled into his bedroom.

"This gets you off?" he asked, sounding equal parts pissed and hopeful.

"Uh, *no*. Lean forward, face on the bed."

He bent, and she zipped his ankles together. She cut the tie on his wrists using the knife and jerked his right arm behind his back before he had time to think about making a move.

"Give me your left," she said.

"No!" He tried to flip over. She hiked his arm up his back until he cried out.

"Give it to me, or I'll snap your arm off."

Whimpering, he gave her his left hand, which she zip-tied to his right behind his back before taking a step away.

"Turn over."

Flopping like a landed fish, he turned to his back and then sat on the end of his bed, his gaze falling to the knife in her hand.

"That's my fish knife," he said as if the worst thing that had happened to him that day was that she'd borrowed his knife.

She jerked open a drawer and hit paydirt on the first try—a long silk tie. She used it to gag him.

"Hutty-a-hant?" he asked as she secured it.

"I want you to lay here quietly while I run a quick errand. No biggie."

She left him and strode outside to the cleat at the back of

the boat, untying the line securing them to the pier and letting it drop into the water with little fanfare.

One down.

Shimmying to the bow, she untied the remaining line. As she squatted by the cleat, she scanned the restaurant on the opposite side of the pier. The captain had disappeared...*no.* There he was with his friends. The party had abandoned the dining table for the bar. They sat with their backs to her.

Excellent.

The captain might hear the boat start, but he'd probably assume Richard was taking his lady visitor on a cruise. Little chance he'd panic and report the boat stolen.

Shee slipped back inside to the tune of Richard's grunting as he struggled to free himself.

"Are you going to make me stab you?" she called through the door.

The noises grew more fervent.

Shee sighed. "Seriously, Richard. Don't make me kill you. Then I have to drag you outside and dump your carcass overboard before you start to stink—"

The grunting stopped.

Richard called out something that sounded like "I'm sorry."

"Good man."

Shee took a seat at the helm.

Okay.

Hm.

While she considered herself a Jack-of-all-trades, boats weren't her strong suit. Once she turned the key, she'd have to be on her way. If she drifted around or backed into the pier, the captain would come running.

She turned the key. The engine roared to life. She pushed the throttle forward, spinning the steering wheel to point away from the pier and in the general direction of YOU.

So far, so good.

She smiled, feeling pretty pleased with herself.

Ah, to be on the sea...wind in your hair—

Something rang, and she cocked her head.

A phone.

Not my phone...

She gasped.

Richard's phone.

She'd left it in his pocket.

She dove for the door of the front berth and flung it open, *just* as Richard managed to shake the phone from his pocket. It tumbled onto the bed.

"Gimme that," she said, lunging for it.

He protested and tried to clip her with his shoulder. She snatched the phone and pounced on him to knock him to his back on the bed. Once she straddled him, he fell limp, as if everything had become too much.

"Don't move," she barked at him.

She searched the bunk's many cabinets to be sure he didn't have anything else useful hidden somewhere—a spare phone or worse, a *gun*. All she needed was to have him pop out of the berth, blazing.

"Hello?" said a tinny voice.

Shee froze.

Who the heck is that?

She glanced at the screen of Richard's phone and realized, during the struggle, that she must have accidentally answered the call.

Oh no. What did they hear? She'd been muttering who-knows-what the entire time.

She realized Richard was staring at her, his eyes like saucers.

He'd heard the voice, too.

"Elk! *Elk!*" he yelped through his gag.

She scurried out of the room, shut the door behind her, and raised the phone to her ear as she reentered the main cabin.

"Hello?"

"Oh. Hey, uh, is Richard there?"

Shee took a deep breath to ensure her voice sounded as calm as possible.

"May I ask who's calling?" she asked.

"It's Ivan, his captain—is that *him*?"

Behind her, Richard wailed.

Sonuva...

After a peek out the front windshield to ensure the boat wasn't about to crash into anything, Shee walked outside and shut a second door behind her. Outside, the sound of the engines covered the sound of Richard's protests.

That was good.

Peering over the back of the boat, she spotted Captain Ivan staring at her as he walked down the pier, phone pressed to his ear.

Oh. Hello there.

She waved to him.

He waved back.

"Are you guys going somewhere?" he asked in her ear. She watched his lips move in real life.

"Richard's taking me for a ride," she said, punctuating the line with a giggle.

"Does he know—I mean—" Ivan stopped walking and perched his free hand on his hip. "Can I talk to him?"

"He's, uh, in the head."

Ivan sighed. "Okay. Um, tell him if he needs anything to give me a call. I'll be here if he needs help docking, okay?"

"Okay. Thank you." She waved again.

He waved back and lowered his phone from his ear before returning to the bar.

Shee smiled.

Returning to the cabin, she pushed down on the throttle as Richard howled.

"Don't make me get stabby!" she screamed at him.

Silence fell.

Shee made a slight directional adjustment and roared toward YOU.

CHAPTER TWENTY-TWO

Shee pulled to the south side of Tantalus Island and cut the cabin cruiser's engine. Drifting three hundred yards offshore, she used Richard's binoculars to scan the small beach Charlotte had referenced.

Thank you again, Richard. So generous...

No sign of her daughter and Xander.

Sweeping left, she spotted a few stragglers wandering around a larger beach, separated from the smaller one by a clump of trees and a rock jetty. Charlotte had described this exact setup.

She had the right spot.

The sun had set three-quarters of the way through her trip. She'd cut the vessel's running lights to keep it from looking like a boat parade as she approached the highly guarded island.

There was nothing left to do but bob in the dark and wait.

She tapped the gas meter to confirm the tank was at a little more than half full. In theory, she'd have enough gas to get back, but she couldn't waste a drop. Maybe Richard kept extra fuel on the boat.

"Hey," she said, opening the door to the front cabin.

She took a quick step back as Richard tumbled toward her like the contents of an overfilled closet, poking his head at her like an angry tortoise.

"What the—"

She reflexively punched him in the face.

He cried out from behind his silk tie gag.

As he twisted away from her, she side-kicked him back on the bed. He landed on his back, moaning.

"What the hell was that Richard?" she asked.

He rolled on his side, blood oozing from his nose, staining the light blue tie in his mouth.

"Ew oke eye ohs!"

She sighed. "I didn't break your nose."

"Ess ooh eh."

"I *didn't.* I know what that feels like when the cartilage collapses, and that wasn't it."

He stared at her with a doleful, basset-hound expression, his eyes watering.

It worked.

She felt bad.

She huffed. "Look, I'm sorry about your nose, but what am I supposed to do when you come charging at me like an angry potato?"

He frowned as best he could with the tie in his mouth. "Uck ooh."

She clucked her tongue. "Richard. *Language.* There's a lady present."

His brows tilted up in the center. The water dripping from his eyes became more persistent.

"Are you crying?" she asked.

"Eh *urtss.*"

Oh for crying out loud.

She'd gone from captor to nurse.

She popped back into the main cabin to grab a rag she'd seen in the galley and used it to wipe away the trickle of blood on his lip.

"I'm sorry, but you have to take some responsibility."

He scowled at her.

"Are ew crayssy?"

"*No.* Think about it. You caused your own problems, and I don't just mean that half-baked attack. You *knew* I was up to no good. You should have *never* let me on your boat. Why would you trust me?"

His gaze dropped to her boobs before bouncing back to her eyes.

"*Exactly*. Why would you endanger yourself for sex?"

He shrugged one shoulder and stared, hangdog, at his belly.

"Aw. Don't sell yourself short. I'm sure you have other charms."

He snorted a little laugh and winced as a blood bubble popped from his nose.

She dabbed him again with the rag and patted him on the foot. "Now, even though you don't deserve to know after that stunt, I have good news for you. Are you ready?"

He nodded.

"I'm *not* going to kill you. I'm not even going to *hurt* you. I needed to borrow your boat to pick up my daughter and a client of ours. I'm a bounty hunter. Okay?"

He frowned. "You already hurt me."

"Fair enough. Maybe a little. I'm sorry. But, doesn't it make you feel better to know I'm not some psycho who brought you to a deserted island to roast and eat you?"

His eyes popped wide.

"Oh. You hadn't considered that possibility." She sniffed. "Well, you can scratch it off the list anyway. You'll be fine. This will all be over soon."

His head dropped to the bed with what looked like resignation.

She tapped a tooth with the tip of her nail. "But I had a question for you...what was it... Oh, I remember—do you have any extra gas on board?"

"In da old."

She hooked a thumb toward the door leading outside. "In the hold? Is that the panel in the floor out there?"

He nodded.

"Cool. Thank you. I'll be back in a bit. Why don't you take a nap?"

He closed his eyes with a quiet whimper.

She shut the door and grabbed the binoculars to scan the beach again.

Still no sign of Charlotte.

Dammit.

While she waited, she scrolled through her phone, searching for an island to return to *other* than Andros. Captain Ivan might be waiting with cops by the time she—

A loud *pop!* split the night air, and Shee sprang to her feet.

That sounded like a gunshot.

Scrambling outside, she cocked her head until two more shots blasted.

Definitely gunfire.

Lifting her binoculars, she scanned the shore.

Nothing.

The shadows she'd seen meandering on the big beach had disappeared. They hadn't seemed like people about to burst into a gunfight. Whoever had the gun didn't seem to be shooting at *her*, which she imagined was a good thing, but there shouldn't be shots ringing from a resort island *at all.*

Nervous energy shivered through her body. She glanced at the paddleboard strapped to the inside wall of the boat, then back at the island, then back at the paddleboard.

I can't just sit here.

She couldn't bob in the water while gunshots blasted on the island. Not with Charlotte there somewhere. The firing had stopped, but it didn't matter. Why would someone be hunting or shooting skeet in the dark?

Plus, the pops had sounded like a handgun.

She ducked back into the cabin and fiddled with the dash until she released the anchor. She heard the clanking of the chain as it ran, steadying herself as it bit into the seafloor and the boat's drifting ceased.

Hopefully, the anchor would hold. If Charlotte was finding it difficult to convince Xander to leave, she could only imagine how hard it would be if they had to paddleboard home because the boat had drifted to Cuba.

The sound of snoring reached her ears, and her attention shifted to the front berth door.

Then there's Richard.

Should she tell him she was stepping out?

Nah.

He'd already tried to escape once.

She'd be right back.

Hopefully.

She plucked the keys from the ignition to ensure Richard couldn't run away if he emerged from the cabin. Wrestling her shirt over her head, she walked outside and released the paddleboard from its straps. She heaved it into the water, grabbed the paddle, and dropped into the sea beside it.

The water was warm. She'd expected a chill. To feel *something.* Instead, it felt as if she'd slipped into a second skin.

Pulling herself onto the paddleboard, she straddled it before oaring her way toward the island. Sitting wasn't the most hydrodynamic way to proceed, but staying low and less noticeable seemed like a good idea.

She paddled, shifting from left side to right. At her current rate, she'd hit the island in—

The board jerked to the left beneath her.

Shee froze, paddle hanging in the air beside her.

Did I hit something?

A thousand tiny alarms rang at the end of every nerve.

She knew why.

That wasn't what *hitting something* felt like.

Something had hit *her.*

She swallowed.

A big fish? A stingray? A shark checking to see if she was edible? She stared at her knees, where her legs disappeared into the warm, dark water below.

Where *anything* could be lurking.

Where *anything* might be staring at her toes, drooling salty spit into the sea.

Oh hell no.

While she and Mason sporting matching missing legs might be *adorable* and make for interesting Halloween couple costumes, she wasn't willing to do *anything* for love.

She pulled her dangling legs from the sea. Standing, she found her balance and started paddling as if her life depended on it—just in case it did.

She arrived at the little beach and pulled the paddleboard to the sand, creeping low against the jetty. The clearing was small—barely big enough to call it a beach at all.

Still no sign of Charlotte.

She checked her watch. It had been two and a half hours since her daughter called.

Something had gone wrong.

Maybe Xander had decided not to play ball?

But wouldn't Charlotte have called to tell her that? She checked her phone.

No missed calls.

Voicemail? There was one.

She cursed herself for not noticing it earlier. Maybe it had popped up when she hit the island—

She recognized the number.

Croix.

Not Charlotte.

She listened to the receptionist's halting voice.

Um... Is this on? Um, call me. Or your Dad. Call the hotel. Xander's girlfriend—um, anyway, call back, like, ASAP. It's important. Okay. Yeah. Bye.

Shee rolled her eyes as she lowered her phone. Croix couldn't have sounded more uncomfortable if she'd left the message with a gun pressed against her temple. It was like she'd never left a voicemail before—

Something rustled deep in the jungle to Shee's left. She turned, hoping to see her daughter and Xander tromping toward her, but instead heard distant male voices.

Shit.

She crouched behind a flowering bush.

The voices were too far away to discern the words, but they

weren't Charlotte's. At least two men, maybe three.

Were they the source of the gunfire?

Shee's phone vibrated in her hand, and she answered it, whispering hello.

"Why are you whispering?" snapped her father, always the charmer.

"I'm on the beach at YOU. There's—" She heard voices again and decided to get into a drawn-out description of her predicament wasn't in her interest. "Dad, I have to go—"

"Do you have Charlotte?"

Her father sounded flustered.

Mick McQueen flustered did not bode well.

"I'm meeting her, but she isn't here yet. Can I call you back? I'm kinda busy—"

"They found her dead."

Shee went rigid. "*Who?*"

"Xander's girlfriend."

All the air leaked from Shee's lungs.

"Jeezus, Dad, I thought you meant Charlotte."

"Why would I mean *Charlotte*? Didn't you get Croix's voicemail?"

As he grew more agitated, she could hear the anger rising in her own hissed voice. "Gibberish, yeah. What happened to Isabella?"

"We don't know yet. They found her buried in the woods where they were camping together."

"Oh." Her nerves jangled anew. "Xander's here. Charlotte found him."

"Hm."

"Right..." Shee swallowed.

Charlotte was with a killer.

"I've got to go," she said. "Anything else I should know?"

"I'm sending Mason."

"What? Why? We'll be gone before he gets here."

Hopefully.

"I'm sending him anyway. Just in case. Croix went to the

Andino's to see what she could get out of them. I think they know more than they let on."

Shee nodded.

No doubt.

Picturing her time at the Andino's, a thought occurred to her. Something that had been eating at her for days.

"Have Croix check inside the iguana," she said.

"What?"

"Check inside the iguana," she repeated, as the voices in the jungle began again, this time closer.

Her phone beeped in her ear, and she glanced at the screen.

Dead. No bars.

It was as if someone had turned off the cell tower.

Did he hear me?

Swearing, she spiked her phone into the white beach sand.

CHAPTER TWENTY-THREE

"Too late," muttered Croix to herself, parking two blocks from the Andino's mansion.

The cops had already set up a perimeter around the senator's home, and news crews from every outlet had gathered like circling sharks. As the sun set, giant white lights burst to life, illuminating the faces of the heavily made-up men and women eager to share sensational updates with their tragedy-hungry viewers.

Croix searched her Jeep until she found a paper bag in the back seat. Ripping it into one flat sheet, she turned to dig a pen from the glove compartment. In thick letters, she scribbled *MCQUEEN SENT ME* on the bag.

Finished with her impromptu art project, she studied the position of the cops, looking for a blind spot in their guarded boundary. She needed to get close enough to hold up the sign and, hopefully, the Andinos would let her in.

Hopping out of the vehicle, she walked around the block and approached the mansion through the yard of the neighbor behind them. Surprisingly, no one had thought to trespass yet, though a drone above her head took an interest in her progress as she hoisted herself up and threw a leg over the stucco yard wall.

She looked up and flipped it off.

It blinked at her.

Croix turned her attention to the large bushes on the opposite side of the wall. They stood where she needed to drop, tall and prickly.

It's never easy...

Balancing herself on the wall like a squirrel, she sprang into the yard, tucking and rolling as she hit the cement pool surround to keep from snapping an ankle. Rough pavement bit at her elbow.

Ow. Ow. Ow.

One arm and half her face slipped into the pool, but not before she'd stopped most of her forward momentum. She sat up, soggy locks stuck to her cheek, and pulled a clusia bush branch from her sneaker.

Graceful like a giraffe.

She stood and brushed off her scraped knees, gaze rising to the collection of slider doors serving as the mansion's back wall.

Whoops.

A woman in a housekeeper's uniform stood staring at her from behind the stormproof glass, her expression obscured by the lights inside that backlit her boney silhouette. Croix jerked her homemade sign from her pocket and hastily unfolded it, walking it forward like a shield until the woman stepped back from the glass and disappeared into the house.

Croix lowered her sign and adjusted her wet curls.

I look like a crazy person. There's no way they're—

A man Croix recognized as Nic Andino strode to the door and slid it open.

"You're with Mick McQueen?" he asked.

She lifted the sign again in response.

MCQUEEN SENT ME.

He scanned the area and hastened her forward with impatient flicks of his well-manicured index finger.

"Come in."

Croix stepped inside, and the man shut the door behind her. Outside, the drone dipped and lined up to peer through at them. In response, Andino smacked a buttoned controller mounted to the wall. Motorized shades dropped from where they'd been tucked inside the window's valances, effectively cutting the drone's view.

"Who are you?" Andino asked. While he didn't snap the words, it was clear it took everything he had *not* to.

"I'm Croix."

"Mick found Xander?"

Croix stared at the man, studying every micro-expression on his face. He seemed genuinely clueless. She'd suspected he knew *exactly* where his murderous son had run, but now she wasn't so sure.

She shook her head. "We haven't got him yet, but with these new developments, Mick wants to know what *you* know."

Nic's expression clouded. "What *I* know? What does that mean? I told your colleague—" He stopped and poked his chest with his finger. "You think *I* know where he is?"

Croix called upon the tact Mick encouraged her to practice. "We think you may know more than you think you know."

"What does that mean?" Andino ran his hand over his head, flattening the black hair there for a moment before it sprang back into place.

"Look, I'll tell you the same thing I told the FBI—I have *no idea* where Xander is, but I know my son isn't capable of murder. I didn't hide him. I'm *not* hiding him. No one wants to find him more than I do. *It's why I hired you.*" He chopped at his hand to punctuate each word of his last sentence.

"Did you tell the FBI you hired us?"

He closed his eyes. "No. I wasn't sure how to handle that. Your contract is clear."

Croix tried not to look surprised.

We have a contract?

Mick didn't pay attention to boring things like paperwork. Angelina probably handled the details.

"Um, which part of the contract?" she asked.

Nic's eyes sprung open again. *"The part where I'm not supposed to tell anyone about you,"* he spat through gritted teeth.

She nodded. "Oh. Right."

Croix looked away, thinking. It didn't seem as if Nic Andino was about to *suddenly* remember his son confessed to murder and that he'd sent the boy to Mexico, but she didn't want to go back to Mick emptyhanded.

There had to be *something*.

"Is there *anything* you didn't tell Shee?" she asked.

Nic shook his now-hanging head.

"Is there anything he brought back from the trip before he left again?"

"Not that I know of..."

"Anything he might have hidden?"

Nic lifted his palms toward the ceiling before letting them drop. "I wouldn't know if he *hid* them, would I? I don't think so."

"Shee searched his room?"

"She did..." He paused.

"What?"

He shrugged one shoulder. "I might have rushed her, but the FBI already went through it, too."

"Did *they* find anything?"

"No."

Croix bit her lip. She was running out of ideas.

"Can I look anyway?" she asked, disappointed to hear her voice growing squeaky.

Nic made a fist with one hand and bumped his lips. He looked trapped somewhere between crying and punching a wall. Either the man was the best actor on the planet, or he really didn't know his son's location.

He took a deep breath and released it. "Sure. You're here. Why not?"

He turned and led the way to a staircase as Croix felt her phone vibrate in her pocket. She pulled it out.

Mick.

"What's up?" she asked.

"Look for a lizard," said Mick.

She stopped and lowered her voice. "Do you feel okay?"

"What? *Yes.* I told Shee you were there, and *she* said to *look for a lizard.* No. Wait. Iguana. She said *look inside the iguana.*"

Croix rolled her eyes and continued her march up the stairs behind Nic. "That doesn't make any sense."

"We got disconnected, but she said it. Just look for a damn lizard, will you?"

"Fine. You talked to her? Did she, uh, find, you know who?"

Nic turned to glance at her as they reached the landing, and she held up a finger, asking him to wait.

"She found him," said Mick. "She's picking them up now."

Croix nodded. "Should I, um, *share*...?" She let her thought die, waiting for Mick to piece together what she didn't want to say in front of the client.

Mick grunted. "No. Don't say anything until we've got the bird in hand."

"Got it."

"Any news *there*?" he asked.

"Not yet. Let me get back to you."

"Yep."

She hung up to find Nic staring at her.

"Did they find him?" he asked. "Was that Mick?"

"It was, but nothing yet."

The man's shoulders slumped. He motioned to a door. "That's Xander's room."

Croix walked inside. She could tell the room had been flipped by the feds. They'd tried to straighten, but everything sat askew, from the desk to the mattress.

She scowled.

Is it me, or does this place feel empty?

"They took stuff with them?" she asked.

Andino's head cocked. "No...? I don't think so."

She rounded the bed and stopped short.

A lizard sat on the windowsill, tucked behind a heavy curtain.

Whaddya know...

Mick *isn't* totally crazy.

She leaned down and touched the creature, finding it made of rubber.

Inside the iguana...

Picking up the toy, she poked her finger into its gaping mouth and felt her fingertip meet the back of its throat. Pushing harder, a thin film of rubber gave way as if it had been sliced to create a tiny trapdoor into the iguana's bowels.

She felt around until something slid beneath her finger. Pressing the thin object to the side of the belly, she dragged it out of the lizard's mouth.

"What is it?" asked Nic, moving in.

Croix tucked the toy into her palm and unfurled a tiny piece of paper.

"L14-R38-L6," she read aloud. She looked at Nic. "Does that mean anything to you?"

He scowled. "Sounds like a safe code. Left, right, left."

"Oh. Good call." Croix nodded. She'd watched a movie about an old-timey safecracker pressing his ear against a metal door and spinning a black dial. She'd asked Mick how the thief knew which way to turn the knob, and he'd looked at her like she was from another planet.

"It's a *safe*," had been his answer.

Whatever. Mick had the *worst* taste in movies. Half the time they weren't even in color.

She returned her attention to Nic. "Where's his safe?"

"He doesn't have a safe." He scoffed and then sobered, glowering at the paper in her hands. "School locker, maybe? Bike lock?"

Both suggestions seemed reasonable but didn't sit well with Croix for long.

"Why would he hide the combination for those in a rubber lizard?" she asked.

"I don't—" Nic's eyes widened as he pointed to the ceiling. "*Upstairs*. There's a safe in the attic, but it came with the house. Locked. We never got around to having someone open it." He squinted at her. "Do you think he had it repaired without telling me? To hide things from me?"

Croix shrugged. "He's your kid, but let's check. Lead the way."

He hesitated and then stormed into the hall, where he pulled down attic-access folding stairs for them to climb into the stuffy uppermost level of the house. Flicking on a light, he pointed to a large standing safe in the far corner of the room.

"Over there. Give me the paper."

Feeling unconfident about her old-timey safe-cracking skills, Croix handed him the combination.

Nic strode to the large metal box and squatted to spin the dial clockwise several times. Croix couldn't believe how fast he was until he leaned in and shifted to a different level of concentration. She guessed the first few turns were to clear the safe's brain and start fresh.

Who knew?

Pulling a pair of glasses from the breast pocket of his linen shirt, Nic proceeded, lining up the numbers until he was finished.

He looked at her, leaned back, and jerked the handle.

The safe popped open.

He spat a word in a foreign language.

Nic shook his head as he plucked a tube from atop a pile of other papers. He unrolled it to reveal a strange, wiggly sketch.

"My Picasso," he muttered, looking at her. "That little *maláka*."

CHAPTER TWENTY-FOUR

Charlotte stole a peek at Xander as they approached his lemon-hued cottage. He seemed a million miles away, with his hands stuffed in his pockets and his head hanging low. She'd asked him about his stay and how many times he'd been to the island, only to be answered with grunts and shoulder shrugs.

He punched in a code and entered his cottage without hesitation and without turning as if he'd forgotten she was there.

She paused on the porch to scan the area, finding nothing but jungle. The bungalows were spaced for the privacy of their famous inhabitants.

If I scream, will anyone hear me?

"You're letting the bugs in," said Xander.

She turned to find him staring at her, a bottle of vodka in one hand and a beer in the other.

"Do you like vodka?" he asked.

She nodded as she shut the door behind her. "Sure."

He put down his beer and slid a glass to the center of the marble counter above the fridge. Cracking open the vodka, he stared at it, glanced at the glass, and then turned to her, looking lost.

"Do you want to make yours? I'm not sure how you like it."

"Sure."

She glanced at the large digital clock on the wall that was hanging in the same spot as the identical one in her cottage. Everything about Xander's room aligned with hers, but for the clothes and other paraphernalia he'd strewn around it.

She had to kill an hour and a half. She needed to get him thinking about home. Maybe plumb the depths of any objections he might have to the idea of heading back, so she could prepare a counterargument.

She stepped to the counter as he retreated with his beer to flop on the loveseat.

"So, what do you do?" she asked, making herself a screwdriver with ninety percent orange juice and ice. The splash of vodka she hoped would calm her nerves.

"I'm nobody," he said. "My dad's a senator."

"Oh. Neat." Silence fell again, and she struggled to fill it. "My parents are in politics, too," she added before she could stop herself.

She had mixed feelings about the comment. *Daughter of a politician* wasn't the backstory they'd fed YOU—identifying politicians and their children was too easy—but she'd wanted to steer Xander toward home and thought sharing a common background might increase his trust in her.

Indeed, he perked. "Yeah?"

She joined him on the sofa, sitting to the far opposite end. "Yep."

"Then you *know*."

"Pssht." She took a sip of her weak cocktail. "Do I *know*."

"You're probably as messed up as me." He chuckled, his first sign of levity. "I guess you already talked to Dr. Lilith?"

She nodded without elaborating. Technically, she *had* talked to the doctor, if not officially.

"What's her deal?" she asked.

Xander showed as much animation in his expression as she'd seen.

"She's *amazing*." He suddenly twisted away from her, staring through the window behind them long enough that Charlotte felt obligated to search for movement outside.

"Do you see something?" she asked.

"No. I thought I did. Probably a bird."

Charlotte took another sip, racking her brain for a way to

change the topic. The conversation had headed in the wrong direction. She needed to make Xander warm and fuzzy about his parents and *less* excited about being on the island.

Maybe she could wax poetic about her imaginary parents.

"Yeah, the whole child of a politician thing is a pain, you know, but in the end, my parents—"

"I'm going to show him," spat Xander.

Charlotte's brow knit. "Who?"

"My *dad*." He finished his beer and tossed the empty can at the trashcan near the minibar area. The can hit the lip, bounced against the wall, and clattered to the ground. "He thinks he owns me. But I have my own mind. My own *destiny*."

Charlotte took a sip from her glass.

This is not going well at all.

"You're being a little, like, *drama queen*, don't you think?" she asked in an attempt to lighten the mood.

What looked like anger rippled across Xander's expression, and she realized *playful mocking* wasn't the direction to take. She changed tack.

"I mean, you already have your own life—"

He stood and paced the tiny room.

"I need to get something cleared up, and then I'm going to make my move," he said, sounding more as if he were talking to himself than her.

"Yeah?" she asked.

"Yeah. I got it all figured out. I'm going to *own* him."

"Own—your *dad*?"

"Yeah."

"Oh." Charlotte wished she had a tranquilizer gun. She could stop his agitated pacing, end his rant, and drag his butt to the beach.

As if he could hear her thoughts, Xander stopped pacing to stare almost dreamily at her.

"We're all different, you know?" he said. "We all fly to different heights, but in the end, we all have wings."

Charlotte took another sip of her drink.

Oh boy.

The guy was losing his mind.

She sneaked a glimpse at her watch. What had felt like forever now felt like not enough time. She only had an hour to get Xander *I'm-going-to-own-my-dad* Andino out the door.

Her chances seemed less promising by the second.

Back at the Loggerhead, she'd imagined herself having a nice, logical, heartfelt talk with a not-drunk, not-emotionally-crippled guy who was enough younger than herself that he'd think she was both a peer and *wise*. He'd see the sagacity of her pitch and agree to head home.

Mission accomplished.

Now, her pre-mission play-acting scenario felt achingly naïve. The assignment felt like a bad fit—more spycraft and less *detective*.

She'd wanted to impress her parents so much that she hadn't taken a moment to honestly assess her limitations.

Stupid.

She wasn't a spy. She wasn't a psychiatrist either, which was clearly what the moody mess in front of her needed for his daddy issues.

He was still staring at her, wide-eyed as if awaiting a response. She felt energy vibrating around him—very different from the black hole he'd felt like when they first met.

She needed to say something.

What did he say? Something about wings?

"Um..."

"Maybe we could do it together," he said, swooping to touch her hand.

She recoiled, pressing herself against the back of the sofa.

This has taken a turn.

"I, uh..." She put her glass down.

Seeming to sense her discomfort, he took a step back.

"How many times have you talked to Dr. Lilith?" he asked.

"Um, just the once..."

Xander laughed as if she were a world-class comedian sticking the punchline.

"That explains it. You probably think I sound *nuts.*"

She blinked at him.

Yep.

She shook her head. "No, of course not—"

He squatted in front of her and grabbed her upper arms to stare into her eyes.

"*You have no idea the power you have.*"

She hoped he was right because she didn't like his grip on her arms.

"Look—"

He continued, releasing one of her arms to thrust his own toward the ceiling. "You *can* fly to the *sun.* You can *be* the power in your life. You don't need others to give you wings."

Something about Xander's delivery hit Charlotte as canned—as if he were repeating a memorized speech.

Something from his dad?

No. That didn't make sense. Why would he talk about how much he resented his father and then quote his bogeyman with such reverence?

Dr. Lilith? He'd just referenced her...

"Did Dr. Lilith tell you that?" she guessed.

He let go of her other arm and dropped the few extra inches to his knees.

"Dr. Lilith's the *best,*" he said. "You'll see." His eyes closed. "Then we'll meet Zeus."

"Who *is* this *Zeus*?" she asked, hoping to get a fresh take from Xander. Rapture hadn't shared much, but she'd certainly shared Xander's expression of reverence.

Xander's eyes popped open. "He's a *genius.* You'll meet him near the end."

"The end of *what*?"

"Your time imprisoned in the bowels of your captors."

Charlotte swallowed.

What the—

Xander took a deep breath. "Daedalus is Dead to Us."

"*Daedalus*?" Charlotte rolled the name around her brain, finding it familiar. Greek mythology, which she'd always found fun to read, was at the forefront of her mind, thanks to all the references to Zeus.

Xander had mentioned *wings*...

That's it.

It had to be. She'd seen a statue of *Icarus* on the island. She'd taken it as just a winged man but—

"Daedalus? Icarus' father?" she asked.

He nodded and stepped back from her to stand.

"Icarus flew with the broken wings his father, Daedalus, gave him," he said. "He fell."

"Um...that's not exactly right..." said Charlotte. "Icarus didn't *listen* to his father's warnings, flew too close to the sun, and the wax on his wings melted."

Xander whirled and pointed at her. "*No.* Don't you see? We're the *new* Icaruses. We're *smarter.* We don't let our fathers drag us to earth." He stabbed a finger toward the ground, his jaw clenched.

Charlotte stared at him.

He's completely lost it.

Xander's eyes flashed. "Daedalus tried to keep Icarus *down.* He built it into the *system.*" He lifted his hands and eyes to the ceiling and boomed his next line. "*Are you ready to fly?*"

Charlotte sucked in a breath as she realized what she was witnessing.

The fervent delivery of the canned speeches.

The anger.

The passion.

The detachment from reality...

It all made sense now.

YOU was a *cult.*

She didn't like to admit defeat, but she didn't imagine she'd be able to erase weeks, months, or *years* of brainwashing in time to get Xander to the boat.

Game over.

She'd meet Shee, report her findings and let *them* figure out the next step. They were the collection of military-trained badasses. They'd figure a way.

She rose to her feet, and Xander lowered his hands, looking as if the spirit possessing him had flown away.

"I'm sorry," he said, patting the air in front of him like it was a horse's whither. "That was a lot to hit you with all at once."

She chuckled. "Kinda—"

"I like you."

"I, uh, like you too." She glanced at the door. "Maybe tomorrow—"

Xander spun off into his thoughts. "I need, like, a *week*. Zeus is going to clear up something for me, and then I'll have everything I need."

He stepped forward to take her face in his hands. She stiffened.

"I'll tell you everything you need to know. Dr. Lilith will help."

He leaned in as if he was about to kiss her.

"Whoa." She maneuvered away from him.

"What? You don't feel it?" he asked.

"I uh…" Flustered, Charlotte spat the first thought that came to mind. "Don't you have a girlfriend?"

He scowled. "She ran—Why would you ask that?"

Charlotte grimaced.

Stupid.

She had to cover.

"I thought I heard—"

Xander's fists clenched. "What did you hear?"

"What? Nothing—"

Without warning, Xander lunged toward her.

She jerked up her fists, and with a quick right jab, popped him in the nose.

He stumbled back, hands rising to his face.

"What the hell?" he asked.

Charlotte kept her balled fists raised.

Time to leave.

"I came to take you *home*," she said, backing toward the

door.

"You *what*?"

"I came to take you *home*. Your dad. He misses you."

Xander lowered his hands from his nose. "Who *are* you—?"

Charlotte was near the front door when someone pounded on it.

Thank God.

She grabbed the knob and flung it open.

A pair of men, carbon copies of the large escorts who'd greeted her boat upon arrival, stood on the porch.

They looked past her to Xander.

"Zeus is ready to see you," said one.

"Zeus?" Xander echoed, his chest swelling. Any expression of anger or confusion clouding his features faded like a dark cloud drifting past the sun.

She'd never seen him so *happy*.

He looked at Charlotte. "I have to go."

She nodded.

Please.

Xander walked past her as the pair of men split to let him pass. One followed him. One remained at the door.

"I, uh, I guess I'll head back," she said.

The brute shook his head.

"Come with me."

CHAPTER TWENTY-FIVE

"We've got trouble," said Croix.

Mick looked up as she walked into the break room. They'd agreed to meet there upon her return from the Andino's, where he'd bring everyone up to speed. Mason sat at the opposite end of the table, pacing with his eyes, looking like a caged tiger. Angelina and Snookie sat tittering about something by his side. He watched the pair with a growing sense of dread.

Snookie.

While the possibilities of working as a contractor for the FBI excited Mick, having his girlfriend's sister hanging around did *not*. Now everything he did would be discussed, rehashed, analyzed, and judged by the *two of them.*

Feeling the weight of his stare, the sisters' attention swiveled in his direction in unison, as if they shared the same brain.

Something he'd long suspected.

"*What?*" he asked.

They dissolved into giggles.

He sighed.

Nightmare.

He had bigger fish to fry for now, though.

Croix dumped a pile of brochures, file folders, and printouts onto the center of the table.

"What's all this?" he asked.

She motioned to the mess. "Turns out our boy Xander had a secret safe in the attic and the combination too. He had his father's Picasso inside."

Mick scowled. "Shee told me about the stolen Picasso. Why wouldn't the kid take the sketch with him? Try to sell it?"

Croix shrugged. "I think he only took it to piss off the old man. The senator let me take the rest of the stuff."

Angelina plucked a newspaper clipping from the pile and scanned it.

"I don't understand," she said. "It's about some kid starting a clothing line?"

Croix pulled out a chair and sat. "From what I can tell, these are all stories about rich kids getting even richer."

Mick pulled a plastic-ring-bound booklet from the pile. "This looks like a company prospectus," he said. "Only..."

Croix tapped the page. "Only it's not. It's full of even more stories about rich kids."

"Still lost," said Angelina.

"Is there a theme?" asked Snookie. "I mean, other than rich kids?"

Croix nodded. "I have a theory. I think they gave Xander that booklet to show him what they've been able to do for other clients, and then he started keeping track himself, printing out articles and whatnot."

"Who's *they*?" asked Mick.

"YOU. I *knew* there was something up with that place."

Mick picked through the pile. "You're saying the resort is involved with these kids? Doing what? Acting as an investment group?"

Snookie held four printouts in her left hand as she read a fifth in her right. "I remember reading about this guy," she said, holding up an article for the others to see. "He's some big music producer. There was a bunch of talk about him and underage girls, and then it all went away when the accuser recanted." She held up her opposite hand. "This is an article about his son opening his studio."

Croix sat up. "Right. *Backed by his father.* Get it? I think someone at YOU is teaching these kids to blackmail their parents—to squeeze them for money and favors." She paused, pulling a handwritten note from the pile. "Except for *these* kids."

"What happened to them?" asked Mason.

Croix pointed the note in his direction. "This is a list of dead or missing rich kids. And look at the handwriting—all the loops. This isn't Xander's handwriting. This is a *girl's*. Someone was trying to show him the dark side of this thing." She focused on Mick. "Someone like—"

"Isabella," he said.

She nodded.

Snookie snatched the list from her hand. "These kids refused to play ball?"

Croix nodded. "Or failed. Or threatened to tell."

Mick held up a hand. "Everyone, hold on." He dropped the printouts he'd been flipping through. "What does this information mean to *us*?"

"It means Xander's in more danger than we thought," said Croix.

"Or his father is," said Angelina. "And *he's* our actual client."

Mason stood, looking agitated. "Am I missing something? Shee and Charlotte are on that island. We need to warn them. *Now*."

"We did about Isabella," muttered Croix.

Mason's attention shot to her.

"What are you talking about?"

"I guess you haven't been watching the news," said Mick, drawing Mason's ire away from Croix.

"No. Why?"

"They found the Andino kid's girlfriend dead under *suspicious circumstances*."

"What kind of *suspicious circumstances*?"

"They found her buried in the woods where they'd been camping," said Croix.

Mason slapped both palms on the table. If he'd been able to shoot lasers through his eyes, Mick suspected he and Croix would have been sliced like lunchmeat.

"So, in addition to the resort killing kids, the *actual* kid

Charlotte is there to meet *killed his girlfriend*?"

Mick shook his head. "We don't know for sure—"

"When were you going to tell me about this?"

"Easy now. We *just* found out. When I called Shee—"

"Is she with Charlotte?"

"Yes, no—" Mick sighed. "We got disconnected. She was picking her up."

Mason straightened and put his hands on his hips. "I'm going to YOU."

Mick nodded. "Agreed. Can't hurt." He turned his attention to Croix. "What's the fastest way to get him there?"

Croix grimaced. "The flight Shee took is the fastest *scheduled* flight, but it doesn't run again until Tuesday morning."

Mick turned to Snookie. "Can we do this through the bureau? Use a private plane?"

Snookie already had her phone in hand. "I can get you cleared to work the case—some of these names look familiar. I think we're tracking these disappearances, so it should be easy to jump on it. But I don't know how fast I can get us a plane."

"You need a plane?" said a voice.

All eyes turned to the door where Ollie stood, shoulder leaning on the doorframe, hands in his pockets.

"You can get us a plane?" asked Mason.

Ollie smiled. "I can get you anything."

Mason pointed at him. "Make it happen."

CHAPTER TWENTY-SIX

The guard opened the solid wood door and pushed Xander into a room smaller than his walk-in closet.

"Sit," said the walking mass of muscle, motioning to the only chair—only furniture—in the room.

Xander eyed him.

Is that a knife scar on his chin?

Feeling flush, he dropped into the chair as the big man left, closing the door behind him.

Only then did Xander notice the wall he faced was a large, dark window.

He stared at it.

Cops.

That's what the room and the window reminded him of—a police interrogation room from a movie. Usually, the police captain or the victim watched from the other side.

But that begged the question...

Who's watching?

His gaze traced to where the wall met the ceiling until it tripped over a camera staring down at him.

Camera.

More watching?

A television occupied another corner, mounted high on the wall.

He rubbed his eyes as the room took a spin around itself.

I didn't think I drank this much.

A soft hiss filled the air, and he tilted back his head to search the space above him for the source.

"We had high hopes for you," said a familiar, male voice. "Zeus is beside himself."

"Whaaa..." Xander's jaw worked as he tried to get his situation assessed in his head. "What did I do?"

"Who was the girl in your room?"

"The girl—" His head flopped to the left, and he righted it. It felt heavy. "Oh. Right. Mac—*something*? *Maxine*, I think?"

"MacKenzie."

Xander pointed at the all-seeing window. His reflection pointed back.

"Yep. That's it."

"Do you know who she is?"

"Max—? No. She—" He shook his head, trying to clear it.

"She asked you to leave."

"Leave? We were in *my* room." A panicky thought rippled through him and leaned toward the window. "Wait. Is she saying I did something to her or something?"

He didn't remember having sex. His father had warned him, long ago, that a senator's son had to be *careful* with girls.

I might have tried to kiss her...

He shook his head. "Everything that happened in there was one hundred percent conceptual. *Conseptional.* Con—" He took a deep breath. "She was *with* me. It was all *cool*."

"Not that," said the voice. "I meant, she asked you to *leave the island.*"

"Did she?" A flood of relief washed over Xander. This wasn't about sex stuff. Fuzzy memories of his time with the girl from the beach filtered into his head like light flickering through gauze.

Hm.

She *had* said something about leaving.

He gasped.

"That's it. I got it. She said my *dad* hired her."

"We know. The point is, we've talked about this."

Now, he was confused again. "About...*tonight?*"

"About your father trying to control you."

He nodded. "Oh. Yeah, I know. *Totally*. I wasn't going to *go*."

"It sounded like you were suggesting she come with you on your mission."

Xander stretched his legs in front of him and crossed his arms against his chest. He didn't remember much, but he remembered how he'd *felt* while he was talking with that girl. Scared. Hopeful. He didn't want Dr. Lilith and Zeus to know how scared he was about what they wanted him to do. He was hopeful the new girl would stay with him the way Isabella did.

The way she *used to*.

Isabella didn't believe anymore. She didn't believe in Zeus or YOU. She didn't believe in *him*.

He felt sleepy.

"Xander?"

Xander realized he'd closed his eyes and opened them.

"Hm?"

"Were you going to ruin everything?"

He slapped a palm to his chest. "Me? Noooo. I was trying to *help*. I told her about flying. I was...what's the word? *Recruiting*. I was *recruiting* her."

"Did we say we needed help recruiting?"

"No, but—"

"You're lucky you're here. Not everyone gets invited back to YOU."

Xander felt the air leak from his lungs. "I know."

The voice continued in a steady, soothing drone. "We chose you because we believe in you. We saw your potential. We saw what your father has *never* been able to see."

Xander's head pulled back as if he'd been slapped in slow motion.

Ouch.

"Isn't it true, Xander? That you're much more than your father thinks you are?"

"Yeah. Yeah, it *is*." He chewed his lip. The weight of his eyelids became unbearable. "Can I go back to my room now? I'm really tired."

He wasn't sure what was going on. Maybe this was the

interview they did before they took someone to see Zeus. Even if it was, he wasn't sure he wanted to meet Zeus right *now*. He wanted to be fresh.

Maybe the girl was still in his room.

She was so pretty...

"Do you need a new girlfriend?"

Xander's head snapped up from where it had started to loll.

Are they reading my mind?

"What?" he asked, buying time as he felt his head for wires that might be tapping into his thoughts.

"Were you *flirting* with MacKenzie?"

He shrugged one shoulder.

"I dunno..."

"Because Isabella's dead?"

Electric fear shot through Xander's body. His arms uncrossed, and he sat up.

"*What?*"

"Isabella. She's dead. It's all over the news."

Xander shook his head. "No, she's *not*."

The television on the wall behind him flickered on, and he twisted in his seat to find his face and Isabella's staring down at him. It was a picture of them from the summer before when they'd flown to California. They cuddled with arms wrapped around each other, smiling for the camera.

A reporter voiced over the shot.

"*...police are looking for her boyfriend, Xander Andino, a person of interest...*"

Xander gasped, his eyes so wide he had to blink to wet them. He spun back to face the dark window.

"This isn't real."

"It's real. You remember."

"Remember *what*?"

"Killing her."

He shook his head so hard he felt dizzy. "Are you crazy? I didn't kill Izzy!"

"Sure, you did. She wasn't joining you here. She was going

to turn you in."

"No, she wasn't. She wouldn't—"

"She threatened to turn you in, and you choked her to death at the campsite."

"I—*no!*" Xander sprang to his feet, a sudden dump of adrenalin clearing his foggy mind. "You're *lying.*"

"You put your hands around her neck, and you heard her gagging. She tried to stop you, but you were too strong for her—"

Xander lunged at the window and pounded on it with the side of both fists. He could hear how thick it was. Too thick to break. It reminded him of the hurricane-proof windows of his home.

Why did I ever leave home?

"I did *not* kill Isabella," he said in staccato, spitting a single word with every strike of his fist.

The voice continued. "You pushed until you felt that bone in her neck snap beneath your thumb. Then the gagging noises stopped. She stopped clawing at your hands."

Xander flung himself away from the windows and looked at his hands. Rolled up his sleeves. There were no scratches. He kicked the chair into the corner of the room with a brain-bruising clatter. Bending at the waist, he put his hands over his ears.

"Stop it! *I didn't kill her.* I left her at the campsite."

"Oh, you left her alright. Her eyes staring at the night sky, wide, unblinking—"

"She's not *dead!*"

"She's dead. It's all over the news. How could we be lying?"

Xander turned to gape at the news clip again. Something tickled his throat, and he coughed until he dry-heaved in the corner. When the spasms stopped, he remained there, catching his breath, head hanging, watching tears drip off his nose and splash to the tile floor below.

This isn't happening.

"Are you going to *command the now*? Or is it too late?" asked the voice.

Xander wiped his eyes and turned to the dark glass.

Command the now.

"Will Zeus help me?" he asked. He could barely hear his voice.

"What did you do after you killed her?"

Xander felt the strength leave his body. Nothing made any sense.

Did I kill her?

He stared at the window, helpless.

"I don't know."

"You packed up everything, and then you had to kill the campfire, so the other hikers wouldn't see it. Remember?"

He nodded. He remembered hearing campers. In his mind's eye, he pictured his feet kicking dirt over the fire.

I did put out the fire.

"Are you remembering now?" asked the voice.

He sniffed. "Yes."

"Then you rolled Isabella from the clearing into a shallow ditch shored on one side by an outcropping of rock."

He looked up.

I remember.

He could see the rocks lining the opposite wall of the ditch.

"Yes."

He righted the chair and dropped into it as the voice continued. His anger and energy had been replaced by unbearable fatigue.

So tired.

"Then you scurried around like a squirrel, gathering armfuls of leaves and sticks and piling them on her body. You didn't have to bury her. Winter is coming. The animals will finish her off, scatter her bones, and the snow will come."

Xander looked up at the television.

Snow was falling on Isabella's grave.

He closed his eyes.

So tired.

CHAPTER TWENTY-SEVEN

Charlotte glared at the man blocking her exit from Xander's cottage and noticed his name had been stitched on his powder blue polo.

Thor.

Seriously?

"I'm not coming with you," she said in her brattiest voice— the way MacKenzie would say it.

It took all her strength to deliver the line. Inside, her stomach felt like jelly.

The man stared at her for a beat and then called someone on his phone, his eyes never leaving her, his large body still blocking the door.

"*Move.* I'm going back to my cottage," she snapped. She attempted to slip around him, but he put up an arm to stop her progress.

She huffed. "What are you *doing*?"

He cleared his throat. "She wants to go back to her room."

His gaze remained on her, though his comment was meant for the person on the opposite side of the line.

Charlotte turned and stomped away from him, planning another way to escape.

He grunted and lowered his phone.

"You're going to need to come with me."

She twirled on her heel to face him again. "You said that before. *Fine.* Whatever. After you."

He turned to step onto the porch.

She spun and bolted for the back of the cottage.

As she flung open the back door, she heard him swear behind her. She headed for the gate in the privacy fence she'd seen on her own property, though Xander's seemed to be obscured by a large, pink-flowered bush.

Please be there, please be there...

She spotted the outline of the gate as she approached.

Yes!

Fumbling with the latch, she glanced over her shoulder to see Thor appear at the back door of the cottage. She threw open the gate and sprinted down a jungle path.

"Stop!" he roared.

She kept running. She needed to get to the beach and find her mother. Shee'd know what to do. Later, someone could come back and pick up Xander. Not her. She'd be busy writing her negative-a-zillion-stars review of YOU.

The food was amazing, accommodations were next level, but security was a little too kidnappy...

She heard Thor slapping away low-hanging, elephant-eared greenery behind her, the thud of his feet growing closer. He ran fast for a side of beef.

A loud bang blasted behind her. Her body jerked.

A gun?

Charlotte made an adjustment she hoped would point her toward the rendezvous beach and sped up as much as she dared across the uneven ground of the man-made jungle.

On her way to YOU, she'd been afraid she'd be caught for *trespassing.*

That seemed like the best-case scenario now.

What is going on?

Certainly, the goon wasn't firing *at* her. That would be—well, *illegal* and seemed like the least of it. She was at a high-end resort, not in a sci-fi movie where madmen hunted humans for sport—

A second gunshot rang out, and she heard something hit a

tree ten feet in front of her.

Her body jolted with adrenaline.

This is real.

She shifted direction, a new panic speeding her pace.

Another shot.

This time she heard the bullet buzz overhead.

No, no, no...

Even if the man planned to scare her, a minor miscalculation—

"The next one is in the back of your skull," called the guard.

He was close. She wasn't winning the foot race.

And he had a gun.

Please let this be the right call.

Charlotte stopped, panting, her hands over her head.

Thor is crazy.

If he shot her, here, in the middle of YOU's manufactured jungle, who knew what would happen? Maybe he'd gone rogue. He might bury her where she fell and tell the boss she ran away.

He was fast. She'd never stay far enough ahead of him that the next bullet might not find her. She could call his bluff, but he'd already proven himself willing to endanger her life.

"I'm here. I stopped," she said, turning.

Thor crashed through the leaves behind her like a rabid rhino, stopping five feet in front of her, his gun raised.

"Do you know who I am?" she asked, hoping to remind him killing rich people came with consequences.

Thor holstered his gun and grabbed her wrist. He wrenched her arm behind her back. Pain shot through her shoulder. She heard the cuffs snap shut.

"You can't do this," she said, genuinely incredulous. "My father will *sue you* into your *next lifetime* for this."

Thor seemed unconcerned. "I'll worry about that later." Grasping her upper arm, he dragged her back down the path.

"Ow! Easy!"

He didn't answer, but the pull on her arm relented.

That was a good sign, she hoped. Maybe it meant Thor wasn't a madman bent on killing the guests. He was following orders.

Maybe she'd made the right choice. Better to end up in YOU jail for misrepresentation than shot in the back of the head.

"Where are you taking me?" she asked.

"The same place I take everyone," he muttered.

She blinked at him.

Everyone? Did he chase people through the jungle all the time?

"Where is that?"

He nodded forward and she followed his sightline to the silver pyramid.

She felt a bubble of fear in her stomach.

"What happens to the people you take there?" she asked.

Thor didn't answer.

CHAPTER TWENTY-EIGHT

Mason, Ollie, and Snookie pulled into the circular driveway of the sprawling rancher. Inside, no lights glowed.

"Your plane is *here*?" asked Snookie.

From his spot in the backseat, Mason shared her concern. He'd expected Ollie to drive them to an airport. Instead, they'd headed west, away from the coast, and ended up in a residential subdivision.

Ollie hopped out of the Jeep, talking as he moved. "It's a fly-in community for seaplanes. There's a lake in the back."

Mason exchanged a look with Snookie before they exited the vehicle and followed.

"How well do you know this guy?" she asked, arriving at his side.

Mason grimaced. "Not well."

Ollie led the way down a pebble path circling the side of the home. As soon as they rounded the corner, Mason spotted the aforementioned lake and a white plane bobbing beside a dock.

That's promising, at least.

"Ollie—"

"Call me *Pony*."

Mason grimaced. "*Ollie*, can you fly this plane?"

Mick had seemed confident in the flim-flam man's acquisition skills, but Mason would have preferred time to do his background checks *before* being thrown into a life-or-death situation—which is what flying a few miles off the ground was.

Ollie seemed confused. "Me? Fly? I was hoping *you* knew how to do it."

He winked.

Mason grit his teeth.

Such a funny guy. I'm going to snap his neck and shove his head—

"Can *you* fly?" Snookie asked Mason.

She looked hopeful, and he understood why. He'd been about to ask her the same thing. Wouldn't hurt to have a backup.

"More of a helicopter guy," he muttered.

Snookie frowned. "I *hate* little planes." She eyed the aircraft and wrapped her thin sweater around her body, though at last check, the balmy air around them hung somewhere around seventy-seven. "I might be able to get a real pilot here pretty quickly..."

Ollie huffed. "I'm messing with you. I am a real pilot. I *swear*. Why do you think I was so good at getting things? Try counting on some joker to deliver genuine Wagu steaks without ending up with a box full of fly bait. You'd be better off strapping them to the backs of donkeys. If some general wants a rare vintage for his wife, you can't sit around *hoping* a bottle shows up."

Snookie sighed.

Mason took a deep breath of his own and tried to trust the man. He needed to get to Shee and Charlotte, and, after all, Ollie would be on the plane as well. Self-preservation *should* keep him from pointing the nose at the water.

The group walked to a small shed near the dock, where Ollie punched in a code to open the door.

The keypad returned his efforts with an ugly buzz.

"Whoops."

He punched in a new set of numbers with the same result.

"Hm... Hold on—" Ollie stared at the keypad as if he was punching buttons with his mind.

"Whose plane is this again?" asked Mason.

"*Mine*," said a voice behind them.

The group turned to find a stout man with a shock of gray hair holding a shotgun leveled at them. The man's shoulders unbunched at the sight of their faces, but his frown grew deeper, even as his gun lowered to the ground.

"*Oliver*," he spat as if the word was a curse.

"Hey, Jim." Ollie stepped forward, hand outstretched, but not before Mason clocked surprise on the con artist's face.

He leaned to Snookie.

"I don't think *Jim* knew we were going for a spin."

Snookie nodded. "You got that impression too?"

Jim stared at Ollie's outstretched hand without taking it.

"What are you doing here?" he asked.

"I—*we* need to borrow your plane." Ollie made a loop in the air with his finger as if he were drawing a circle around them. "It's an *emergency.*"

The information didn't seem to put Jim at ease.

"It didn't occur to you to call me?" he asked.

"I didn't think you were in town."

Jim stomped a slippered foot. "I *knew* it. I *knew* someone had moved the damn plane last week. That's why I changed the code."

Ollie swept an arm toward Snookie as if Jim had won her on a game show. "This is Snookie, uh..."

"*Moore*," said Snookie. "*Ava* Moore."

Ollie blinked at her. "You mean Snookie's not your given name?"

Mason tapped his watch.

"*Ollie...*"

"Sorry." Ollie returned his attention to the man holding the shotgun. "Snookie's with the FBI. Snook, this is Jim Paretsky."

Jim and Snookie met halfway to shake hands.

"FBI?" he echoed.

She nodded. "Retired, now serving as a private contractor."

Jim nodded his approval.

"Jim's retired NYPD. That's where we met," added Ollie.

Mason cocked an eyebrow at Ollie. "You were a *cop*?"

Jim barked a laugh. "*He* was a juvenile delinquent. His dad was my partner."

Ollie nodded, apparently agreeing with both statements.

Mason took his turn shaking hands with the retired officer. "Mason Connelly."

"You FBI, too?"

"Retired Navy."

Jim nodded again.

"What are *you* doing with these fine people?" he asked Ollie.

"I'm helping them on a case. A missing child."

Snookie and Mason exchanged a look, but neither corrected Ollie's use of the word *child* to refer to twenty-one-year-old Xander.

"Missing child?" Jim furrowed a brow in the direction of his plane. "You remember how to fly it?"

"I just flew it—" Ollie stopped short.

"*I knew it*," muttered Jim.

"I flew one *just like it* a month ago," Ollie corrected.

Jim looked at Snookie. "You in charge?"

She nodded. "I suppose I am."

"Do I get reimbursed by the FBI if I let this nitwit commandeer my plane?"

She nodded. "Of course."

A plump woman with short gray hair and a thin floral robe approached from the house.

"Jim?" she asked.

Paretsky turned. "It's okay, Jessie. I'll be back in a second. It's Ollie. He needs the plane."

Jessie searched the faces of the group until she spotted Ollie. "Hello, Ollie," she said as if he had once left her at the altar.

"Hi, second Mrs. Paretsky," said Ollie.

The woman's mouth pinched. Without another word, she turned and stormed back to the house. Jim watched her until she stepped inside and then glared at Ollie.

"I told you not to call her that."

Ollie shrugged. "It's not like I'm *lying*."

"That's not the *point*."

Mason glanced again at his watch. "Mr. Paretsky, I'm sorry, we need to get on the move. Can we borrow your plane? If we can't, we need to make other arrangements."

Jim sighed. "I guess. Where are you going?"

"Andros Island."

Jim poked a finger at Ollie. "She's full. Be careful. If I see one scratch—"

Ollie stepped forward to embrace the man. "Not a scratch. I promise."

Jim stiffened, submitting to the hug until Ollie released him and stepped back.

"You don't need the code. I've got the key here," said Jim, thrusting a hand into the oversized pocket of his robe.

He scowled. "I did have it..."

He patted his hip before switching the shotgun to his opposite hand and fishing in the other pocket.

"I *thought* I grabbed them..."

Ollie held up a set of keys. "These?"

CHAPTER TWENTY-NINE

Shee plucked her phone from the sand and tried to call Charlotte. She had no bars. It was as if the island's cell tower had been plucked like a flower by King Kong.

Can't call Charlotte. Can't call Mick.

Shee took a deep breath and released a fluttery, nerve-syncopated exhale.

She needed to focus and make the right move.

The gunfire she'd heard was probably nothing. Even if Xander killed Isabella in a crime of passion, he wouldn't have a gun on the island—and if he did, why would he shoot Charlotte?

Unless he was full-blown crazy...

Did I send her after a maniac?

No. There had to be an explanation. Maybe they had a gun range on the island for the rich kids. Or maybe there was a gun-use demonstration? Or someone had to scare birds away from the pool? There were a million innocuous possibilities that weren't *someone shooting at Charlotte.*

That was the least likely option. They were snatching Xander off of Tantalus Island, not breaking him out of Rikers Island.

She listened again, hearing only the gentle lapping of the water behind her. If the gunfire was an oddity, surely by now there'd be a commotion.

Right. Definitely.

She felt a *little* better. She checked her watch.

Charlotte was an hour late. The sun had snuffed itself over

the horizon. A large, low-hanging moon illuminated the area with a soft blue light.

Maybe Charlotte decided to wait until after dark?

Shee peered into the inky jungle. Cocked her head.

Still nothing.

Dammit.

She needed to give Charlotte more time. Getting Xander to surrender himself wasn't an easy task—

She froze as a head popped above the rock outcropping at the far side of her little beach. Shoulders appeared, then a torso—until soon a full man stood on the jetty in silhouette.

Shee squinted at what *had* to be a semi-automatic rifle in his hands, its unmistakable outline traced by moonlight.

Boy, they hate paparazzi around here.

Shee pressed herself against the tree line as the guard scanned her beach. He raised binoculars and pointed his attention at her borrowed boat, bobbing in the distance.

Shit.

"Boat!" called the man to someone she couldn't see.

Shee crouched lower.

The guard swung his arm in the air as if he were trying to flag down a partner. A moment later, he flopped his hand to his thigh, clearly frustrated his friend wasn't paying attention.

Shee glanced at her paddleboard.

She could stay and wait for Charlotte, but she'd probably get caught for trespassing—not to mention *kidnapping*—once someone found Richard tied up in his forward berth.

That could be a problem.

She didn't know much about Caribbean prisons. Did they have air conditioning?

She didn't want to leave the island and leave Charlotte with Xander a second longer than necessary. Not after Isabella.

On the other hand, she'd be no help to Charlotte in jail. Even YOU jail.

She could head deeper into the island, but she had no idea where to look, and she might miss Charlotte on her way to the beach...

She tapped the sand with the side of her fist, trying to think of alternatives.

No option felt ideal.

Maybe the island *had* blocked phone signals? Maybe she could get some bars back on the boat?

She peeked over the foliage at the guard. He'd grown tired of waiting for his friend. With one last glance at her craft through his binoculars, he scrambled down the rocks and disappeared.

Shee seized her chance. Running to the paddleboard, she snatched it from the sand and slid into the water. She stroked on her belly, paddle tucked beneath her, all the while praying the warm water sharks didn't know what a seal looked like from below.

She peeked over her shoulder. No one was chasing her. No sign of Charlotte on the beach.

Shee grunted with frustration but kept paddling.

Reaching the boat, out of breath, she climbed in and hauled up the board. The guard hadn't returned to his rock perch, but that didn't mean good things. He might be getting into a boat, planning to head out and investigate.

Shee heard Richard's muffled protests from inside the cabin as she scrambled to the helm and flipped the switch to haul in the anchor.

"Save your voice. It's me," she said, firing up the engine. The roar sounded much louder than it had the first time.

She shoved the boat into forward motion, moving slow and steady in the opposite direction of the jetty where she'd seen the guard. She waited until she was around the island, out of view, and then slammed into a higher gear, tearing off into the sea until she was sure she was too far out for anyone on the island to see her.

She put the boat in neutral and cut the engine.

Her phone still showed no bars. She checked Richard's.

Dead.

She flopped back into the captain's seat, head hanging.

I have to get back to Charlotte.

How had everything gone so wrong? *Had* Xander killed Isabella? Had she endangered her daughter after decades of keeping her safe from her insane life?

She's with me five minutes and already—

Richard pounded against his door. With his head, by the sound of it.

Shee slid off the chair to her feet.

"Dammit, Richard, I have to *think*."

She pulled open a kitchen drawer to retrieve a steak knife before pounding on his door with the palm of her hand.

"I'm coming in."

The pounding on the other side ceased.

She paused. "If you try to run at me, I'm going to stab you in the throat and drag you back to Andros like shark bait. You got it?"

There was a pause, followed by a muffled, "Uh-huh."

She opened the door to find her captive sitting on the bed. He moaned.

She assessed the situation.

"Your hands hurt? Shoulders?" she asked.

He nodded.

"Okay. Look. If I let you go, do you promise to be good?"

He nodded enthusiastically.

"You understand I'm *not* stealing your boat, right? And that I don't want to hurt you?"

He nodded again, but his head tilted to the left as he looked away. It seemed he wasn't one hundred percent sold on her good intentions.

Fair enough.

"I know it *looks* like I'm doing horrible things, but I have to save my daughter. She's on an island with a criminal. A man who kills women."

Saying the words made her feel ill. She'd begun hyperbolizing to gain Richard's trust—no small feat after you steal a man's boat and leave him tied up for hours on his bed— but as the words fell from her lips, she realized she wasn't exaggerating at all.

Richard's eyes widened. He seemed sympathetic.

She untied the gag in his mouth.

"My arms are killing me," he said.

"I know. I'm sorry. I am. Hold on."

She cut the zip ties around his feet and wrists and backed out of the room, holding the knife in front of her.

"Come out here and have a seat at the table."

Richard did as he was told. Being tied up had wreaked havoc on his muscles. Rather than worrying he'd try to attack her, she wondered if she'd need to help him navigate the stairs leading from the berth to the main cabin.

He wobbled to the dining area and slid along the booth to tuck himself in behind the table.

Perfect.

"If what you're saying is true, you could have just asked," he muttered, rubbing his wrists.

She rolled her eyes. "Sure. You would have *given* me your boat."

"Maybe not, but I might have driven you where you needed to go." He looked out the window. "Where are we?"

"Near Tantalus. YOU resort."

"I've heard of that. For rich kids, right?"

"Trust fund types, yes." Shee leaned against the wall, trying to decide her next move. She was grateful to Richard for distracting her from her self-pity spiral, but she still had to devise a plan.

"What are you going to do?" he asked.

"I don't know. She's there. I need her here. But there are guards on the island and—I don't know. A growing list of complications. You, for instance."

"Me?" He seemed surprised. "What if I help?"

Shee squinted at him. "Why are you so nice all of a sudden?"

He shrugged. "Except for the sore arms and getting bashed in the nose, this is all pretty exciting. Believe it or not, hedge fund managers don't get involved in things like this very often."

Shee chuckled. "Yep, my main goal was your entertainment. Mission accomplished."

Richard continued without commenting. "I do think you're telling the truth, and I have a daughter of my own."

"Yeah?"

"Yes." He smiled in an almost coquettish manner. "Plus, you *are* pretty—"

She held up a hand. "Seriously, Richard? Will you never learn?"

He nodded. "Sorry."

She pulled her phone from her pocket.

"Are you calling your daughter?" he asked.

"I can't. No bars. I had them and then nothing. It's like the island shut off their service."

"Did you check my phone?"

She nodded. "Nothing."

"I mean the sat phone?"

Shee perked up. "Huh?"

He pointed to a closed cabinet on her right. "I have an emergency satellite phone."

Shee slid open the door to reveal an orange phone plugged into a wire running through the back of the cubby. After a quick inspection, she flipped a switch, and the device sprang to life.

"How does this work?" she asked.

"It works through an app on my phone. Give me my phone, and I'll get it working for you."

Shee squinted at him. "This isn't a trick?"

"No. I *swear*." He pressed his index and next two fingers together and held them aloft.

She recognized the gesture.

"Are you Boy-Scout-pledging me?"

He nodded. "I was an Eagle Scout back in the day."

"No kidding." She grabbed his phone from the helm where she'd left it. "I guess I *have* to trust you, then."

She handed him both phones. He fiddled with them for a moment before looking up. "Okay, what's the number?"

"Give it to me. I'll just talk to her," she said.

"It doesn't work like that. You can't talk. It messages other phones. I need the number and the message."

She considered her options and then rattled off Mick's number. If she only got one try, better to get him into the loop. Then, he could continue to try Charlotte with his working phone.

Richard typed in the number. "Go ahead. Keep the message short. Like a telegram."

"Okay." She took a deep breath. "It's Shee—"

He looked up. "*She*?"

"*Shee*. S-H-E-E."

He seemed confused. "That's your name?"

"Yes. Short for Siofra. It's my grandmother's name. Can we do the genealogy search later?"

"Yes. Sorry. Go ahead."

She started again. "It's Shee. No cell. Charlotte MIA. Try to reach her."

"That's your daughter? Charlotte? Pretty name."

She nodded. "Type."

He typed. Shee waited, her teeth grinding tighter with every second.

Richard jumped in his seat as if he'd been given a shot of electricity.

"What is it?" she asked.

"He wrote back." He grinned at her. "This is exciting. Who's Mick?"

Shee made fists to pound the air in front of her. "What did he *say*, Richard?"

"Oh. Sorry. He said, *Mick. Straight to voicemail. Will keep trying.*"

Frustrated, Shee turned to stare out the window.

"Mick is a tough guy name," said Richard. "Is he a bounty hunter, too? Is he your boyfriend?"

"He's my *father*."

"Oh. Is he tough?"

She turned back to him. "Yes, Richard, he could kill you fifty different ways with a *spoon*, just like I'm going to if you don't keep your eye on that phone."

Something beeped. He dropped his gaze back to the sat phone.

"There's more. He said. *What's your location?*" Richard perked. "This thing has tracking. Can I send him our coordinates?"

Shee blinked at him. "*Yes.*"

He typed. She pointed to the phone.

"Tell him I'm on a boat. Tell him the stupid name."

Richard looked up. "The name? *Hedge Fun*? I thought that was pretty clever—"

"*Type.*"

"Sorry."

Now that her captive had stopped trying to impress her, she saw his deep, undeniable *dorkiness* and felt better about his eager participation. He wasn't a bad guy.

Richard tapped away. A few seconds later, she heard a beeping tone she knew, now, meant a reply.

"What'd he say?"

"*Extraction.*" Richard's brow knit. "What does that mean?"

Shee grimaced. He wanted her to *go get Charlotte*?

Good.

She'd planned to do that as soon as they were done with the sat phone anyway—

Richard held up a hand. "Wait...there's more...*Mason on the way. ETA fifty minutes.*"

Richard looked up at her.

"Who's Mason?"

Before she could answer, his attention dropped back to the phone.

"This part is all in caps," he said.

"What?"

"*WAIT. STAY OFF ISLAND,*" he read.

Shee's nerves strummed like a shredding guitar.

Why? What's up with the island?

She rubbed her face with both hands. Her father didn't want her to go get Charlotte. He wanted her to wait for Mason.

Waiting was the worst thing he could have asked of her.

"Tell him I got it and then send another message. A new number," she said, giving him Charlotte's number. "This one is going to my daughter."

"Okay...go ahead."

"Go to little beach NOW. Without Xander. We're coming."

Shee waited, her anxiety multiplying itself with every second like mold spores. Richard's eyes remained locked on the screen.

"Zander with a Z?" he asked.

"X."

He stopped typing.

She didn't hear a beep, but she asked anyway.

"Did she answer?"

He shook his head.

Shee slapped the table with the tips of her fingers, and an errant spoon lying there clattered to the ground.

She wanted to go get Charlotte—but to *not* wait for Mason, the extraction specialist would be crazy.

She looked at her watch.

This was going to be the longest fifty minutes of her life.

CHAPTER THIRTY

Lilith plucked a grape from the bunch sitting in a glass bowl beside her.

"What do you want to do, *Zeus*?" she asked.

Zeus frowned, pacing the penthouse of his pyramid. "Don't say it like that."

"Like what?"

"The way you said *Zeus*."

She snickered. "Sorry."

"We need to figure out what's going on. How did you not see this coming?"

Lilith shrugged. "I hadn't talked to MacKenzie yet."

"Why not? Isn't that your job?" he snapped.

"She said she wanted to wait. She said she'd call me this afternoon." Lilith sighed. "Half these kids have been in and out of therapy for years. They aren't always clamoring to have one more person crawling around in their heads. I have to take it slow."

Zeus sat in the swivel chair he had installed in front of the floor-to-ceiling window overlooking the island. It's where he did his best thinking.

"You should have sensed she wasn't one of our kids. She shouldn't have even made it to the island," he grumbled.

"She had a *referral*. Everything looked normal."

Lilith tossed a grape at him. It flew past his line of vision and rolled beneath a corner table.

"Cut it out," he said. "Pick that up."

Lilith's eyes flashed. "You're getting a little full of yourself there, *Zeus*."

He glared at her for a moment and then looked away. "You're acting like this wasn't a major slip-up. We have to get her out of here and keep her quiet."

"Or toss her to the sharks."

Her comment pulled Zeus' gaze toward the sea. "We don't know enough about her. We don't know who would miss her or who knows she's here."

"I was *kidding*."

He grunted.

I wasn't.

He swiveled to face her. "She was here to take him home. She's *got* to be working for his father."

"I assume." Lilith's head lolled to the side. "What about Xander? Should we cut him loose?"

"No. He's our first politician's kid. He's important to our growth."

Lilith's nose crinkled as if she smelled something awful. "You are *no* fun anymore."

Zeus gripped the arm of his chair.

"You always knew this was about something *bigger*."

She frowned. "Can't you let it go? We live in *paradise*. We've got more money than we could spend in a lifetime—let's just run a resort like normal people."

Zeus felt his anger growing. "They need to *pay*. There have to be *consequences*, or they'll never learn. They're destroying society. The planet. *Everything*."

"They're never going to learn. You're kidding yourself."

"They *will*. I'll stop them."

She shook her head. "You sound like some moronic, misguided superhero. Listen to yourself."

He fumed.

She stood and walked to him, kneeling to look him in the eye where he sat.

"I'm serious. Let's *go*," she said, placing a hand on his knee.

He slapped it away.

"Are you crazy?"

She stood, her face flush.

"Right. *I'm* the one who's crazy." She turned away and then back. "You can talk about how you're saving the world all you want, but you're just angry. This is all just *revenge*."

He stood. "How *dare*—"

Someone knocked on the door. Zeus shut his mouth.

"Come in," he barked.

Lilith returned to her spot on the sofa.

Talos, Zeus' personal guard, appeared.

"It's about MacKenzie. She ran, but we have her," he said.

"She *ran*? Why?" Zeus looked at Lilith. "What does she know?"

Lilith shrugged. "Who knows? You should have sent me to get them instead of sending those goons." She glanced at Talos.

Zeus recalled hearing a loud bang. Maybe more than one. It had been faint through the pyramid's hurricane glass, and at the time, he hadn't thought much about it, but—

He turned his attention back to the guard. "Was that gunfire I heard?"

Talos nodded. "Thor said it was necessary. She wasn't hit."

Zeus groaned and dropped his head into his hands.

"Put her in one of the observation rooms."

The guard left, and Zeus looked at Lilith. "They shot at her."

She nodded. "Yup. Empty-headed ogres."

He pulled his shirt over his head and swapped it for another that had been draped over the back of his chair—a light blue polo with *Gregory* written on the left chest.

"Where are you going?" she asked.

"Just stay here," he said, heading for the door.

CHAPTER THIRTY-ONE

"Hey," said Mick, answering the knock on his apartment door.

Angelina stood in the hall with Harley tucked under one arm.

"You look like shit," she said.

He frowned. "Thanks. You come all the way up here to tell me that?"

Leaving the door open, he walked back into his living room.

Angelina followed. "Sit on the sofa," she said, in one of her bossier tones.

Mick glanced at his lounge chair.

"Why?"

"Just do it."

With a huff, he sat. Angelina perched beside him and let Harley scamper to the cushions.

"What are you doing?" he asked.

She tapped her palms on the top of her thighs. "Lay your head in my lap."

"What?"

"Seriously? For retired Navy, you don't take orders well *at all*."

Mick grimaced. "Angie, I've got things on my mind. Shee—"

"Are you going to get on a plane and fly there?"

"Where? To Shee? No. I sent Mason—"

He looked away.

Should I have gone?

Angelina talked over his second-guessing. "Then let Mason do his thing, and you lay down for a second. Just do it. You used to love it."

Struck by what she said, a flicker of memory fanned in his mind. He saw himself and Angelina on a beach somewhere, his head in her lap as she ran her impressive fingernails through his hair and over his scalp.

I remember that.

Without another word, he laid back and let his head rest on Angelina's thigh. She raked through his hair.

"Close your eyes," she said.

He did.

"Tell Mama what's wrong."

His eyes popped back open.

"You know what's wrong. Shee and Charlotte could be in trouble."

Angelina dragged her palm over his face, pulling his eyelids shut again.

"Shh. I know. But you were upset *before*. Get it off your chest."

He sighed.

"My head hurts. Sometimes, I feel like I don't have my sea legs. Sometimes, my thoughts are fuzzy."

Angelina's fingers danced over the large scar on the side of his skull.

"You were shot in the head," she said. "I'm sure Doc Cough told you these things could happen."

"He did. It's just..."

He felt his jaw tighten.

"I'm not afraid to die," he said.

Angelina snorted a laugh. "Who said anything about *dying*?"

"It's just—This place is *important*. I need to finish this mission."

"What mission?"

"To help...maybe atone..."

"Atone for what?"

His body tensed. "For *everything*."

Angelina placed her hand over his eyes to slide them shut again.

"Cut that out," he said.

He needed to sit up. He didn't want to tell Angelina every thought in his head, but it was as if someone had taken the cork out of the bottle. He couldn't stop his fears from spilling everywhere.

"Breathe," she said.

From the darkness beneath her hand, he sucked in a deep breath of air and started again, measuring his words.

"The hotel is running. Shee is back. You're here with me—I need to keep *living*. A little longer. For them, for her…"

He pulled Angelina's hand away from his open eyes and stared up at her.

"…for *you*."

Angelina's eyes widened, suddenly glistening. The trembling tears gathering along her lower lids mirrored how *he* felt inside.

Wobbly.

His thoughts drifted to a Jell-O mold his mother made once when he was young. He'd poked it, and it vibrated. He poked it again, and his finger broke through the membrane minutes before the first party guests were due to arrive. The more he tried to fix the hole, to smooth over the scar, the worse it looked.

Panic welled in his chest, and he shook his head.

Why am I thinking about Jell-O?

Something wet struck his cheek.

When he refocused, he found Angelina staring down at him, petting his face.

So beautiful.

A little of his panic stripped away with each stroke.

"Aw, come on," he said, secretly pleased. "Don't get all emotional-Italian on me."

She leaned down and kissed him on the forehead.

"That's the sweetest thing you ever said to me," she said.

"Don't get emotional?"

She huffed. "That you wanted to stay alive for me."

He scoffed.

"I'm glad you got shot in the head," she said, kissing her way from his forehead to his mouth.

"That's the nicest thing you've ever said to *me*," he muttered.

She giggled. "I'm serious. I think it brought you in touch with your feelings. You never would have admitted this stuff to me before."

Mick frowned.

I'm brain-damaged. I knew it.

She kissed his lips, and Mick felt a calm run through his body like a slow-rolling stream, rivulets of peace trickling down his arms and into his toes—

It didn't last long.

There was a *bang!* and he shot up as if he'd been electrified, smacking his skull into Angelina's forehead.

"Ow!" she barked, throwing back her head.

"I got it," announced Croix as she burst into the room, out of breath.

Mick glared at her as he adjusted himself to a sitting position on the sofa. He and Angelina rubbed their noggins.

"What the hell?" said Croix, her euphoria replaced with what looked like a combination of surprise and horror.

Mick squinted at Angelina. "You didn't secure the door."

Angelina turned to say something and, instead, burst into laughter.

"*What?*" he asked.

"Nothing." She stood and walked into his bedroom.

Harley stopped dancing at Croix's feet and shot after her mommy.

Mick turned his attention to Croix.

"We don't knock?"

"Sorry. It was opened."

She seemed a little deer-in-headlights.

"What's so important?" he asked.

She held up her phone. "I got one of my guys to do a deep dive on the YOU resort."

"I told you. The resort isn't our concern."

"But it *should* be," said Croix, moving to sit on the sofa beside him. "It's got *everything* to do with what's going on with Xander."

"How so?"

"Get this." Croix took a deep breath as if she were about to give a presentation. "The island was built by some billionaire—Douglas Coleman—as a retreat for rich guys with all sorts of weird exotic stuff they couldn't get legally in the states—"

"A scumbag with money."

"Basically. But halfway through construction, the guy was thrown into jail for sex trafficking, kiddie porn, and a list of other gross stuff. *His son turned him in.*"

"Like those newspaper stories you found in Xander's safe, where the kids were turning on their parents?"

"*Exactly.* And in this case, before the cops can throw Daddy's rich ass in jail, he shoots himself."

Mick grunted. "Understandable. His type doesn't fare well in jail."

"True. But here's another fun fact: he ate the gun *in the son's bedroom.*"

Mick winced. "Trying to make a point?"

Croix held up a hand. "Probably, but don't feel too sorry for Junior. Daddy forgot to take him out of the will."

"That doesn't make any sense."

"Nope. Son gets everything, including the island. And then—" Croix paused. "—wait for it..."

She kept him hanging until he couldn't take it any longer.

"Dammit, Croix, you know I hate it when you do—"

She passed her splayed hands in front of her like a magician. "He *disappears.*"

"Who? The son?"

"Yep. Dougie Jr. Like the earth swallowed him. No trail. His mother, who left the dad years ago, had people looking for him."

"Had?"

"She stopped a year and a half ago, right before YOU opened."

"You think she's involved?"

"Let's just say around the same time, she bought a house in Aspen and got herself a boyfriend fifteen years younger."

Mick scowled. "Someone paid her off to stop looking for her own son?"

Croix held up a finger. "Maybe her own *son* paid her off."

"But what does all this have to do with Xander—"

Mick turned as Angelina reentered the room with a towel and something shiny in her hand.

"What's that?" he asked.

"Aw, why?" Croix whined at Angelina. "You're going to ruin it."

Angelina held a hand mirror in front of Mick's face. He saw smeary, ruby-red lip prints dotting his forehead, cheek, nose, and mouth.

"Jeezus," he said, snatching the towel from her and rubbing his face.

Croix giggled.

"Were you ever going to tell me?" he asked.

She shook her head. "Too funny."

Angelina held the mirror until he had the mess cleaned off, and he returned the towel.

She smiled, made a kissy face at him, and returned to the bathroom, Harley on her heels like a tiny shadow.

Mick returned his attention to Croix. "Okay, smartass. Cut to the big reveal. So the kid is running YOU and getting other rich kids to turn on their parents?"

"Nope. The Big Kahuna is Marcus Gregory Nilsson."

"Who the hell is that?"

"Once I figured out Dougie was involved and followed a few threads, Marcus popped up. He *was* his classics professor at Cargill Academy, Dougie's rich-kid private school. But Marcus crossed the wrong kid and got himself fired."

"I imagine that comes with the territory."

"Sure. But he *flipped out*. Threatened to take the school down, punched a kid—" She fiddled with her phone and then held it up for him to see. "A kid recorded some of one of his meltdowns."

Mick watched the screen as a man in a sweater and jeans screamed at a gathering crowd of well-dressed teenagers. Spit flew from his mouth as he railed against the privileged class.

"You're monsters," he screamed, fists clenched. *"You're all monsters. Look at yourselves! You're destroying the world, and you don't even care as long as you get your Bugatti and your own brand of vodka and your celebrity DJs—"*

Mick squinted at Croix. "You're telling me this nut's running YOU? An island retreat for *rich kids*?"

She nodded. "And guess who bought him the best lawyer money could buy to get him out of his arson and assault charges?"

"Dougie?"

Croix nodded. "Bingo."

Mick mulled a moment. "This guy Svengali'd the kid."

"Huh?"

"He *brainwashed* the kid, got control of the island, and is using it as a base to brainwash more rich brats."

"Oh, right. That's my guess."

"And Dougie?"

She shrugged. "Dead? Kidnapped? A few more years, and he'll be presumed dead. What are the chances the professor is mentioned in his will?"

Mick nodded. "Pretty damn good."

Before Mick could decide what Croix's information meant for Shee and Charlotte, his phone dinged, and he picked it up to read a message.

It's Shee. No cell. Charlotte MIA. Try to reach her.

CHAPTER THIRTY-TWO

Sitting on the only chair in the room—an uncomfortable metal folding chair—Charlotte stared at the ground, trying to make sense of everything that had happened in the last two hours.

She'd been on the cusp of delivering Xander and impressing everyone at Loggerhead to such a degree they'd require her services regularly. Maybe they'd create a west coast arm of Loggerhead and put her in charge of it...

Nope. Not anymore.

Now, instead of being hoisted on the Loggerhead's collective shoulders and carried around in victory, she was locked in an interrogation room—empty, over-air-conditioned, with one hard chair and a large dark window that looked suspiciously like a one-way mirror.

Oh, and she'd narrowly avoided being shot by a trained ape named Thor.

Boy. When YOU stopped showering someone with lavish attention, things went bad *fast*.

She hadn't counted on Xander being part of an island cult. After their talk, he'd been whisked off for reprogramming, she was locked in a room, and her mother was waiting for a daughter who would never come.

Total fail.

Charlotte hung her head and bounced the butt of her palm against her forehead.

Think.

She needed to figure a way *out*. Escaping to the beach with Xander wasn't an option anymore. Getting herself off the island, *alive*, would be the new priority.

She could have blown off Xander and his cult nonsense as drunken ravings if it hadn't been for Rapture. In retrospect, everything the pop singer told her during their brief time together suggested YOU *had* to be a cult.

"Zeus" and Dr. Lilith were brainwashing the guests. To what end, she didn't know. All she knew for sure was the good doctor had vilified Xander's father, a classic cult technique for becoming the young man's *new* family.

Zeus, whoever he was, was probably the cult's leader.

Who calls themselves Zeus? She should have known something was up the moment Rapture mentioned his ridiculous name.

That being said, for what it was worth, she'd spotted a theme. *Mythology*. In addition to *Zeus*, there was the statue of Icarus and Xander's Greek-mythology-laden ramblings.

Though, the cult's "brand" didn't skew exclusively Greek. The Egyptian pyramid was a mixed metaphor, so to speak. Then there was the Jupiter room in the clubhouse—*Jupiter* was the Roman version of the Greek God, Zeus.

Cult leaders often portrayed themselves as gods, so she didn't find Zeus' choices all that odd. Ancient lore and symbols worked to win the hearts and minds of millions in their day. Why wouldn't they work on a bunch of pampered rich kids now?

Charlotte's stomach growled. It was hard to think when she was hungry—

That's it.

She gasped as a thought occurred to her.

Tantalus.

Back on the plane ride over, she'd thought the name of the island sounded familiar. Her musings on mythology had jiggled the reference loose in her memory. *Tantalus* was a king who'd secretly fed his son to the Greek gods. The gods realized what he'd done and punished him to spend eternity *starving* while fruit and water hung just out of reach.

Ol' Father of the Year, Tantalus... Icarus and Daedalus. The island's theme wasn't only mythology, it was *fathers and sons.*

Zeus was even part of the theme—Zeus' dad was Chronos the Titan, who'd swallowed his children after a prophet told him he'd be usurped by them. Chronos' wife hid baby Zeus, giving her hungry hubby a stone to swallow instead. When Zeus grew up, he tricked his dad into vomiting up the other children, who then joined Zeus to take down their father.

This can't be a coincidence.

The only story that didn't stay on the bad-dad theme was Icarus. The *kid* was the jerk in that tale. Icarus died because he ignored his father's warnings and flew too close to the sun.

But that hadn't been how Xander related it.

He thought Daedalus kept Icarus down, building into the wings a way to keep his son from flying too high. Translated that way, the story *could* strike a chord in rich children living in the shadows of powerful parents.

Xander hadn't struck her as a mythology scholar. The new translation of the Icarus story had to have come from Zeus and Dr. Lilith.

Lilith.

There's another one.

A character from Jewish biblical lore. Charlotte remembered reading that singer Sarah McLachlan had named the music event "Lilith Fair" after the character because *Lilith* represented feminism—though some stories made her out to be a baby-killing demon.

Right on theme.

But why turn rich kids against their parents?

Charlotte imagined it had something to do with money—everything did.

She smiled.

The next time someone back in Pineapple Port made fun of her for being a book nerd, she'd have to point out how handy all her useless knowledge had been on this mission.

She needed to tell Shee what the island was up to—

A sound pulled Charlotte from her thoughts. Somewhere

outside her locked door, shoes shuffled on the tile floor.

Crap.

She'd spent the last ten minutes patting herself on her bookish back instead of developing an escape plan.

Dead detectives rarely get credit for being clever.

"Hello, MacKenzie," said a voice from a speaker in the ceiling.

She turned to look at the dark window in the wall.

She recognized the voice.

"Dr. Lilith?"

"Yes. Tell me why you were interfering with guests?"

"Interfering?"

"You were trying to take Xander back to his father."

Charlotte did her best to show no reaction, but inside, she felt the thud of disappointment in her stomach.

They know.

Either Xander had told them, or they'd been listening in on the conversation she had in Xander's room—probably the latter. After all, it was suspicious Thor and his partner had shown up the moment they did.

Thor. Another name from mythology, this time, Norse.

Way to beat a dead horse—

"Why were you trying to take Xander to his father?" repeated Dr. Lilith.

Charlotte gripped the sides of her chair.

Good question. Think, think...

"It was a lie," she blurted.

"You *didn't* tell him you were here to take him home?"

Charlotte wished she could go with that, but she had to assume Dr. Lilith had overheard her conversation with Xander.

She couldn't deny what she'd said.

But she *could* deny what she *meant.*

"No. I *did* say that, but I was lying about what I want," she admitted.

There was a pause. Maybe Dr. Lilith was thinking. Maybe conferring with someone. Maybe Zeus himself stood behind that glass.

"What do you want?" asked Dr. Lilith after a moment.

Charlotte swallowed.

Here goes nothing.

"I want your help," she said, trying to look as puppy-eyed as a Dickensian orphan.

"My help?"

"YOU's help. I—I *hate* my parents." Charlotte flashed anger through her feigned sadness. She hoped she'd read the cult's intentions correctly. If she had, being eager to destroy her parents would be a huge selling point.

"I'm not sure I know what you mean," said Dr. Lilith, sounding stiff.

Concentrating on the childhood memory of a dog she'd lost to old age, Charlotte worked up some tears. "I wanted to get Xander talking, so I could find out how to get your attention. That's why I kinda blew you off this morning. I wanted to get *ready*."

"Ready for what?"

"I wanted to impress you so you'd help me take down my parents. I need you to let me climb the levels like Rapture—"

She sniffed as if overcome by emotion.

"Just a moment," said Dr. Lilith.

Charlotte couldn't be sure, but she thought she'd heard an exasperated sigh.

She hoped that mentioning Rapture had caused Dr. Lilith's disappointment. She hoped the doctor assumed Rapture spilled the beans about YOU's unusual services. Charlotte couldn't say she'd come to the island and then pieced it all together from a winged statue and the guard's names.

Charlotte stared at the window, trying to look anxiety-ridden.

It wasn't hard.

The speaker crackled.

"Please be aware you *cannot* interfere with another guest."

"Yes. I'm sorry. I don't know what I was thinking."

"Xander is on his path."

"I know. He started talking about everything, and I got excited—" Charlotte paused. "Wait, does that mean you're going to help me?"

There was a buzz, and the door popped open. A different guard, not Thor, stood there waiting. His shirt said *Talos*. She wasn't familiar with that name, but she assumed it was from some mythology or another.

"Come with me," he said.

"Where? Am I going up the pyramid?" said Charlotte, starry-eyed.

"You're going to your room," he said.

She tried to look disappointed.

Inside, she was *thrilled*.

CHAPTER THIRTY-THREE

Richard had asked if he could change, and Shee had let him go, unsupervised. She'd already searched the area for weapons and put him through enough. He'd been more than helpful getting her messages to Mick, and if he'd wanted to escape, he would have alerted the authorities then.

It almost seemed as if Richard enjoyed—

Shee looked up as he returned from his bedroom.

Her jaw dropped.

"Richard, what the hell are you wearing?"

She could only *assume* the man before her was Richard. The black hood he wore added an element of mystery.

He cocked his covered head. "What?"

"When you said you wanted to change, I assumed you meant into..." At a loss for words, she motioned to him. "*not that.*"

Richard glanced down at himself. He wore black sweatpants and a navy, long-sleeve tee, both with turquoise marlins stitched on them. Over his head, he wore a black balaclava. Only his eyes and the bruised bridge of his nose remained visible.

Strangely, Shee found herself *less* intrigued that he was wearing a balaclava and *more* fascinated that he'd brought one on a cruise around the Caribbean.

"Why do you have a mask?" she asked.

"I wear it when I work on the engine," he explained. "The

gas smell irritates my sinuses."

This information alarmed her. "Is there something wrong with the engine?"

"No."

"Then w*hy* are you wearing the mask *now*? You know I already know who you are, right?"

She couldn't see his mouth, but she could tell he'd smiled by the way the fabric moved.

"I'm going to spy with you," he said.

She shook her head. "We've gone over this. I'm not a spy."

"*Whatever.* I'm going to *bounty hunt* with you.

She snickered. "Looking like Tommy Bahama Batman?"

Through the window of his balaclava, Richard's tilting eyebrows implied she'd hurt his feelings. She reminded herself only Richard's largess had gotten her this far. She needed to keep him happy.

She decided to change the subject.

"Tell me more about the engines. You can fix them if something goes wrong?"

He nodded.

Shee clucked her tongue. "Richard, you are *full* of surprises."

Her comment seemed to buoy his mood.

"I didn't hire Captain Ivan because I don't know anything about boats. It's just I don't know anything about this area. There are lots of shallows and reefs to navigate around here."

She nodded. "Okay. Maybe I can find something for you to—"

She stopped as a low rumbling sound rolled in the distance. Moving to the deck, she scanned the heavens and spotted plane lights blinking above.

"Hm."

"Is that your friends or the bad guys?" asked Richard.

"I don't know. Go turn on the boat in case we have to move fast."

He nodded and scrambled back into the cabin.

Shee tucked herself against the outer wall of the cabin as the seaplane approached, circled, and then landed a hundred yards from the boat.

Richard stuck his head out of the cabin.

"Who is it?"

She thrust a hand in his direction.

"Binoculars."

Richard disappeared and returned to place binoculars in her waiting hand.

"Stay inside," she said.

He closed the door on his head, tucking all but his cloaked face behind it.

Raising the binoculars to her face, Shee scanned the plane as its engines cut. The aircraft didn't have a *YOU* logo painted on the side of it or anything obvious that might make her life easier.

That was a step in the right direction.

The plane's door opened, and Shee slunk closer to the side of the boat.

No horde of armed frogmen spewed from the aircraft.

Instead, a single, tall man appeared. He wore black swim trunks and a black rash guard.

The bright moon glinted against the titanium leg below his right knee.

Yay!

Shee waved.

Mason slipped back into the belly of the plane and then reappeared, sans leg, to dive into the water, graceful as a dolphin. Ollie took his place at the doorway to cup his hands around his mouth.

"Mason's coming!" he called.

Shee stepped out of the shadows, elated she could kick out of standby mode.

"Who's Mason again?" asked Richard, appearing behind her like a pudgy phantom.

"He works with me," she said, moving to the stern. "Help me get him onboard."

"There's a platform," muttered Richard. "He can get right up if he has any strength at all."

Shee saw he was right. Mason approached with powerful strokes and popped up on the platform like the sexiest, most wonderful penguin she'd ever seen.

Together, they would get Charlotte.

She had no doubt.

"Hey," he said, as she unlatched the access door to let him hop into the cockpit. His eyes were locked on something behind her.

"You know he's there, right?" he asked.

She turned to find Richard behind her, still wearing his balaclava. She pointed to him and then to her face.

"You can take off, the, uh..."

"Oh," he said, pulling off the mask. The wisps of the remaining hair on his shiny pate swirled in the evening breeze.

Mason cocked an eyebrow. "Should I ask?"

Shee shook her head and proceeded with introductions. "Richard, this is Mason. Mason, Richard."

Mason nodded to him as he pulled off the watertight bag strapped to his back and plucked his artificial leg from it.

"Richard's been very helpful," added Shee as Mason reattached the prosthetic. "He lent me his boat and helped me get a message to Mick."

Mason finished and pulled a gun and a long black elastic strap from his bag.

"Your weapon and belly holster," he said, handing it to Shee.

She grinned and wrapped the belt around her waist. "Thank you. I've been feeling naked without it."

Richard's eyes grew wide as he watched her.

"You are *amazing*," he mumbled.

Mason took a step between Richard and Shee to shake his hand.

"Thank you for your help. Nice boat."

Richard snapped from his awe-induced trance and tilted

back his head to gawp at Mason, looking like a chubby child meeting his football hero.

"Are *you* a spy?" he asked.

"None of us are *spies*, Richard," said Shee.

He nodded and took a step back.

"Charlotte's still on the island?" Mason asked Shee.

"Yes. I couldn't call her. Lost the cell connection. It's like the whole island went down."

Mason glanced again at Richard before refocusing on her. "We need to talk," he said.

She caught his meaning. "Richard, could you pop inside for a bit?"

He pouted. "But—"

"It's for your safety," she added. "I promise to keep you in the loop as much as I can."

His shoulders slumped. With one last stink-eye in Mason's direction, he shuffled toward the cabin. "*Fine.*"

When they were alone on the deck, Mason smirked. "You're keeping him in the loop?"

Shee sighed. "I stole his boat and left him tied up in his cabin for hours. After all that, all he wants in return is an *adventure*. I'm letting him play along so he doesn't press charges."

Mason rubbed his neck. "Okay. I have to get you caught up."

"I know. Xander might have killed his girlfriend."

"It's more than that," he said, resting against the gunwale. "The island itself is sketchy at best. Croix says it's some kind of trap for rich kids."

"Trap?"

"They're turning kids on their parents—probably brainwashing them. We don't know for sure, but bottom line is, we don't know how desperate they might be to protect their operation. We have to proceed with caution. If *any* of what Croix uncovered is true, these people have secrets to protect."

"I heard *gunshots*," said Shee, staring in the direction of the island, willing herself back in time to find the source of the gunfire. "Three. While I was on the island."

"You don't know the source?"

"No. I chalked it up to...*whatever*. A car backfired. Someone was scaring birds off a roof. I didn't want to dive into the jungle on a wild goose chase and miss Charlotte on the beach." She rubbed her upper arm as her nerves returned. "If these people are what you say they are, we have to *go. Now*."

Mason motioned to the plane. "I brought Ollie and Snookie. The FBI's involved now. We're contracting for them."

"We are?"

"Your Dad cut a deal with Snookie."

"After I told him to take it easy," muttered Shee.

"It was a no-brainer. Some of the missing rich kids are on the FBI's to-do list."

"Missing?" Shee closed her eyes. "I shouldn't have left the island. I should have found her."

"You didn't know the place had an agenda. I'm as much to blame. I greenlighted her, too."

Shee swallowed. "We can't lose her. We just got her back."

He reached out and pulled her to him. "We won't."

She took a moment to rest against him and then stepped back.

"Let's make one thing clear—*she's* the priority. Xander doesn't matter anymore. We're not at war. We can abandon the mission."

"Agreed." Mason's attention moved to the water. "How far to the island?"

"A mile. Maybe two."

"Let's get going. I've got weapons."

He moved toward the cabin, and Shee put a hand on his arm to stop him.

"Wait. We can't take the boat. They've got guards on the beaches and some crazy lookout tower shaped like a pyramid. They already spotted us once, so they'll be ready."

"Did you dock the first time?"

"No. I stayed a hundred yards offshore and took the

paddleboard." She pointed to the board propped against the sidewall of the cruiser.

Without hesitation, he leaned to unfasten it from its straps. "This'll work."

Shee nodded to the seaplane bobbing in the water a football field behind them. "If YOU is the nefarious operation you say they are, maybe we should take Ollie?"

Mason frowned. "We don't need him."

"You *brought* him."

"He got us the plane. He knows how to fly."

"But he's *here*. Why wouldn't we take him? Dad vetted him, and it never hurts to have backup."

Mason took a moment to think, his steely eyes focused on the plane. "Fine." He fished in his waterproof gear bag and pulled out a small walkie-talkie.

"Come in, Snookie, over."

"Go for Snookie, over," came the response.

"We're going to the island. Ollie's coming. You watch the plane, over."

Ollie appeared at the doorway of the aircraft as Snookie's voice crackled over the walkie-talkie.

"How do I watch something I can't fly? What if it starts to drift? Over."

Without hesitation, Mason strode to the cabin door and pounded on it as if he were trying to knock it down. Richard slid it open, his eyes wide.

"Do you have a line?" asked Mason, before the cherub-faced man could speak.

"A—*rope*?"

"Yes. On the boat."

"I know it's called line," said Richard, looking sheepish. "I just didn't know if you meant, like, a *phone line* or—"

"*Where is it?*" asked Mason, in a controlled but insistent voice.

"Oh, right," he pointed. "There's a mess of it under there." He waddled past Mason to lift a hatch embedded in the decking.

Mason produced a small, powerful flashlight from

nowhere and pointed it into the hold below. Seeming satisfied, he raised the walkie to his lips.

"Snook, we're going to paddle to you with a line and secure you to this boat. Over."

"Copy. I guess that makes me feel a little better. Over," returned Snookie.

Richard grinned at Shee. She didn't know if he was excited about being tied to the plane, being useful, or all the cool walkie-talkie lingo flying back and forth, but he looked *giddy*.

Back at the plane, Ollie held up a thumb to show he'd heard the plan and approved.

Shee stood chewing the inside of her lip, trying to recall everything she'd seen on the island. She didn't want to miss a single detail that might be useful.

Mason pecked her on the forehead. "We'll have her back here in an hour."

She nodded.

Richard's smile dropped as he looked away.

CHAPTER THIRTY-FOUR

Charlotte pointed to the stitching on the chest of the guard marching her back to her cottage. Talos had turned her over to another guard with a more familiar name from mythology.

"Your given name is *Apollo*?" she asked.

He didn't answer. Instead, he mounted the stairs and opened the door for her.

"Don't leave," he said, making it clear he wanted her inside.

She paused on the porch. "I was thinking of going to the clubhouse. I'm so *awake*."

He shook his head. "Stay here. Don't leave."

She pouted. "Am I on house arrest or something?"

He nodded. "Something."

"Seriously?"

"Yes. Until Dr. Lilith comes to get you."

Charlotte's shoulders slumped. She didn't have to fake her disappointment.

Her escape plans were crumbling.

"Can I at least have my phone back?"

He shook his head. "No."

"If it wasn't for Zeus, I would *destroy* you online," she growled, storming past him into the room.

She turned to find him still in the doorway, staring at her, stone-faced.

"Is there anything else I can do for you?" he asked.

"When is Dr. Lilith coming to get me?"

"That's above my paygrade." He motioned to the bench on her porch. "I'll be here for the rest of the night."

Charlotte gaped in bratty horror as he shut the front door and disappeared from view.

She flopped against her bed and rubbed her eyes.

What a day.

She stared at the door, her mind racing.

Being MacKenzie was *exhausting*, but she knew one thing—she couldn't break character, not even in her room.

Xander's room probably wasn't the only one with a listening device.

Maybe a camera.

She stretched her arms above her head and yawned as she turned a three-sixty, scanning the room. A few spots stood out, locations where hiding a camera made sense. The light fixture. The television area. The art. The problem was, she didn't want to be caught on camera, *searching for the camera.*

She needed to hunt without being seen. It was like punching someone in the face, without being seen, while they stared at you.

How could she move around, doing odd things, without looking *odd*?

Her eye fell on the room's personal assistant smart speaker.

An idea clicked.

Time for a dance party.

"Play dance music," she commanded it.

A chirpy beat swelled.

Here we go.

She bounced around the room, trying to look like a girl joyful she was about to meet the cult leader of her dreams.

Moving toward her first object of interest, she picked up a ceramic parrot and pretended to dance with it. Twisting and turning it, she checked and double-checked. No camera lay hidden inside.

She moved on.

There were multiple rooms. Wouldn't there be multiple cameras? What did every room have in common?

She swayed her way into the bathroom, chagrinned to

think there would be a camera there. Maybe not there. It seemed clean.

Shifting to the back room, she bebopped around, picking up random objects to swirl in her hands like dance partners. Throwing back her head, she scanned the ceiling for imperfections. There were recessed "high hat" lights in every room. She'd always called them *can lights*, but an electrician she'd hired to install some in her own house had repeatedly corrected her. He seemed *really* annoyed when she called them *cans*.

I guess electricians have hang-ups of their own.

She reeled back her wandering thoughts.

Stop it. Focus.

There were enough people on this island with issues. No time to psychoanalyze her electrician.

If the cameras were hidden inside the *high hats*, how could she ever tell? She couldn't dance up a ladder and dismantle the lights.

The music faded, and a slower tune began.

She dropped into a chair to catch her breath and stared at the 3D, LED digital clock on the wall, its large white numbers reminding her how little she'd accomplished during her time on the island—

Charlotte blinked.

Did the corner of that number just snuff out?

She stood and stretched, keeping her eye on the clock. The tiny white pixel she thought she'd seen blink out glowed back to life.

Hm.

She sat again.

After a moment, the pixel died.

Jackpot.

Standing again, she moved into the main room where the wall clock's twin hung across from the bed. As she entered, she watched a white pixel pop on.

Charlotte turned away and smiled.

Motion cameras.

With so many guests to watch, the cameras were set to motion-activate, so the guards watching them would know what room to focus on at any given time.

I can work with this.

She had to prepare.

The music changed to something more upbeat, and Charlotte resumed her one-woman dance party as she prepared for bed. She'd brought a thin, panted pajama set that would work for both escaping and looking as if she were going to bed.

They were dark and had pockets.

She'd accidentally brought the perfect PJs.

She pranced to her suitcase and gathered the pajamas, her passport, license, and a small flashlight, all the while blocking the view of the clock.

She boogied into the bathroom to change. Not trusting that no camera lurked there, she slipped the items into her PJ pockets before pulling them on.

Returning to the bedroom, she cha-cha'd to the side window and opened it. The evening came with a breeze, so it wouldn't seem odd. She slid open two more windows in the back and slid open the back patio slider.

She held her breath.

Would opening the back door set off alarms?

She shuffled back into the bedroom and poured herself a shot of rum, keeping an eye on the back slider as she pretended to throw it back. A shadow passed by a window, so she sang to the music, loud and so off-key it was almost impressive.

"*I'm going to the pyramid, yeah yeah, gonna meet the Zeus, uh-huh...you know it...*"

Apollo stuck his head through the open back door. She held the bottle of rum in the air and pretended to drink directly from it as she twirled. Giggling, she dropped into a chair as if she'd lost her balance.

"Dance with me, Apollo!" she called.

She popped up to pretend-swig some more, peeking from one eye at the porch.

Apollo had disappeared.

She waltzed to the front to peer out the window.

Apollo had reappeared at his post, holding his wrist to his mouth as if he was talking to someone like a secret service agent.

A giddy thrill ran through her body.

He's letting me keep the door open.

Hopefully, that was mission control, confirming for him that she was in her pajamas, dancing and getting sloshed.

Nothing to see here. Just a drunk rich girl who thinks she's going to see the wizard tomorrow.

She glimpsed out the back window, her gaze settling on a break in the back fence of her property.

The gate.

Damn.

What if opening the gate set off an alarm?

She'd have to take care of it now.

After pantomiming more drinking, Charlotte pranced out the back door, singing.

Certain a camera watched the back yard as well, she put her foot in the pool and then stumbled toward the back gate. Opening it, she took a step beyond her perimeter. She didn't run, though everything in her body begged her to bolt.

Instead, she made retching noises and then stumbled back into the yard, leaving the gate ajar behind her.

Apollo was rounding the corner of the cottage by the time she reached her pool.

She raised a hand. "Sorry, sorry, my bad. I had to barf."

He poked a finger at the cottage. "I said *stay inside*."

"I am, I am," she said, trying to sound both annoyed and sick. "I'm *celebrating*. Don't be such a buzz kill." She put her hand to her mouth, and in an exaggerated whisper, said, "I didn't want to be sick in my pool. *Not a good look*."

He frowned.

"Get back in the house."

She threw him a wobbly salute.

"Sir, yes, sir."

Reentering the cottage, she moved to the bed and arranged the pillows into one long body pillow beneath the covers. She left the music playing.

It couldn't hurt to have cover music.

Pulling the sheets over her, she hugged the makeshift body pillow so that her body and the pillows would appear to be the same object.

She watched the clock's white pixel die and let out a long steady breath.

Here we go.

Moving agonizingly slowly, she slid her foot over the edge of the bed, her eye never leaving the pixel.

She'd need to crawl, in super slo-mo, out of the bed, across the room, out the back door, across the yard, and through the gate.

If at any point she triggered a motion camera and they spotted her on the ground crawling like a commando, the gig would be up.

She oozed from the bed to the ground.

One arm forward, *slide the body.*

Other arm forward. *Slide the body.*

She slithered into the back room and onto the back porch, the sliding door's track eating into her flesh as she crossed the threshold, half an inch at a time.

Outside, she realized she had a decision to make.

There *had* to be a camera outside.

She didn't know if it was motion-activated or not.

Should she keep moving slowly in the hope it wouldn't trigger? Or should she bolt for the tree line behind the cottage?

She suspected she knew the answer.

She hated it.

Go slow.

A foot past her pool, a moth danced around her face, and she pressed her nose into the grass to avoid it.

Please don't sneeze. Please don't sneeze.

She crept through the grass like a hunting lizard, until the gate remained the final obstacle between her and the jungle.

The wrought-iron port was still open, but not far enough for her to move through without touching it.

Please don't squeak.

She dragged herself through and into the jungle overgrowth, praying she wouldn't surprise a *real* snake.

When she felt sufficiently engulfed by the jungle, she stood, rising beside a tree as if she were a sprouting limb.

I should have been a ninja.

The world remained silent but for the faint sound of her music playing back in the cottage.

No alarms. No bellowing guards.

Time to run.

She bolted in the direction of the little beach.

CHAPTER THIRTY-FIVE

Charlotte remained deep in the jungle, regretting she hadn't thought of a casual way to go to bed with her shoes on. Every step toward freedom proved both terrifying and painful. YOU had done an amazing job creating their lush paradise, but in the center of all the greenery, much of the island's original rough, dry landscape remained. When she wasn't worrying about critters in the underbrush, she was tearing her arches on shells or stubbing her toes on petrified coral outcroppings.

Though she'd seen nothing larger than a lizard during her short time on the island, rustling noises in every direction implied larger things roamed. She gripped the unlit LED flashlight in her hand, terrified to turn it on lest she'd be seen, or *she'd* spot something she didn't want to see.

Am I even going in the right direction?

She stopped and listened, hoping to hear a boat or water lapping against the shore.

Instead, she heard a faint whine. Almost as if someone was crying.

She moved in the direction of the noise, slowing her progress to stay silent. After ten feet, she noticed a glow beyond the foliage.

Hopefully, she'd found the beaches.

She continued until it became apparent she hadn't found the sea.

Had she found a utility building?

Surrounded by jungle stood a small square structure.

Unlike every other cottage on the grounds, it was *not* swathed in teak. No effort had been made to beautify the concrete block.

Her heart sank. A utility shed meant she wasn't that far from the core of the resort.

She was about to head in the opposite direction when something else caught her eye.

The building had square windows, high on the wall, from one end to the other, about ten feet apart.

All of them had *bars*.

Who would try to steal YOU's lawn equipment? Had landscaping pirates stopped by in the past?

The crying noise that first attracted her to the building began again in earnest. This time, she could tell the sound was human.

"Let me out!"

A female voice sobbed.

"Shut up!" barked someone else. "We're trying to *sleep*."

Charlotte straightened.

We're?

Did YOU have a *prison*?

Her nerves danced. If what she'd found *was* a prison, guards would be nearby. She'd love to be a one-woman rescue team, but there was no way she'd overcome probably-armed prison guards with a mini-flashlight, bare feet, and pajamas.

And who knew? Maybe the people inside were actual criminals. Maybe that's how YOU afforded the island—they rented half to a private prison.

She doubted it, but again, the prison would have to remain a mystery for another day.

"I need to talk to Zeus," called a male voice.

Charlotte cocked her head to listen.

The voice sounded familiar.

"I wasn't going anywhere with that girl. I *swear*. I need to talk to Zeus."

Charlotte raised a hand to her mouth to stifle a gasp.

Xander. The voice *had* to be Xander's.

They'd sent him to YOU prison?

Why not me?

It took her a moment to work it out.

Because I haven't been recruited yet.

Xander was being punished for not following the rules. *She* needed to be indoctrinated first. For that to happen, YOU had to keep pretending they were a benevolent group, pledged to help young heirs succeed.

It didn't matter.

She still couldn't raid the prison. Not even for Xander.

No, she'd find Shee and report what she'd found.

Charlotte tilted back her head, taking a moment to ask the heavens how her mission had gone so terribly, terribly *wrong*. YOU had more secrets than Xander. YOU was—

Stars.

She saw stars. This close to the prison clearing, the trees had thinned enough that she could see stars in the cloudless Caribbean sky. She pivoted on her heel until she spotted the Little Dipper and the North Star at its tip.

If that's North, then...

She pointed west. The beach had to be in that direction. The direction she'd been heading.

Back in the jail, a girl wailed until the wracking sobs made her cough.

Time to go.

Charlotte slipped back into the inky blackness of the jungle.

CHAPTER THIRTY-SIX

"Uh oh," Lilith sat up in bed, staring at her phone.

Marcus Gregory "Zeus" Nilsson snuggled deeper into his silky bed sheets.

"Go to sleep," he grumbled.

"We've got trouble."

Zeus huffed. Lilith had spent all night trying to talk him into leaving the island. She was *insane*. Why would he ever leave Tantalus? Things were only getting better. Soon, he'd have all the money and power he could ever want from the parents, and then he'd use it to destroy their idiotic spawn.

"I don't care," he said. "I told you, we're not going anywhere."

Something touched his nose, and he cracked open an eye as Lilith dangled a phone in front of his face.

"You don't understand. This is the *girl's* phone," she said.

"What girl?"

"*MacKenzie.* This is her phone. I took it from her, just in case."

"So?"

"So, she got a message."

"*So?*"

"It came through while the cell towers are shut down."

He snorted. "They're still down? The staff's been dealing with complaints all day."

"They're back up *now*, but this message came through when they were *down*. Some emergency message system."

Zeus sat up and took the phone from her to read the message on the screen.

Go to little beach now. Coming for you. Explain later.

He looked at her. "Who sent this? Who's coming?"

"I don't know."

Zeus sighed. "Well, my guess is she *is* working for Senator Andino. She played you."

"*Us*," corrected Lilith. "She played *us*. What are we going to do?"

"I'll kick her off the island for misrepresentation."

"That's not enough. They'll be back. It could be the FBI, for all we know."

He chuckled. "If that was the case, the place would be crawling with Feds by now. No, this is good. His father doesn't want the Feds to know, and he sent in a private team."

"But he shouldn't even know about us at *all*."

Zeus ignored her to continue playing out his thoughts. "MacKenzie will tell the senator that Xander's alive, and he'll let it drop. The boy's safe here. I'll make sure he knows."

Lilith shook her head. "Let him *go*."

Zeus rubbed his eyes with the butts of his palms. "No way. We have massive leverage, and I have plans for him."

"*He killed his girlfriend.* I don't even want his creepy ass on the island. It isn't even safe to have him here around the other guests—"

"He didn't kill her." Zeus winced, regretting the words even as they spilled from his lips. Lilith had hit that tone that made his head hurt, and he'd just wanted her to stop.

She scowled. "How do you know?"

"He doesn't seem like the type," he said, hoping she'd let it go.

Not a chance.

Her anger only grew. She poked a finger at him. "*No.* You *know.* What do you know?"

He sighed. "I sent men to pick him up, and one of the boys might have gotten a little rough with the girlfriend."

Lilith's eyes saucered. "Are you saying one of our people killed her?"

"She was going to go to the police."

"So we *killed* her? Who? Who killed her?"

"Thor."

Lilith groaned as if she'd been belly shot. "I should have known. I told you to fire that psychopath."

"He's good at the kidnappings."

"Oh yeah, he's *fantastic*." She made fists with both hands and spoke through gritted teeth. *"He killed a girl."*

"It had to be done. And, it worked in our favor. We framed Xander. He and his father will do *anything* to keep him from going to jail."

"Do you hear yourself?" Lilith rose to her knees, wobbling on the mattress as she took Zeus' face in her hands and stared into his eyes.

"Listen to me. This has gone too far. Blackmailing a billionaire for his island was genius. It should have ended there."

He slapped her hands away.

"Get off me."

Rolling out of bed, he strode to the closet to get dressed. "You knew what you signed up for."

"I knew you wanted to throw a little chaos and heartbreak into the lives of these entitled children and their enabling parents—I'm all for that—but I thought the end game was *money*, not your stupid obsession."

Zeus popped his head through his light blue *Gregory* work polo to arch an eyebrow at her.

"Why would you ever think it's about *money*?"

"Why *wouldn't* it be? Why would we risk our lives to make a bunch of kids miserable?" Why—"

Zeus saw red. He strode forward and grabbed Lilith by the jaw before she could scramble away.

"Shut up," he said.

"*Ow!* Let *go*—" She writhed, struggling against him. He squeezed harder. She chopped at his wrist. He squeezed *harder*.

Her whine became a squeal.

He eased his grip. She fell still, her watery-eyed gaze locked with his.

"This isn't about *revenge*," he said in a measured tone. "This is about a small group running the planet into the ground. I'm not going to sit by and watch it *happen*."

He released her, and she scrambled backward on the bed to cradle her jaw in her palm.

"You hurt me," she said.

"Every time you belittle my mission, you hurt *me*."

He returned to dressing.

"Where are you going?" she asked.

"Everyone trusts 'Gregory,'" he said, running a quick comb through his hair. "I'm going to handle this myself."

He grabbed his phone and called the guard room. "Is Xander Andino in the prison like I asked?"

"Yes, sir."

"Good. Patch me through to Apollo."

There was a click on the line. Apollo answered.

"Sir?"

"The girl lied. Bring her here."

"Yes, sir."

Lilith stared at him from the bed, shaking her head.

"She's going to talk," she said. "They're going to put the pieces together. We need to *go*."

He tucked in his shirt. "She's *not* going to talk."

"You can't just kill anyone who threatens to tell. It's *over*."

He leveled his gaze on her. "That's where you're wrong. It's not over until I say it's over."

His phone rang, and he answered.

"She's gone," said Apollo.

"*Gone*? What are you talking about? Aren't you guarding her?"

"I didn't see her leave. The cameras never picked up any

movement—"

Zeus roared at the ceiling.

"Who's gone?" asked Lilith. "MacKenzie? Her people have her?"

"*Shut up.*" Zeus shot her a look and returned to the problem at hand.

He had to think.

He raised the phone to his ear.

"Listen to me. Send men, *armed men*, to the little beach, that sandy blank spot next to The Cove."

"Yes, sir. You think she's there?"

"I have reason to think so, yes. Someone's coming to pick her up. Grab her and anyone else who shows up."

"Yes, sir."

"Shoot them if you have to."

"Yes, sir."

Zeus hung up and stood with his chin against his chest.

"You're not who you used to be," said Lilith, her voice soft.

"No," he said, heading for the door. "I'm who I'm *supposed* to be."

CHAPTER THIRTY-SEVEN

Mason took the helm of Richard's cruiser and reversed until the boat bobbed fifty yards away from the plane.

"Still too far to toss the rope," called Shee.

He cut the engine and rejoined her outside.

"That's okay. I'll take her the line. I don't want things too close."

Leaving his leg on the boat, he took the paddleboard and one end of the line to the plane to pick up Ollie.

"I'm supposed to be running this mission," said Snookie, as Ollie lowered himself onto the paddleboard behind Mason. "How am I going to do that babysitting a plane?"

Mason busied himself tying the line to the plane. "We need you to stay here and keep an eye on Richard."

"Who the hell is Richard?"

His knots secure, Mason motioned back to the vessel. "He's the owner of the boat Shee commandeered."

"*Commandeered*? She stole his boat?"

He nodded. "And we don't want him stealing it back."

Snookie huffed. "What do you want me to do? Keep him at gunpoint?"

"Nah. He's loving this. Tell him FBI stories. He'll eat them up."

Before Snookie could ask why she'd be telling a grown man bedtime stories, Mason turned to Ollie, whose hands were gripping his hips as if he were trying to crush them to dust.

"We're heading back. You good?" he asked.

Ollie offered a stiff nod. "Not a big fan of water."

Mason paddled back to Richard's cruiser. When they reached the boat, he steadied the paddleboard against the platform to pick up Shee.

"Hop on. Bring my bag," he called to her.

"What about me?" asked Richard.

"You and Snookie keep each other company," said Shee.

"*Snookie*?" A crooked smile popped onto Richard's face as he squinted in the direction of the plane.

Shee shook a finger at him. "Do *not* harass her. She's an FBI agent, not a stripper. She *will* shoot your ass."

"Really?" Richard went starry-eyed again.

"Let's go," said Mason.

Shee lowered herself onto the paddleboard behind Ollie and wrapped her arms around his waist.

"I feel like the sexy meat in the middle of a sexy sandwich," said Ollie.

"Do you have to make this weird?" asked Shee.

"Here we go," said Mason.

He pushed off and paddled toward the island, finding his rhythm, working left and right, the muscles in his arms and shoulders warming as they flexed and released. It felt good to have a real *need* for his upper body strength, after struggling for so many months against his handicapped lower half.

"Do you want me to take a turn?" asked Ollie.

Mason kept paddling. "No."

"I was hoping he'd say that," he heard the Captain quip to Shee.

He continued paddling. When they neared the island, Shee spoke up.

"To your right is the main beach. There could be guards there. We want to point to the left. That little beach over there."

Mason adjusted.

A light flashed on the little beach three times in rapid succession.

Mason pulled the paddle from the water and froze.

"What's that?" he asked.

"I don't know," said Shee.

The light flashed again. Three times, but each held longer. After that, another quick succession of three flashes.

"It's an SOS," said Mason, paddling harder.

"It's got to be Charlotte."

He could hear the excitement in Shee's voice.

The light continued blinking until they were twenty yards away. In the moonlight, Mason saw a single person on the beach. Female. She stopped flashing her SOS and instead waved her arms over her head.

She'd spotted them.

Charlotte.

Mason's dark mood lifted like dissipating fog as he stroked toward her.

The paddleboard rocked. Shee was waving back.

Another light flashed, and Mason's body went rigid.

"Hold," he said.

The paddleboard's rocking stopped.

The new light wasn't Charlotte's. It glowed steadily *behind* their daughter, partially obscured by foliage.

It grew brighter.

"Someone's coming," he said, digging in.

"*No,*" said Shee. "*No, no, no...*"

Two large figures appeared on the beach behind Charlotte. She turned her arms in the air.

"They've got guns," said Shee.

One of the men on the beach peeled off from the other to walk toward the waterline.

"We've been spotted," said Mason, still paddling.

Mason saw the flash of the man's gun before he heard the pop.

"In the water. *Now,*" he barked, counting on his sharp tone to make the others move without second-guessing.

The three of them dropped into the sea.

"They've got her," said Shee, sputtering.

"Give me my pack," said Mason.

Shee pulled his waterproof bag from her back, and he slipped the strap over his head.

He tapped the paddleboard. "Hold on to the board. Try and make progress to the beach when it's safe. I'll be back."

Without waiting to hear a response, Mason swam, cutting the water with smooth, strong strokes. He could feel his remaining leg pulling toward the missing space below his right knee. He'd practiced swimming with one leg during his rehab, but as a thirty-year SEAL veteran, the movement of his reconfigured body would never feel natural.

And once he hit the beach...

He couldn't flop on shore like a beached whale. He needed to buy himself time.

Everything in his heart pulled him toward Charlotte, but he forced the rest of his body to the left, pointing toward the larger beach and the jetty there.

The guard continued to sporadically fire in Shee and Ollie's direction. The one holding Charlotte called to his partner. He wanted to go.

Mason hit the beach, unseen, on the opposite side of the jetty. He swung the pack from his back and reattached his leg in record time.

Retrieving his gun from the pack, he peered over the rocks. The other guard had started toward his trigger-happy partner at the shoreline. He still held Charlotte by one arm. Her hands seemed to be pinned behind her back.

Mason needed to act before they regrouped.

He took aim and fired, striking the guard with the gun in the upper thigh.

The man yipped and collapsed as Mason scrambled over the rocks. The guard holding Charlotte wrestled his weapon from his hip.

"Hold it right there!" he said, raising his pistol as the SEAL slowed to a stop.

If the guard had thought to point the gun *at Charlotte*, he might have had a chance.

"Drop it. I'm not messing around." The man's voice

dropped lower, but his hand shook.

"I promise I'm not either," said Mason. He raised his weapon's muzzle, his aim shifting from the man's chest to his head. "Let her go."

The guard's attention flicked in Charlotte's direction. His elbow bent, drawing her closer.

"Drop it or—"

Charlotte pushed from her captor, creating the perfect distraction. Mason fired, striking the man in the shoulder farthest from where Charlotte had stood. The force of the bullet spun the guard, and his gun tumbled end over end into the sand ten feet away.

The wounded man at the shoreline grunted, and Mason turned to find him dragging himself toward his weapon.

Mason fired again, purposely missing the man in the sand by a foot. The guard abandoned retrieving his weapon and threw his arms over his head.

"Okay, okay, okay," he chanted.

"Don't move," said Mason.

Grimacing, the man gripped his wounded leg.

"I'm going to bleed out," he said through gritted teeth.

Mason recovered the man's gun and rolled his eyes.

"Oh, come on. It's through and through in the meat above your knee. I've had worse papercuts."

Mason turned to Charlotte, who seemed much calmer than he'd expected to find her.

"Am I glad to see you," she said.

Mason's heart swelled. He couldn't remember ever being so distracted during a mission. All he wanted to do was drop his weapon and throw his arms around her.

"Step away from them," he said, picking up the second gun. "I need to focus a second."

She did.

Mason put the other pistols into his bag and tucked his own into his waistband. He patted down the man with the leg wound, finding one empty holster on his hip and no other weapon. He took the walkie-talkie from his belt and added it to his pack.

"Put your hands over your head. Straight up."

The guard gaped at him. "Why? I have to keep pressure—"

"Just do it, or I'll give you a hole you have to worry about."

The guard lifted his arms, and Mason jerked his light blue polo off.

The other guard, who had been moaning and writhing in the sand, suddenly fell silent.

"He's got a walkie-talkie, too," said Charlotte, pointing.

She moved forward, and Mason hustled to swoop in front of her.

"I've got it."

He punched the man hard in the jaw just as he tried to raise the speaker to his lips. The guard went limp, collapsing back to the sand.

"Oh God," said Charlotte. "I think I heard *bone*."

"Sorry," he said, suddenly aware of the spectacle unfolding before his daughter.

She's too old to be scarred for life from this, right?

He wasn't entirely sure how kids worked. She *seemed* fine...

She raised her cuffed hands. "I need his key."

Mason chucked the second walkie-talkie into his bag and found the guard's key on his belt. He used it to set his daughter free.

"*Thank you,*" said Charlotte.

He surveyed the fallen. Relief to have Charlotte safe had left him breathless. Before he could overthink the situation, he wrapped his arms around her and squeezed her against him.

"We had no idea—"

"I *know*," she said, chuckling.

"*Charlotte!*"

Shee ran toward them from the water. Barely past the shoreline, Ollie dropped to his knees in the sand, looking stunned. He spotted Mason looking at him and waved.

Idiot.

Mason released Charlotte as her mother plowed into her.

Shee gripped the girl by her upper arms and shook her.

"Are you okay?"

"*Yes*," said Charlotte, laughing. "You're rattling my *teeth*."

"Sorry. *Sorry*." Shee let her go and huffed a loud exhale.

Charlotte told them about being chased and shot at, her experience with YOU, and Xander's brainwashing.

"Quite a day," said Shee.

Charlotte nodded and pointed to the man with the leg wound. "I think he's the one who shot at me. *Thor*."

Mason bristled, swiveling toward the guard. "Oh yeah?"

Shee put a hand on his arm.

"You already shot him," she said.

Mason cracked his knuckles and tried not to think about wrapping his hands around Thor's neck.

"One other thing," said Charlotte. "I stumbled on a prison in the jungle, and I think I heard Xander inside."

Mason refocused at the sound of Xander's name. "A prison? Where? How far?"

Charlotte pointed into the jungle behind them. "That way, dead east, not far."

He nodded.

Shee's head tilted as she motioned at Charlotte's clothing.

"Are those *pajamas*?"

"Yes." Charlotte laughed and then sobered as she looked past them. "Hey—what's wrong with him?"

Mason and Shee turned.

Ollie had curled into a fetal position on the beach, the warm Caribbean sea lapping at his ankles.

CHAPTER THIRTY-EIGHT

Shee jogged toward their fallen comrade.

"Ollie?"

He didn't respond. The man's arms were wrapped around his body, his expression twisted with what looked like pain. His olive-skinned hand had turned fish-belly white, and though the liquid glistening on his forehead could be water, it seemed more like sweat.

"Are you okay? Are you shot?" she asked, squatting beside him, searching for blood.

He looked up at her, sand speckling his dark eyelashes, apparently unable to talk. Holding up a hand, he motioned for her to wait.

Charlotte and Mason arrived beside her.

"Is he shot?" asked Mason.

"No. I don't think so, but there's something wrong with him," said Shee.

"Almost done. Just a sec," Ollie croaked.

Mason scowled. "We need to *move*."

Shee clucked her tongue. "Give the man a *second*."

Ollie's features relaxed as he took a deep breath.

"Okay," he said, sitting up to meet their gazes with a wobbly grin. "What's next?"

"Ollie, what the hell was that?" asked Shee.

"Heartburn."

She smacked his shoulder. "Shut *up*. That was *not* heartburn."

He pressed his lips into a tight smile.

"You're affecting the safety of the team," said Mason. "Spit it out, *now*, Captain."

After a measured beat, Ollie spoke a single word.

"Angina."

Shee scowled. "Nerves?"

He shook his head. "Nervous people *say* they have angina, but they don't. Believe me."

"Like a heart attack?"

"It's a blood flow to the heart issue. It can start a heart attack. I have medication," he reached into his pocket and produced a tiny pill tin.

Mason swore. "Why didn't you tell us?"

He shrugged. "You wouldn't have let me come. You needed a plane. I'm a pilot. You needed to get to—" He glanced at Shee before returning his attention to Mason. "I'm going to guess *your* daughter? The math was pretty simple."

Mason rubbed his head between his hands.

Shee guessed he wanted to throttle Ollie, but it was hard to be mad at a guy who'd helped him save his daughter.

A thought occurred to her.

"If this is an issue, why didn't Mick stop you from coming?" she asked.

Ollie frowned. "Um..."

"He doesn't know?"

He winced. "I *might* have lied about that part."

"What did you tell him?"

"Cancer."

Mason muttered something unrepeatable.

Ollie brushed the sand from his face and chest. "I was working my way to the truth. In my defense, I didn't think there'd be paddleboards and gunplay on day *two*."

Shee stood. "We'll come back to this. For now, you *breathe* or do whatever you have to do. Is there anything we can do to help?"

"No. Really. Nitro kicked in."

Shee clapped her hands together. "Good. I need you to get

Charlotte back to the boat."

This caught Mason's attention and his focus swung to Shee. "*You're* going back to the boat, too."

Shee shook her head. "Nope. I'm going with you to the prison. Ollie's going back to the boat with Charlotte."

Mason's jaw muscles bulged as he grit his teeth. "You're asking the soldier who just *had a heart attack* to paddle a mile to the boat?"

"Not a heart attack," mumbled Ollie.

"*Charlotte* can paddle. She's strong. *He* just needs to be able to sit upright."

"I can paddle," chimed Charlotte. "Though I *could* stay and show you where the prison is—"

"*No*," said Mason and Shee together.

They exchanged a glance and then Shee took a deep breath before addressing Mason in a calmer tone.

"Look, it's not ideal, but she said Xander's in a prison. These people have guns. We should make the effort to save the kid."

Mason put his hands on his hips, his chest flexed, neck spattered with salt water, sweat, and sand—looking very much the SEAL.

"*Fine.* As long as she's off the island. More guards will be on the way once these don't return."

Shee nodded. "Agreed."

"You're *sure* you don't need me?" piped Charlotte. "I know where the prison is..."

"*No*," said Shee and Mason in unison again."

Charlotte held up her hands. "*Okay.* Fine. Message received."

Shee couldn't help but smile.

Man, I love this kid.

"Go with Ollie. *Now.* We won't be any good if we're worried about you." Shee picked up the paddle and held it out to her daughter. "You're sure you're okay with this?"

Charlotte took it. "I'm sure."

Mason hung his head as if he were trying to turn the sand into diamonds with the sheer weight of his glare.

"I don't know—"

Shee cut him short. "*Stop.* You're not going alone, and I can't send Captain Coronary with you."

Ollie scowled at her as he stood.

"It wasn't a freaking heart attack..."

Mason caught Shee's eyes, imploring her to reconsider with a look.

Shee sighed. "It's *fine.* I promise. It's an island full of rent-a-cops. How bad could it be?"

He pulled his gun and she could tell he'd given in.

"Let's get moving."

After a collection of hugs, Ollie and Charlotte took the board into the water.

Shee watched as Charlotte paddled away.

"She'll be safe on the boat," she said to reassure herself.

She turned to Mason.

"Okay. What's the plan, Extraction Jackson?"

He offered her a withering gaze.

"Step one, skip the nicknames."

"Sorry, Big Guy."

He sighed.

"The plan's pretty simple—we find the prison, breech it, find Xander, and bring him home."

She smiled. "Easy peasy."

CHAPTER THIRTY-NINE

Zeus looked at his watch. The guards and *MacKenzie*—or whoever she really was—should have been back by now.

He'd been sitting behind the glass in the observation room for nearly twenty minutes, plotting how to trick the little bitch.

This wasn't his job. Lilith had picked a hell of a time to fight him. He needed her psychiatric skills.

He looked down at the name stitched on his light blue polo shirt. He'd lean on his Gregory persona to get MacKenzie talking.

Hopefully, she was some dippy girl and not an undercover cop.

She didn't *seem* like a cop. Maybe she was a *friend* of Xander's? He hadn't thought to ask the boy if they'd known each other before. Maybe she was who she said she was, and the senator had tapped her to quietly bring back his son, without the press getting wind.

He needed to find out who she was, who sent her, and who knew she was on the island. Once he had that information, he could find what she held dear and use it for leverage.

With the rich kids, it didn't take much. The slightest obstacle and they fell to pieces. He'd flipped one girl by threatening to post offensive things on her social media accounts. She was so scared of losing followers she'd agreed to bring them her parent's bank account information.

Everyone had something they wanted to protect. MacKenzie wouldn't be any different.

He took a cleansing breath.

He felt better.

What did MacKenzie know, anyway? Only that Xander, a *wanted murderer*, was on the island.

Period.

Lilith was worrying about nothing.

Another hour with Xander, and they'd figure out the perfect way to shut his father up. That would take the heat off them. MacKenzie would have nothing to report and nothing to accomplish.

Life on the island would go back to normal.

Lilith was right about one thing, though. Maybe it was time to start taking revenge on the brats who had inspired him in the first place. He'd punished the parents for raising their little monsters, but the monsters needed to pay, too.

If the guards ever showed up with MacKenzie, he could start with her.

He looked at his watch again.

Definitely taking too long.

He stood and strode to the communications room.

"Zeus, sir," said the guard there, straightening in his seat.

Zeus ignored him, grabbed a walkie-talkie from the rack, and spoke into it.

"Ra, come in."

Nothing.

He looked at the guard. "Have you heard anything from Ra or Thor?"

He shook his head.

Zeus tried again, this time calling for Thor.

"Go for Thor," said a voice.

"*Thor*. What's going on? What's taking so long? Do you have her?"

"On our way."

Zeus took a deep breath and released it. "Good. Hurry up."

He tossed the walkie-talkie back on the counter.

"Have them bring MacKenzie to observation room two."

"Sir—"

Something about the guard's tone made Zeus pause.

"Hm?"

"We had reports of gunfire."

He nodded. "I know. It was Thor."

"No, that was earlier. I mean, about fifteen minutes ago. A couple of the guests called it in."

Zeus gaped. "*Fifteen minutes ago?* Why didn't you tell me?"

"I called your room—"

With a huff, Zeus grabbed the walkie-talkie again.

"Thor, come in."

Nothing.

"Thor. Were you shooting again?"

Still nothing.

He tried twice more with no success.

"Dammit!" Zeus dashed the handheld to the ground, sending three pieces spinning across the floor.

Xander.

He had to check on Xander. If something was up, it probably had something to do with him. He couldn't let anyone get him. The idiot wouldn't hold up to scrutiny. *Not yet.* Usually, the angry kids like him made the most compliant followers, but he wasn't *ready.* He was willing but weak.

He grabbed a second walkie.

"Who's at the prison tonight?" he asked.

"Kraken," said the guard, cleaning the chunks of plastic from the floor.

Zeus rolled his eyes. Dougie Jr. had been allowed to choose his mythological name recently, and he'd chosen *Kraken.*

"Kraken, come in."

"Kraken here."

"This is Zeus. How are things there?"

There was a pause.

"Fine?"

Zeus scowled. "*Are* they fine? You don't sound sure."

"No. They're fine. I mean, are you asking about something in particular?"

"*I'm asking if the prison is secure.*"

"Oh. Then yes."

"You haven't seen *anything* strange?"

"No. I heard gunshots, though."

"Did you report them?"

"No. I figured you knew?"

Zeus sighed. "Just keep your eyes peeled."

"Okay. I mean, yes, sir."

Zeus put down the walkie-talkie and turned to the guard.

"Let me know if anything else strange happens. And let me know the second you hear from Thor or Ra."

"Yes, sir."

Zeus wandered into the hall and stared at the clock on the wall.

One a.m.

This night is never going to end.

CHAPTER FORTY

A few steps into the jungle, the walkie-talkie Mason had taken from the guards on the beach crackled to life in his bag.

"Come in, Thor," said a voice.

Mason swung the pack from his shoulder and retrieved the device.

"You're going to answer it?" asked Shee.

He held his hand aloft, requesting silence.

"Go for Thor," he said into the walkie.

"You forgot to say *over*," whispered Shee when he'd released the button.

He bobbed a shoulder. "*He* didn't. I'm guessing they don't do that."

The voice on the other end continued. "*Thor*. What's going on? What's taking so long? Do you have her?"

Mason cleared his throat. "On our way."

"Good. Hurry up."

They waited in silence. It seemed the voice on the other end was happy with the exchange and had moved on.

Shee released the breath she didn't realize she'd been holding.

"I guess we bought ourselves a minute."

Mason turned off the walkie-talkie and dropped it at the foot of a scrub pine that had managed to survive among its new, more tropical neighbors.

"You don't want to hang on to that?" asked Shee as Mason continued forward without it.

He shook his head. "I don't want it chirping, and if I turn it off, it's useless anyway."

The jungle around them grew darker until a glow appeared through the trees. They headed toward what turned out to be a floodlight attached to a stout concrete block building.

"Looks like a prison," whispered Shee.

Mason nodded. "Stay behind me."

They crept forward until they spotted a single man leaning against the wall of the prison, his face downturned but illuminated by the glow of the phone in his hand.

"One guard?" whispered Mason as they crouched at the edge of the man-made jungle.

"That's all I see," she confirmed.

The young man wore the same uniform as the men they'd left back on the beach.

"Gun." Shee pointed out the holster on his hip.

Mason nodded.

"Do your stuff," she said, patting him on the back.

He turned to scowl at her. "I'm not going to *shoot* him."

"He looks armed..."

"He's doing his job. He isn't a soldier."

"In the calf or something?"

Mason sighed.

"You shot the other guards," she added.

"They were shooting at *us*."

She sniffed. "Fine. You used to be *fun*."

He squinted at her and noticed she was smirking.

She'd been teasing him.

He shook his head.

"You're a first-class weirdo," he muttered, refocusing on the prison so she wouldn't see his amusement.

"So, what *are* you going to do?" she asked.

"I'm *thinking*." He *was* thinking, but in truth, removing gunplay from the equation had left him momentarily stumped.

"Maybe distract him, and I'll see if I can sneak in?"

He bobbed his head from side to side, considering. He didn't like the idea of Shee entering the prison alone, but he liked the idea of her being the distraction even less.

He pulled his pack from his back and set it beside him. "I've got it."

He retrieved the shirt he'd taken from the guard on the beach and slipped it over his own. Disguised as *Thor*, he pointed to the jungle directly across from the guard's post.

"I'm going to create a distraction there," he said. "You cover me from behind."

"You mean sneak into the prison."

"No, I mean *cover me*. From *here*."

"Fine." Frowning, she pulled her weapon from her shoulder harness. "Am I waiting on any kind of signal?"

"You'll know it when you see it."

He looked at Shee. Her pretty face was lit by the soft glow of the prison's lights, and he fought the urge to kiss her.

As Shee stared at Mason, trying to pull the plan he'd refused to divulge from his mind with telepathy skills she didn't possess, his mouth curved into a strange, lopsided smile.

It made Shee want to kiss it.

"Do you ever kiss your sailors during a mission?" she asked.

He didn't seem to react. Then, when she'd started to doubt her joke, his crooked smile grew.

"Only the really dangerous ones," he said.

He leaned in and kissed her on the lips, lingering as she fell from her squatting position to her knees to bring him closer.

"What was that for?" she asked as he pecked his way across her cheek.

His kisses slowed as they reached where her neck met her shoulder.

"You read my mind," he mumbled.

She pulled back. "Did I? I was *trying* to."

She'd hated to interrupt him, but if he hadn't stopped, she would have thrown him to the forest floor and pounced on him like a jungle cat.

"Now who's no fun?" he whispered, his breath on her ear making her shiver.

With a final kiss below her ear, he pulled back, and she reached out to grab the collar of his borrowed shirt.

"Be careful," she said, staring into his eyes, willing him to listen to her.

He nodded and then ran through the underbrush with considerable grace for a large, one-legged man. His growing mastery of his appendage made her wistful. Soon, she'd hardly be able to tease him at all, and that would be a shame.

She waited, fanning her face with her hand. She still felt flush. She wasn't sure what had come over them but suspected they were giddy from getting Charlotte back.

Soundlessly cuffing a bug as it bounced off her cheek, she heard a man's voice cry out.

"Help! Help me!"

Shee straightened.

Who the hell is that?

It sounded like Mason, but—

Mason spilled from the jungle directly in front of the guard.

"Help! It bit my leg off! I'm bleeding!"

He crawled forward on his side, holding up his stump, knee poking into the air.

Shee covered her mouth with her hand to stifle a laugh.

He didn't...

She could hear the guard gasp from her position twenty yards away. He could see—or rather, *not* see—Mason's missing right shin.

The guard put a hand on his gun.

"What? Where?" he asked. He sounded terrified.

"It's gone now," moaned Mason. "Please, *help me.*"

"I should call for backup," said the guard, fumbling for the walkie-talkie on his hip.

Shee's eyes widened.

Oh no. If he calls for help—

"I already called them," said Mason, writhing in feigned agony. "I just need your help until they get here."

The guard abandoned the walkie and started forward, his head on a swivel as he searched for signs of whatever had nipped the leg off the poor bastard screaming at the edge of the jungle.

"What is it? Is it still out there?" he asked.

"No..." Mason moaned.

The guard broke into a jog.

"Are you sure? What happened?"

Mason crawled toward him, stabbing his elbows into the dirt and dragging himself forward.

Shee broke from the shadows and moved toward the building, gun drawn. It seemed like the thing to do, though she suspected her motivation came from wanting a better view of Mason's theatrics.

I will never let him live this down...

She watched as the guard hunched over him.

She smiled.

I wouldn't do that...

In one deft motion, Mason's giant paw rose into the air like a cobra preparing to strike. He jerked the guard to the ground and placed his sizable forearm around the man's throat.

Shee moved in, pistol pointed at the guard's chest.

"Hands up," she said.

He did as he was told. Mason relieved him of his weapon and walkie-talkie.

"Watch him," said Mason, shifting to the tree line to grab his pack and reattach his leg.

"Is this a drill?" asked the guard. He was younger than Shee had first assumed, staring up at her with wide, frightened eyes, like a bush baby in headlights.

"Not a drill," she said.

Mason returned to his full height and motioned to the prison building.

"Cameras. How long until backup gets here?" he asked the guard.

The boy looked as if he might cry.

"I'm Douglas Coleman, Jr.," he said.

"Nice to meet you. *How long*?"

"Maybe fifteen minutes?"

"Let's hustle." He pushed the young man toward the building.

When they reached the door, Shee poked Dougie Jr. in the shoulder blade with the muzzle of her Glock.

"Open the door."

"Are you here to take us home?" he asked.

Shee and Mason exchanged a look.

"*Us?*" asked Mason. "Who's *us?*"

The young man looked over his shoulder at them, biting at his bottom lip with such fervor Shee wondered how he managed to speak at all.

"I'm Douglas Coleman, Jr.," he said.

She frowned. "You mentioned. *Open the door.*"

"Oh—" He complied, his hands shaking as he punched a code into a keypad. He didn't seem as eager to die in duty as a cult leader might hope.

Once in, Douglas turned, his teary eyes glistening beneath the prison's harsh lighting.

"I'm Douglas Coleman, Jr.," he repeated a third time. "*Dougie.*"

Shee's gaze dropped to the name stitched on the chest of his uniform.

Kraken.

"Dougie Kraken?"

He glanced down. "That's my code name."

"*Kraken?*" She eyed the boy. He'd weigh a hundred and fifty pounds with a baboon clinging to his back.

She let it go and scanned the large open room into which they'd entered. It had the feel of an ASPCA, with one long hallway flanked by cages on each side. The only difference was that instead of pit bull mixes, the cages were populated with young men and women. Five that she could see.

"This is my father's island," said Douglas, sounding more insistent. "He took it."

This caught Mason's attention.

"*That's* why your name sounded familiar."

A flash of excitement rippled across Dougie's face, only to be obliterated by a racking sob.

"I don't think I want to do this anymore," he said.

Shee looked at Mason. "What's going on?"

"His professor stole the island from his father." Mason looked to the boy for confirmation. "Right?"

Dougie mumbled something, looking as if he were about to collapse to the ground.

Mason leaned in. "What?"

The boy swallowed.

"He made me *kill* him."

Shee's eyes opened wide. "Your father?"

Dougie nodded as Mason put a hand on the boy's arm.

"It's okay."

As Dougie melted back into tears, Mason guided him to a plastic chair.

"He said this was the last step—giving me responsibility," said Dougie. "Then Zeus would make me his Right Hand."

"His *right hand*?" Shee rolled her eyes.

Dougie continued to cry, though his sobs blended with the cacophony now erupting from the cages. The prisoners wanted out. They called for help and banged things against their bars like Attica inmates.

"Who are these people?" Shee asked Dougie.

He sniffed. "They're traitors to Zeus."

Shee recognized the name from Charlotte's story of her time on the island.

"The man who had you *kill your father*? You still call *them* traitors?"

Dougie looked away. "My dad wasn't a good guy," he muttered.

"I've got a newsflash for you—neither is *Zeus*," she said.

Dougie appeared pained.

"Leave him alone," said Mason. "We've got to get what we came for and go."

Shee turned away, muttering. "Weak-minded idiots...shooting at my daughter..."

Mason headed down the hall. "We didn't come to break up a cult. We're getting Xander and getting out of here."

At the sound of his name, Xander called out from the last cell, his face pressed against the bars.

"I'm here!"

"Open the cell," barked Mason.

Shee spotted a panel and smacked the button corresponding to Xander's cell.

"I need to explain. I need to talk to Zeus..." Xander babbled as Mason pulled him toward the exit by his arm.

Shee scowled at the boy. Since hearing of Isabella's death, she'd been haunted by the memory of the girl's sister and mother. She wanted to throttle him for what he'd done.

"I want to leave," said Dougie. "Take *me*."

Mason turned to him. "You want to get off the island?"

Dougie nodded. "More than anything."

Mason motioned to the cells. "Wait five minutes, and then let them all out."

Shee looked at him. "Are you sure?"

He nodded and returned his attention to the boy. "Do you know the cove next to the tiki bar beach? On the other side of the jetty?"

Dougie nodded, eager as a puppy.

Mason pointed. "It's due west of here. Go through the jungle. Hide and wait. We'll pick you up."

"Just take me with you," he whined, glancing with what looked like envy at Xander. "Don't make me take *them*. They hate me. It isn't *fair*."

"Don't make me say it," muttered Mason, heading for the door with Shee in his shadow.

"Say what?" called Dougie.

Mason sighed and called over his shoulder.

"*Life* isn't fair."

Shee snorted a laugh and muttered.

"It just takes some people longer than others to realize it."

CHAPTER FORTY-ONE

"Sir, wake up."

Zeus opened his eyes. He'd nodded off in the observation room. He sat up, trying to shake the cobwebs from his tired brain. "Is she here?"

"Who?"

"MacKenzie?"

The guard seemed no less confused. "Oh. No. But there's someone in the prison."

"What? What are you talking about?"

"Someone's in the prison. They took Xander Andino."

"*What?*"

Zeus sprang out of his chair. "What about the guard? Who—?"

He grimaced as he remembered.

Dougie.

The weakest link.

He should have moved one of the *real* guards to the prison with everything going on, but he never dreamed anyone would find the prison—

"Who is it?"

"Sir?"

"*Who took Xander?*"

"I don't know. A big man and a woman. I've never seen them before."

Zeus cocked his head. "Why'd you say a *big* man? Like, *unusually* big?"

The guard nodded. "Like *The Rock* big."

"Shit." Zeus scratched his head with his hand. Someone that big *had* to be a professional. Senator Andino wasn't messing around. And as soon as that kid got back to Daddy, he'd crumble like a cracker. He'd spill everything he knew.

What does he know?

Zeus groaned.

The prison. He was in the prison with the others.

"I should have never put him in there."

"Who?" asked the guard.

Zeus looked up. He'd forgotten the guard was there.

"Shut up. Go away," he said, motioning out the door.

Looking bewildered, the man left.

Zeus rubbed his eyes.

Think, think, think.

By now, Xander was probably already on a boat. Ra and Thor hadn't been at their posts watching the shoreline. They'd been getting MacKenzie.

He sighed.

MacKenzie had to be the key. She'd called for help. Those messages Lilith showed him—the ones that worked with the cell off.

He hit himself in the skull with the palm of his hand.

I should have listened to her.

He took a few breaths and tried to focus.

Okay. It isn't too late. Even if he lost the island, he had time to get away *and* a stunning amount of money in offshore accounts.

Zeus ran out of the room and took the elevator to the penthouse, shaking with nervous energy.

He felt awake now.

Bursting through his door, he sprinted to the bedroom and grabbed a suitcase from his closet. Throwing it open on the bed, he packed.

"Lilith!" he called.

He punched the code into his safe, the code he and Lilith used for everything as a joke.

2-2-3-7-3-3-3

It spelled B-A-D-S-E-E-D on a phone keypad in honor of all the little dicks he'd taught at the school, all the little spoiled princes and princesses he now spent his life trying to ruin.

"Lilith!" he called again, tossing a stack of cash into his suitcase.

"She isn't here," said Talos, appearing at the doorway.

"What are you doing here?"

"I heard you," he said.

Something felt odd to Zeus. It took him a moment to realize what it was.

"You're fully dressed."

"Yes, sir?"

"Why?"

"I just came back from the docks."

"Why were you there? Did you hear what happened at the prison?"

"No, sir. What happened?"

Zeus huffed. "It doesn't matter. We have to go. I need Lilith to start packing."

"She already packed."

"What?" Zeus whirled and strode to Lilith's closet. He threw open the doors.

It looked as if a tornado had ripped through it.

Panic shot through him. "Where is she?"

"She left on the Valor."

He spun to face Talos. "Where? I mean, where was she going?"

"She didn't say."

"By *herself*?"

"With the captain."

"She took *Phil*? You didn't think it was weird she needed a captain in the middle of the night?"

Talos shrugged. "She said you'd be going later."

"Going *where*?"

"She didn't say."

The Girl Who Killed YOU

Zeus threw back his head and roared.

She left.

And if her treachery wasn't bad enough, she'd left in the getaway boat *he'd* been planning to take.

"I need another boat. Do we have another one?"

"There's the Sea Ray."

"That'll do. I'll take that."

"Do you need a captain?"

He thought.

No. He didn't want anyone to know where he was going. He could figure out how to drive the boat. How hard could it be?

"No. I'll drive it. Make sure it's got a full tank."

"Yes, sir." Talos' brow knit. "Is that all? Is there anything I should know?"

Zeus stared at the man who'd been his loyal bodyguard for almost two years.

How much does he know?

He glanced into the suitcase where his pistol lay.

CHAPTER FORTY-TWO

"Where are we going? What's the plan?" asked Shee as they pushed through the jungle.

Mason glanced back to be sure Xander was still moping along on their heels. The boy hadn't seemed *thrilled* about his release into their custody, but he hadn't fought them either. Zeus had done quite a number on him.

He turned his attention to Shee.

"Our little beach might be hot by now," he said, pointing south. "Snookie got us a satellite shot of the island, and I noticed a dock area. We'll find a boat there."

No sooner did he say the words than the jungle spat them out onto a lit, pebbled path promising civilization ahead.

"We're leaving the island?" asked Xander. "Where are we going?"

"I imagine *you're* going to jail," said Shee.

Mason saw her wince as she realized her mistake. The last thing they needed was Xander running away.

Xander stopped.

Mason turned, readying himself to grab the kid if he made a break for it.

"Keep moving," he said.

Xander stared at him, wide-eyed. "So it's true? I killed Isabella?"

A tear rolled down the boy's cheek. Mason found himself wondering what was wrong with all the young men on the island. As far as he could tell, all they did was cry.

Shee's brow knit. "What do you mean *is it true*? You don't remember?"

Xander bit a quivering lip and shook his head. "*They* told me—"

"*Who* told you?"

"A voice. Zeus, maybe. I don't know. They showed me the news—"

Shee and Mason exchanged a look.

"Are you crazy?" asked Mason.

Xander seemed surprised by the question. "What?"

"I mean, *medically* crazy. Do you have episodes? Do you forget things you've done? Are you on medication—?"

"Or maybe *off* medication?" interjected Shee.

Xander ran a hand through his hair. "No. I mean, I've been depressed. I used to take medication for that, but it made it worse—"

"Have you ever lost time? Forgotten things?" asked Shee.

Xander shrugged. "No. Maybe if I was drunk, a *little*, but nothing like..."

He seemed unable to continue his thought.

Mason sighed. "Do you think you could forget killing your girlfriend?"

Xander's tears came faster. "*No*. But they told me *how* I did it. They told me—"

Shee rolled her eyes. "They told you so you'd be able to incriminate yourself."

The boy squinted at her. "*What*?"

"They told you facts only the killer would know. Get it? If the police questioned you and you told them the right facts..."

Xander gaped at her. "So you don't think I did it?"

"I think you'd *remember*," said Mason.

Shee nodded. "We'll get it worked out. Everything works out in the end, right?"

Xander nodded and they started forward again. Mason could tell by the kid's expression that he knew Shee's words to be true. Things did always work out in the world of a fortunate son.

It was smart of Shee to remind him.

"*Stop.*" Shee suddenly hissed the word. She threw out her hands to block Xander's progress, smacking Mason in the stomach in the process.

Mason's head snapped in the direction of Shee's gaze. She'd been a stride ahead when the path ended, and they stepped onto a pebbled area leading to a long pier. Standing fifteen feet away, a muscular man wearing one of the island's trademark blue polos stooped to pick up luggage piled there.

He turned to look at them.

"Stay here," said Mason.

The guard dropped the case in his hand and reached for the gun on his hip.

Mason had no time to play quickdraw. He sprinted forward. Diving, he crashed into the man's chest like a linebacker. They hit the ground with a grunt of air knocked from the guard's lungs. The gun in his hand skittered across the ground to tuck out of sight beneath a row of bushes.

As he fell, Mason saw Shee bolt down the longest of two docks, screaming something he couldn't make out.

Where the hell is she going?

He didn't have time to process the possibilities. The guard twisted him to the side to free his arm and threw a glancing blow at his jaw. In the same motion, he seized Mason's gun hand. Mason jerked free, but as they fought for control, the weapon tore from his fingers and flew into the air.

Mason watched it arc behind him and land in two feet of water.

Mother—

The guard took the opportunity to roll out from under him. Mason scrambled to his feet to square off. They stood, glaring at one another, each rocking weight from foot to foot in an anticipatory dance.

Beneath the glow of the lamps lining the water's edge, Mason saw the man's light blue shirt had *Talos* stitched on the chest. Talos was taller than he'd thought and muscular. More than likely a professional.

Mason glanced behind him and considered scrambling over the rough coral coastline and sloshing into the water to grab his gun. The math didn't work. If he made a move for *his* weapon, Talos would snatch his own from beneath the bush. Probably, much faster.

"So, Talos," said Mason. "Can I call you Talos?"

The man scowled. "Sure."

"Great. I was thinking, we don't need to do this."

The man's eyes bobbed to the left, and Mason glanced in that direction. One small boat remained tied to the smaller pier.

Talos wanted the last ride out of town.

"I suppose you want that boat," said Mason.

Talos kept his fists aloft. "I do."

His gaze dropped, and Mason regretted not changing into long pants. Talos had spotted the metal leg.

"Unfortunately, I'm going to need that boat," said Mason. "There's got to be another somewhere. Why don't you toddle off and take that one?"

Talos shook his head. "That's the last one."

"Hm. Then we have a situation."

Talos nodded. "Yep."

Mason glanced at Xander, who remained just past the edge of the jungle, staring dumbly at them.

"Xander, could you be a pal and grab me the gun out of the water?" he asked.

Talos locked in on the boy. "Move, and I'll kill you."

Xander looked at Talos, the water, Mason, Talos, and back to Mason.

"I dunno..."

Mason sighed. There was almost no chance Talos could touch Xander before he caught him but supposed getting the boy involved *could* complicate things. By now, Talos was probably realizing taking the boy hostage and walking him to the remaining boat wasn't a bad idea.

"Okay. Tell you what. You tuck back down the path there for me."

Xander nodded and backed away.

As if someone had shot a starter's pistol, Talos spun and bolted for the bushes.

Mason sprinted after him. Talos dropped to a squat and lunged for the gun a second before Mason plowed into him. Branches cracked. The two of them rolled across the ground, exchanging blows. During one of his turns on top, Mason missed and punched the ground. He swore.

Luckily, Talos could only respond with his own bloodied knuckles. He hadn't found the gun in time.

Grappling like circus bears, Mason caught Talos across the cheek with an elbow, only to catch knuckles on his jaw and three quick rabbit punches to the ribs.

Mason lifted his good leg in time to kick Talos off of him, and the men scrambled to square off again.

Talos wiped the blood from his nose.

"Army?" he asked.

"Navy," said Mason. "You?"

"Ranger."

Mason nodded his approval.

Talos squinted at him. "Frogman?"

Mason nodded.

Talos chuckled. "Shit."

His eyes flicked downward.

That's it. Do it.

This was what Mason had been hoping for.

Talos had tried to catch him off-guard with chit-chat, but now he swept for Mason's leg.

Mason shifted his weight onto his prosthetic limb and lifted his good leg as the man dipped. Using all the torque he could summon with his hips, he caught the man in the head with his knee.

The effect was instantaneous. One-hundred percent gravity. Talos collapsed on his face in the dirt, his leg outstretched behind him like a ballet dancer captured in mid-leap.

"Ooh, *damn*," said a voice.

Mason turned as Xander appeared.

"Give him a wide berth," he said. He didn't expect Talos to wake up any time soon, but better safe than sorry.

Mason twisted, scanning the area for Shee. They had to get to the boat and—

She was nowhere to be found.

"Where's Shee?" he asked as Xander arrived beside him.

"Is that the chick?" the boy asked as he peered down at Talos. He kicked the man's outstretched foot with his own.

"Cut that out," said Mason. "Yes. The *chick*."

Xander pointed to the dock. "She jumped on a boat."

"She *what*?" Mason stared across the empty Caribbean. "She took a boat?"

"No, she *jumped* on the back of a boat that was taking off."

Mason gaped at him and watched Xander smile for the first time.

"It was pretty badass," said the kid.

CHAPTER FORTY-THREE

Running down the dock after the guard in the boat had *seemed* to Shee like the thing to do at the time.

Less so now.

As Mason leaped on the man on the beach, she'd spotted the other guard on the Sea Ray motorboat bobbing halfway down a long dock and jutting into the moonlit Caribbean.

Afraid he'd take a potshot at Mason, she pointed herself at him, pulling her weapon as she ran, screaming for him to drop a gun she hadn't seen.

Seemed like the thing to do.

Then the Sea Ray roared to life. The boat moved along the dock.

She should have let the guy *leave* and returned to help Mason, but, inexplicably, she ran *faster*. She'd almost caught up to the boat when she ran out of dock. She'd meant to stop, but the boat turned right and cut directly in front of the dock and—

She jumped.

Why? She didn't know. Something about the boat's flat back platform being right in front of her, the head of steam she'd built chugging down the dock, the fact that this guy belonged to the group who threatened her daughter and probably killed Isabella Candella.

It was all a blur of anger and stupidity.

It hit home how stupid jumping off the dock was when she found herself clinging to the back of a speeding boat.

The boat's nose rose higher as it roared away. The back end, where her fingers had managed to sink into and grip a teak grate, dipped, pulling her weight toward the churning water of the boat's wake. Her naked toes, fully revealed when her flip-flop flew off mid-jump, had somehow stuck in a plastic vent, embedded in the floor of the platform.

She marveled at her luck. If the universe had followed any sort of rules during that jump, she would have hit the platform and bounced right into the water.

I'm Spiderman. Who knew?

But was she *lucky*?

One big toe away from hitting the water, she had a decision to make. Should she let go and tumble off the back before the boat motored too far from shore, praying she didn't wrench off a digit in the process?

Or should she try to climb into the boat?

She grimaced.

I hate swimming.

She loved islands, beaches, and being *near* water. Bobbing around a shallow pool on a hot day was delightful.

But *sink or swim?*

No thank you.

Adding to her decision were the additional factors of darkness, amputated digits, and sharks—who would be *very* interested in the bloody stumps where her toe once wiggled...

No brainer.

She'd go *up*.

Straining, Shee reached up, feeling for a cleat on the transom above her.

Polished metal glided across her palm.

Got you.

A new sense of stability allowed her to pluck her toes from the platform. She shuffled forward, squatting low.

She peeked over the transom to see if the driver was on his way back to shoot her in the head and let her body tumble into the sea.

Nope.

The focus of the man at the helm remained locked on the

open water. He didn't seem aware of his stowaway.

Shee stood, wind blasting her face, and stepped into the boat.

Lifting her shirt and reaching for her gun, her fingers passed through the spot she'd expected to feel her pistol grip.

Her gaze dropped to her belly holster.

Empty.

She swore under her breath.

Lucky with the toes, *unlucky* with the gun. She'd had the stupid pistol in her hand when she jumped. Her jarring landing had left her weapon to be eyeballed by curious parrotfish as it drifted to the bottom of the sea.

Okay. Plan B.

Shee evaluated the guard wearing the resort's signature powder blue polo. He wasn't big like the thugs she'd seen while dropping off Charlotte. This one stood maybe five-nine and a hundred and sixty pounds. Maybe he wasn't a guard at all. Maybe he was a spooked server. She felt good about her chances in a fair fight—

Without warning, the man at the helm turned the wheel. Centrifugal force flung Shee against the starboard side of the boat. She caught herself against the gunwale, but not without a considerable thud and an involuntary yelp of surprise.

The man turned.

Shee recognized him, and her gaze dropped to the name stitched on his shirt for confirmation.

"Gregory?"

He blinked at her.

"Stop the boat," she yelled over the motor. She straightened from the hunched position she'd dropped into to avoid flying over the side of the boat and braced herself for the boat's momentum to stop.

Gregory remained frozen.

She lifted her shirt to give him a peek at the gun belt around her middle, but not so high he could see she had no gun.

She cupped her hand around her mouth to create a

makeshift bullhorn.

"Stop the boat, or I'm going to shoot you."

He pulled back the lever, and the nose of the boat dropped. Blessed silence fell upon them.

"Ah. That's better, huh?" she said. "Are you running?"

Gregory swallowed and nodded. "He's nuts. I had to get out of there."

"Who's nuts?"

"Zeus."

"So I've heard. Where are you headed?"

Gregory ran his hand through his hair, looking sheepish. "I don't know. I just wanted off the island. I saw you guys, and I panicked."

She nodded. "Tell you what. I've got the FBI on the west side of the island—"

His eyes popped wide. "You do?"

"Yes. One of them, anyway, and they're good at multiplying. Let's turn the boat around and head back. We'll pick up my guy and then meet up with the others. You can tell them what you know and let them take care of the rest."

Gregory didn't answer.

"You need to tell the authorities what they're up to," she added. "It's the best way to keep yourself out of trouble."

He nodded. "Yes. Of course. To be honest, I'm a little scared."

"Don't be. He can't hurt you now."

He nodded and walked toward her. "I'm so grateful." He reached out as if he wanted to hug her.

She held out her hand to stop his approach. "No need for that. Just—"

Ignoring her, he continued forward, a large smile plastered across his face. His outstretched arms pulled closer to his body.

Every alarm bell in Shee's brain rang at full blast. The frozen smile, the way he'd tucked his arms, the way he'd swung wide to approach her from the direction most perpendicular with the nearest edge of the boat...

He's going to shove me off the—

Gregory must have seen something change in her expression. He rushed, lunging forward.

Shee saw it coming. Dodging to the side, she used his momentum against him, sending him over the side.

Without bothering to check on him, she scurried to the helm and put the boat in gear to pull away. She knew how easy it was to grab hold of the back platform.

Fifteen feet from where they'd been, she dropped to neutral. Only then could she hear him.

"Help!"

"Why would you do that, Gregory?" she called back to him.

He swam toward her.

She put the boat back in gear to remain out of reach.

"Stop!" he screamed, treading water.

"Are you brainwashed? Are you trying to help Zeus?" she asked.

"No!"

He sounded *offended*. Shee scowled. The big guy on the beach…he'd been about to carry luggage to the boat…

A pop of air left her throat as she realized the truth.

"*You're Zeus.*"

"No, I'm *not*," he said, swimming toward her. "I'm the manager. I guess—I guess I *am* brainwashed."

"Nope, nice try. Too late for that. You're Zeus. Are you prepared to tread water forever? Zeus?"

"I'm not Zeus."

"Okay. You keep telling yourself that while you're swimming back to the island." She put the boat into gear and jumped forward another ten feet.

"No, no, wait!" He waved his hands over his head, and she dropped to neutral again.

"Fine. Yes. I'm Zeus. But YOU isn't a bad thing. I'm saving the world."

"From spoiled rich kids?"

"Yes." He tread water, sputtering. "You think they're just spoiled rich kids, but you don't know them like I do. They grow up to be rich men and women of power, with no moral compass, no humility—narcissists determined to never do anything that doesn't benefit themselves. They're *literally* destroying the world."

"And you're going to change all that by getting them to blackmail their parents?"

He shook his head. "That's step one. To create a war chest for the rest of the plan."

She strolled to the back of the boat. "And what's the rest of the plan?"

"I'm going to teach them a lesson. Ensure they do the right thing."

"You're going to blackmail them. Like Dougie. If he steps out of line, you'll tell the authorities he killed his father. You made that boy *kill his own father*."

Zeus floundered. "*Please.* I can't keep swimming."

Shee sighed.

"Are you going to help me?" he asked.

She nodded. "In a manner of speaking."

"What does that mean?"

She smiled. "Are you familiar with the term *keelhauling*?"

Shee spotted Mason at the end of the dock as she puttered back to the island with Zeus dragging behind the boat. He'd found a comfortable position on his back that kept him both breathing and, *eventually*, quiet.

For a guy who considered himself the "god" of his little world, he exhibited zero divinity. He'd started the ride threatening to destroy her, alleged his innocence, claimed he was the only person capable of stopping the end of the world, and, his voice failing him, concluded by blaming everything on his partner Dr. Lilith. By the time he'd finished *that* lie, he'd become the hero in a short story about Lilith's capture—seems she had family in Nassau, and he could lead the authorities to her in exchange for clemency—*even though he hadn't done anything wrong and was, in fact, the savior.*

He didn't want her to forget that part.

Somehow, Shee couldn't picture *Jesus* throwing the apostles under the bus the way Zeus had gleefully chucked Lilith beneath those metaphorical tires.

She pulled the boat to the dock, and Mason leaned down to hold it fast.

"I see you have yours wrapped up," she said, motioning to a bound man on the beach.

Mason glowered at Zeus, who now clung to the boat's platform like a drowning rat.

"I see you've been trolling with yours," he said.

She nodded. "Nothing biting. Ah well. Hop on. We'll take him to Snookie and send her people in for the rest of his minions."

Mason and Xander stepped into the boat, and the SEAL hoisted Zeus inside to secure him.

"You're making a terrible mistake," sputtered Zeus. "These rich kids are going to destroy the world—"

"Said the guy from his private island," said Shee, pulling from the dock. "Shut *up.*"

CHAPTER FORTY-FOUR

One Week Later

Mick sat on the porch and sipped on his end-of-the-evening bourbon. Beside him Croix sat, eyes locked on her phone, as usual.

"Find us any more people?" he asked, watching a bat flutter past their landscape lighting.

Croix looked up. "Maybe. Tech dude."

"Like your hacker friend?"

She shook her head. "More like an engineer type. I was thinking he could be our Q, like in the James Bond movies."

Mick chuckled. He and Croix had watched a fair number of James Bond movies together. He had all the older DVD titles. Once Croix finished teasing him for *owning DVDs*, she'd enjoyed the movies.

Shee strolled onto the porch, the screen door banging shut behind her.

"What are you two up to?" she asked.

"Chillin' like Bob Dylan," said Mick.

Croix giggled.

Shee leaned against the porch railing. "Any word on Xander?"

Mick shrugged a shoulder. "Nic says it looks like he'll be cleared. They know the island guards were in the area, and one seems eager to flip on the other."

She nodded her approval. "Good. Kid's a little addlebrained, but he isn't a murderer."

"Oh, and Snookie let me know that Zeus character is threatening to sue you for dragging him behind his boat."

Shee rolled her eyes. "Pfft. We were *water skiing*."

"Without skis?"

"Not my fault if he didn't come prepared."

Mick chuckled. "How's Charlotte?"

Shee's face lit at the mention of her daughter. "She's great. Loved every minute of it."

Mick sipped his bourbon. "She's her mother's daughter."

"Might have something to do with her father's blood, too," said Shee, laughing.

"Probably mostly," muttered Croix.

Mick perked, remembering more news he'd heard from Snookie. "Speaking of Charlotte, some of those kids you found on the island came with rewards on their heads."

"Yeah?"

"Yep. I thought maybe you'd like to share the cash with Charlotte since she found the prison."

"*Hey*," said Croix, scowling. "When you offered that job to me, you didn't mention *rewards*."

Shee shrugged. "Guess that'll teach you to be a little less picky with your assignments."

Croix pouted. "You *suck*."

Shee grinned at Mick and then glanced at her watch. "Well, I guess I'm going to head up. Watch a little TV in my room."

Mick nodded. "Okay. Have a good night."

"Good night. Good night, Croix."

"I hope you get bedbugs," muttered Croix.

Shee patted Mick on the shoulder and disappeared into the hotel.

Mick leaned over the arm of his Adirondack chair to elbow Croix.

"Watch this," he said.

"What?"

"Just wait. You'll see. Sometime in the next ten—"

The porch door creaked, and Mason appeared with Archie.

The dog shot down the stairs to the yard to piddle, his white coat almost glowing in the darkness.

"Hey, guys," said Mason, spotting them. "Whatcha doing out here?"

"Oh, nothing," said Mick.

His singsong tone inspired Croix to eye him. As Mason watched Archie, Mick held up a finger, asking her to be patient.

He turned his attention back to Mason. "Going to bed?"

"Hm? Oh. Yep. I've got some organizing I've been wanting to do. Just letting Archie out."

"Uh-huh."

Finishing his business, Archie jogged back up the porch stairs, and Mason opened the door to let him into the hotel.

"I'll see you in the morning," he said.

"Yep," said Mick.

"Good night," said Croix.

She watched him go and then locked in on Mick.

"*What?*" she asked.

He smirked, bouncing his eyes in the direction of the hotel. "Coincidence, wouldn't you say?"

Her expression tightened. "That they're going to bed?"

He tilted his head, eyebrows bobbing toward his hairline.

"Oh..." Her eyes widened, and she pointed skyward. "Are you saying they're hooking up?"

Mick took a sip of his bourbon. "That's the third time this week they've done that."

Croix's lip curled.

"*Ew.*"

~~ THE END ~~

WANT SOME MORE? FREE PREVIEW!

If you liked this book, read on for a preview of another Shee McQueen Mystery-Thriller Series AND the first Pineapple Port Mystery (which shares characters with Shee McQueen's world!)

THANK YOU!

Thank you for reading! If you enjoyed this book, please swing back to Amazon and **leave me a review** — even short reviews help authors like me find new fans!

ENTER THE SHEE SWEEPSTAKES!

Enter the Shee McQueen Sweepstakes for a chance to win a Kindle Reader and get free books! https://amyvansant.com/giveaways/enter-to-win-kindle-shee-mcqueen-books

Enter the Shee McQueen Sweepstakes!

ABOUT THE AUTHOR

Amy Vansant is a *Wall Street Journal* and *USA Today* best-selling author who writes with a unique blend of thrills, romance, and humor.

BOOKS BY AMY VANSANT

Pineapple Port Mysteries
Funny, clean & full of unforgettable characters

Shee McQueen Mystery-Thrillers
Action-packed, fun romantic mystery-thrillers

Kilty Urban Fantasy/Romantic Suspense
Action-packed romantic suspense/urban fantasy

Slightly Romantic Comedies
Classic romantic romps

The Magicatory
Middle-grade fantasy

FREE PREVIEW!

PINEAPPLE LIES

A Pineapple Port Mystery: Book One – By Amy Vansant

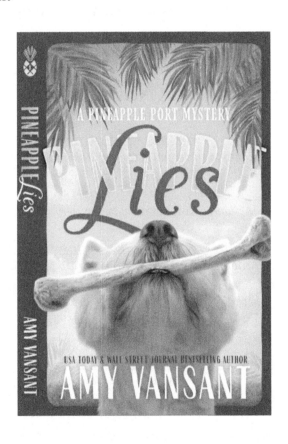

CHAPTER ONE

"Whachy'all doin'?"

Charlotte jumped, her paintbrush flinging a flurry of black paint droplets across her face. She shuddered and placed her free hand over her heart.

"Darla, you scared me to death."

"Sorry, Sweetpea, your door was open."

"Sorry," echoed Mariska, following close on Darla's heels.

Charlotte added another stroke of black to her wall and balanced her brush on the edge of the paint can. Standing, her knees cracked a twenty-one-gun salute. She was only twenty-six years old but had always suffered bad knees. She didn't mind. Growing up in a fifty-five-plus retirement community, her creaky joints provided something to complain about when the locals swapped war stories about pacemakers and hip replacements. Nobody liked to miss out on that kind of fun.

Charlotte wiped the paint from her forehead with the back of her hand.

"Unlocked and open are not the same thing, ladies. What if I had a gentleman caller?"

Darla burst into laughter, the gold chain dangling from her hot-pink-rimmed glasses swinging. She sobered beneath the weight of Charlotte's unamused glare. Another pair of plastic-rimmed glasses sat perched like a baby bird on her head, tucked into a nest of champagne-blonde curls.

"Did you lose your other glasses again?" asked Charlotte.

"I did. They'll turn up."

Charlotte nodded and tapped the top of her head. "I'm sure."

Darla's hand shot to her head.

"Oh, there you go. See? I told you they'd show up."

Mariska moved closer, nudging Darla out of the way. She threw out her arms, her breezy cotton tunic draping like aqua butterfly wings.

"Morning hug," she demanded.

Charlotte rolled her eyes and relented. Mariska wrapped her in a bear hug, and she sank into the woman's snuggly, Polish-grandmother's body. It was like sitting on a favorite old sofa, rife with missing springs, and then being eaten by it.

"Okay. Can't breathe," said Charlotte.

"I'm wearing the top you bought me for Christmas," Mariska mumbled in Charlotte's ear as she rocked her back and forth.

"I saw that."

"It's very comfortable."

"This isn't. *I can't breathe.* Did I mention that? We're good. Okay there..."

Mariska released Charlotte and stepped back, her face awash with satisfaction. She turned and looked at the wall, scratching her cheek with flowered, enameled nails as she studied Charlotte's painting project.

"What are you doing there? Painting your wall black? Are you depressed?"

Charlotte sighed. Darla and Mariska were inseparable; if one wasn't offering an opinion, the other was picking up the slack.

"You're not turning into one of those dopey Goth kids now, are you?" asked Darla.

"No, it has nothing to do with my mood. It's chalkboard paint. I'm making this strip of wall into a giant chalkboard."

"Why?" Darla asked, her thick, Kentucky accent adding syllables to places the word *why* had never considered having them. Her mouth twisted and her brow lowered. Charlotte couldn't tell if she disapproved, was confused, or suffering a sharp gas pain. Not one guess was more likely than any other.

"Because I think I figured out my problem," she said.

Darla cackled. "Oh, this oughta be good. You have any coffee left?"

"In the kitchen."

Darla and Mariska lined up and waddled toward the kitchen like a pair of baby ducks following their mama. Mariska inspected several mugs in the cabinet above the coffee machine and, finding one, put it aside. She handed Darla another. Mariska's mug of choice was the one she'd given Charlotte after a trip to Colorado's Pikes Peak. She'd bought the mug for herself, but after Charlotte laughed and explained the double entendre of the slogan emblazoned on the side, *I Got High on Pikes Peak*, she'd thrust it at her, horrified. Mariska remained proud of her fourteen thousand foot spiraling drive to the peak, however, so she clandestinely drank from the offending mug whenever she visited.

Charlotte watched as she read the side of the mug, expelled a deep sigh, and poured her coffee. That heartbreaking look was why she hadn't broached the subject of Mariska's *I Got Baked in Florida* t-shirt.

The open-plan home allowed the two older women to watch Charlotte as she returned to painting the wall between her pantry door and living area.

"So are you pregnant?" Darla asked. "And after this, you're painting the nursery?"

"Ah, no. That's not even funny."

"You're the youngest woman in Pineapple Port. You're our only hope for a baby. How can you toss aside the hopes and dreams of three hundred enthusiastic, if rickety, babysitters?"

"I don't think I'm the youngest woman here anymore. I think Charlie Collins is taking his wife to the prom next week."

Darla laughed before punctuating her cackle with a grunt of disapproval.

"Stupid men," she muttered.

Charlotte whisked away the last spot of neutral cream paint with her brush, completing her wall. She turned to find Mariska staring, her thin, over-plucked eyebrows sitting high on her forehead as she awaited the answer to the mystery of the chalkboard wall.

"So you're going to keep your grocery list on the wall?" asked Mariska. "That's very clever."

"Not exactly. Lately, I've been asking myself, what's missing from my life?"

Darla tilted her head. "A man. *Duh.*"

"Yeah, yeah. Anyway, last week it hit me."

Darla paused, mug nearly to her lips, waiting for Charlotte to continue.

"What hit you? A chalkboard wall?" asked Mariska.

Charlotte shook her head. "No, a *purpose*. I need to figure out what I want to *be*. My life is missing *purpose*."

Darla rolled her eyes. "Oh, is that all? I think they had that on sale at Target last weekend. Probably still is."

Charlotte chuckled and busied herself resealing the paint can.

Mariska inspected Charlotte's handiwork. "So you're going to take up painting? I'll take a chalkboard wall. I can write Bob messages and make lists…"

"I'll paint your wall if you like, but starting a painting business isn't my *purpose*. The wall is so I can make a to-do list."

Darla sighed. "I have a to-do list, but it only has one thing on it: *Keep breathing.*"

Mariska giggled.

"I'm going to make goals and write them here," said Charlotte, gesturing like a game show hostess to best display her wall. "When I accomplish something, I get to cross it off. See? I already completed one project; that's how I know it works."

There was a knock on the door and Charlotte's gaze swiveled to the front of the house. Her soft-coated wheaten terrier, Abby, burst out of the bedroom and stood behind the door, barking.

"You forgot to open your blinds this morning," said Mariska.

"Death Squad," mumbled Darla.

The Death Squad patrolled the Pineapple Port retirement

community every morning. If the six-woman troop passed a home showing no activity by ten a.m., they knocked on the door and demanded proof of life. They pretended to visit about other business, asking if the homeowner would be attending this meeting or that bake sale, but everyone knew the Squad was there to check if someone died overnight. Odds were slim that Charlotte wouldn't make it through an evening, but the Squad didn't make exceptions.

Charlotte held Abby's collar and opened the door.

"Oh, hi, Charlotte," said a small woman in a purple t-shirt. "We were just—"

"I'm alive, Ginny. Have a good walk."

Charlotte closed the door. She opened her blinds and peeked out. Several of the Death Squad ladies waved to her as they resumed their march. Abby stood on the sofa and thrust her head through the blinds, her nub of a tail waving back at them at high speed.

Mariska turned and dumped her remaining coffee into the sink, rinsed the purple mug, and with one last longing glance at the Pikes Peak logo, put it in the dishwasher. She placed her hands on her ample hips and faced Charlotte.

"Do you have chalk?"

"No."

She'd been annoyed at herself all morning for forgetting chalk and resented having it brought to her attention. "I forgot it."

Darla motioned to the black wall. "Well, there's your first item. *Buy chalk.* Write that down."

"With what?"

"Oh. Good point."

"Anyhow, shopping lists don't count," said Charlotte.

Darla chuckled. "Oh, there are *rules*. The chalkboard has rules, Mariska."

Mariska pursed her lips and nodded. "Very serious."

"Well, I may not have a chalkboard, but I have a wonderful sense of purpose," said Darla putting her mug in the dishwasher.

"Oh yes? What's that?"

"I've got to pick up Frank's special ED pills."

She stepped over the plastic drop cloth beneath the painted wall and headed for the door.

"ED?" Charlotte blushed. "You mean for his—"

"Erectile Dysfunction. Pooped Peepee. Droopy D—"

"Got it," said Charlotte, cutting her short.

"Fine. But these pills are special. Want to know why?"

"Not in the least."

Mariska began to giggle and Darla grinned.

"She's horrible," Mariska whispered as she walked by Charlotte.

Darla reached into her pocketbook and pulled out a small plastic bottle. She handed it to Charlotte.

"Read the label."

Charlotte looked at the side of the pill bottle. The label held the usual array of medical information, but the date was two years past due.

"He only gets them once every two years?"

"Nope. He only got them *once*. Ever since then I've been refilling the bottle with little blue sleeping pills. Any time he gets the urge, he takes one, and an hour later, he's sound asleep. When he wakes up, I tell him everything was wonderful."

Charlotte's jaw dropped. "That's terrible."

Darla dismissed her with a wave and put the bottle back in her purse.

"Nah," she said, opening the front door. "I don't have time for that nonsense. If I'm in the mood, I give him one from the original prescription."

Darla and Mariska patted Abby on the head, waved goodbye, and stepped into the Florida sun.

Charlotte shut the door behind them and balled her drop cloth of sliced trash bags. She rinsed her brush and carried the paint can to the work shed in her backyard. On her way back to the house, she surveyed her neglected yard. A large pile of broken concrete sat in the corner awaiting pickup. As part of her new *life with purpose* policy, Charlotte had hired a company to jackhammer part of her concrete patio to provide room for a garden. The original paved yard left little room for plants. With the patio removed, Charlotte could add *grow a garden* to her chalkboard wall. Maybe she was supposed to be a gardener or work with the earth. She didn't feel particularly *earthy*, but who knew?

She huffed, mentally kicking herself again for forgetting to buy chalk.

Her rocky new patch of sand didn't inspire confidence. It in no way resembled the dark, healthy soil she saw in her neighbors' more successful gardens. Charlotte returned to the shed to grab a spade and cushion for her knees, before kneeling at the corner of her new strip of dirt. It was cool outside; the perfect time of day to pluck the stray bits of concrete from the ground before the Florida sun became unbearable. She knew she didn't like sweating, so gardening was probably not her calling. Still, she was determined to give everything a chance. She'd clean her new garden, shower, and then run out to buy topsoil, plants, and chalk.

"Tomatoes, cucumbers..." Charlotte mumbled to herself, mentally making a list of plants she needed to buy. *Or seeds? Should I buy seeds or plants?* Plants. Less chance of failure starting with mature plants; though if they died, that would be even *more* embarrassing.

Charlotte's spade struck a large stone and she removed it, tossing it toward the pile of broken concrete. A scratching noise caught her attention and she looked up to find her neighbor's Cairn terrier, Katie, furiously digging beside her. Part of the fence had been broken or chewed, and stocky little Katie visited whenever life in her own back yard became too tedious.

Charlotte watched the dirt fly: "Katie, you're making a mess. If you want to help, pick up stones and move them out of the garden."

Katie stopped digging long enough to stare with her large brown eyes. At least Charlotte *thought* the dog was staring at her. She had a lazy eye that made it difficult to tell.

"Move the rocks," Charlotte repeated, demonstrating the process with her spade. "Stop making a mess or I'll let Abby out and then you'll be in trouble."

Katie ignored her and resumed digging, sand arcing behind her, piling against the fence.

"You better watch it, missy, or the next item on the list will be to *fix the fence*."

Katie eyeballed her again, her crooked bottom teeth jutting from her mouth. She looked like a furry can opener.

"Fix your face."

Katie snorted a spray of snot and returned to digging.

Charlotte removed several bits of concrete and then shifted her kneepad a few feet closer to Katie. She saw a flash of white and felt something settle against her hand. Katie sat beside her, tail wagging, tongue lolling from the left side of her mouth. Between the dog and her hand sat the prize Katie had been so determined to unearth.

Charlotte froze, one word repeating in her mind, picking up the pace until it was an unintelligible crescendo of nonsense.

Skull. Skull skull skullskullskullskuuuuulllll…

She blinked, certain that when she opened her eyes the object would have taken its proper shape as a rock or pile of sand.

Nope.

The eye sockets stared back at her.

Hi. Nice to meet you. I'm human skull. What's up, girl?

The lower jaw was missing. The cranium was nearly as large as Katie and had similar off-white color, though the skull had better teeth.

Charlotte realized the forehead of this boney intruder rested against her pinky. She whipped her hand away. The skull rocked toward her, as if in pursuit, and she scrambled back as it rolled in her direction, slow and relentless as a movie mummy. Katie ran after the skull and pounced on it, stopping its progress.

Charlotte put her hand on her chest, breathing heavily.

"Thank you."

Her brain raced to process the meaning of a human head in her backyard.

It has to be a joke... maybe some weird dog toy...

Charlotte gently tapped the skull with her shovel. It didn't feel like cloth or rawhide. It made a sharp-yet-thuddy noise, just the sort of sound she suspected a human skull might make. If she had to compare the tone to something, it would be the sound of a girl about to freak out, tapping a metal shovel on a human skull.

"Oh, Katie. What did you find?"

The question increased Katie's rate of tail wag. She yipped and ran back to the hole she'd dug, retrieving the lower jaw.

"Oh no... Stop that. You sick little—"

Katie stood, human jawbone clenched in her teeth, tail wagging so furiously that Charlotte thought she might lift off like a chubby little helicopter. The terrier spun and skittered through the fence back to her yard, dragging her prize in tow. The jawbone stuck in the fence for a moment, but Katie wrestled it through and disappeared into her yard.

"Katie no," said Charlotte, reaching toward the retreating dog. "Katie—I'm pretty sure that has to stay with the head."

She leaned forward and nearly touched the jawless skull before yanking away her hand.

Whose head is in my garden?

She felt her eyes grow wider like pancake batter poured into a pan.

Hold the phone.

Heads usually come attached to bodies.

Were there more bones?

What was worse? Finding a whole skeleton or finding *only* a head?

Charlotte hoped the rest of the body lay nearby and then shook her head at the oddity of the wish.

She glanced around her plot of dirt and realized she might be kneeling in a *whole graveyard*. More bones. More *heads*. She scrambled to her feet and dropped her shovel.

Charlotte glanced at her house, back to where her chalkboard wall waited patiently.

She *really* needed some chalk.

Get *Pineapple Lies* on Amazon!

Made in United States
North Haven, CT
15 April 2024

51353199R00163